"Christina Suzann Nelson offers readers a compelling and well-written story in *If We Make It Home*. The characters are clearly distinct in personality and life circumstances, but bonded by a friendship that survives the toll of years and the battering of their crises. Nelson skillfully draws readers into character emotions in a way that sets us up for what lies ahead. No neat and tidy bows at the end, but hope-filled and courageous conclusions. Nelson's storytelling is a gift to her readers."

—CYNTHIA RUCHTI, author of twenty-two books,
including *A Fragile Hope*

"If you love discovering new authors with a lyrical, literary voice, then you're in for a treat. If you like those voices to also deliver a powerful, engaging story with true emotional depth, then you're in for a feast. Highly recommended."

—JAMES L. RUBART, best-selling author of *The Five Times I
Met Myself* and *The Long Journey to Jake Palmer*

"I turned the final page of *If We Make It Home* with a sigh of satisfaction. Christina Suzann Nelson is a writer to watch! The adventure these three friends found themselves on had me wide-eyed and holding my breath, but their inner journeys were even more breathtaking. High stakes for each of the characters, yes, but a payoff that is so worthwhile."

—DEBORAH RANEY, author of Christy Award finalist
Home to Chicory Lane and the Hanover Falls series

"*If We Make It Home* is a powerfully well-written novel layered with complex characters, witty dialogue, and superbly plotted collision courses of divine destiny. Three estranged friends, reunited decades after college, make an unusual wilderness journey so life-changing that readers can't help but be changed alongside them. Christina writes with an unpretentious poetry and finesse that charmed me from the first page to the last.

A life-and-death drama brimming with tension and wry humor, *If We Make It Home* moved me with its gut-wrenching honesty and profound wisdom. It's beautifully raw. Elegantly real. Simply stunning. Christina Nelson has created an absolute must-read masterpiece."

    —CAMILLE EIDE, award-winning author of
       The Memoir of Johnny Devine

IF WE MAKE IT HOME

*A Novel of Faith and Survival
in the Oregon Wilderness*

CHRISTINA SUZANN NELSON

Kregel
Publications

If We Make It Home: A Novel of Faith and Survival in the Oregon Wilderness
© 2017 by Christina Suzann Nelson

Published by Kregel Publications, a division of Kregel, Inc., 2450 Oak Industrial Dr. NE, Grand Rapids, MI 49505.

ISBN 978-0-8254-4495-1

Printed in the United States of America
17 18 19 20 21 22 23 24 25 26 / 5 4 3 2 1

To my grandpa and my dad,
the men who raised me to love stories.

Chapter 1

IRELAND JAYNE

The scents of wood, essential oils, and accomplishment float over me as I enter my office. I take a moment to savor the view from my third-story vantage point. Old-growth fir trees shade my window from the harsh sun and give me a glimpse of the private college campus. They stand like guardians, keeping me safe in my oasis, protected from the hurt and chaos of people.

I ease down onto the ball that serves as my desk chair as it strengthens my core. My woven-hemp bag is packed for my trip, and I only have a couple hours today to work on the article I'm writing about the changes in the environmental movement. The picture at the corner of my desk defines so many of these shifts in my own lifetime. The image of me in my twenties, my hair hanging in dreads, my face decorated with piercings. In those days, saving the planet was more than my passion; it consumed me, surrounded me, insulated me.

For many of my students, this is still the truth of their existence, but I've grown older. My finger glides over the small bump below my lip where a metal hoop used to hang. It's been years since I chopped off the dreads, replacing them with short curls that tumble over my head.

Today's movement is no less valuable. It's intellectual. It's in my writings, my academic talks, and my teachings.

Pulling in a deep breath, I lay my palms over my diaphragm, feeling the expansion of my lungs. The air whistles out of my pursed lips as my shoulders drop and the tension in my neck begins to rest, my body and mind sinking into tranquility.

The calm is extinguished with a hard knock at the door. It opens without my invitation, and Dr. Doogan steps into my space. I jump to my feet, the ball crashing into a potted aloe behind me. He's about the last person I would have expected to come to my office. Any meetings we've had in the past have taken place in his domain.

I pull the gauzy scarf from my head and run my fingers through my curls.

His wiry eyebrows press together, and he grips his elbows.

"Professor, I'm sorry, I wasn't expecting you. Please, have a seat." I step around my desk and offer him the only real chair in the office, a second-hand recliner that barely fits in the corner.

He eyes the chair, then shakes his head. "This won't take long. I know you have a train to catch, but it is important."

Something in his tone pushes me back until my legs bump into my desk and I sit on its smooth, cold surface. "Is there a problem?"

He nods. "Unfortunately, there is. McCormick Wilson came to see me yesterday."

A muscle above my right eye twitches. Mac, as the other students call him, has been a waste of this institution's time from the first class he attended. His heart has never been in the cause. When he completed his graduation requirements, I was glad to see him go. Even if it meant sending him into the world to make money off people who legitimately cared about the future of the planet. "What did he want?"

"He claims his entrance to the master's program was denied for unsavory reasons."

"The boy is a fraud. I call *that* unsavory, don't you?"

"Those aren't the reasons he's claiming." Dr. Doogan sucks his lower lip into his mouth, chewing it, then turns to my sacred window. "He says he was denied based on his refusal to have a physical relationship with you."

I lean forward as I absorb the punch. "No." There are no other words. I feel Mac's attack as if he were in the room with me now. As if he's actually reached out and assaulted me. The pain and shock leap from the shadows and pull me down.

"Don't say anything else. I'm not here to get your statement. In fact, I'd rather you keep your side of the story to yourself for the time being. If we play our cards right, maybe this will blow over. Mr. Wilson could see the error of his ways and let it go. The last thing we need to do is antagonize him."

Tingles run down the length of my arms. I shake out my hands, trying to restore control. "Okay. But what is he even doing here? He graduated."

"He's talking about filing a lawsuit to force us into admitting him to the program." Dr. Doogan huffs out a breath. "And he'll want restitution for . . . suffering."

Fire spreads over my skin. His *suffering*? What a joke. A very unfunny joke.

"We can't let him do this. What if other students get the idea that they can bully the university into whatever they want? Grades, classes—anything? How am I supposed to teach when Mac is trying to destroy my reputation?"

"That's the thing. You won't be. At least not for the time being. Ireland, I've talked to the university's attorneys. They strongly suggested putting you on leave. Call it sabbatical if it feels better."

"Where exactly am I supposed to go?"

"You have your speaking engagement at the University of Northwest Oregon. You can still do that. Maybe enjoy some time at your alma mater."

My heart sinks further. If only it were that easy. Going back. It's not the same. There's hurt in the loss. Why that loss should hurt any more than the other hundreds, I don't know.

"Just don't mention this situation to anyone. I mean it. Anyone. We don't want the media getting hold of this any sooner than necessary." He laces his fingers, tucking them beneath his chin as his narrowed eyes drill into me. "Your job is on the line here."

"My *job*?" I step back, building an invisible wall between us. "What do I care about this place anyway? This may be just the catalyst I need to go somewhere else and start over. There's nothing here for me." I can't calm the waver in my voice.

He scoops his fingers through thin gray hair. "Ireland, you know better than that. You're getting too old to run when life doesn't go your way. Remember, I've seen your résumé. This is the longest you've stayed in one spot. Don't throw away all you've built because you're scared."

His words hang in the air like cloying humidity. I fight the urge to brush at my arm in an attempt to escape their grip.

I yank my duffle bag from the floor and fling the strap over my shoulder. Grabbing my phone, computer, and charger, I take off. I don't even bother to wait for Dr. Doogan to go. I don't lock my door, set my voicemail to "out of the office," or turn off the salt lamp.

I just leave.

❖ ❖ ❖

A kid screams in the seat in front of me. Great. I take the train for the peace. The *clack, clack, clack* of the rails. To see the scenery outside the window, from waterfalls to open fields. I am not here to listen to someone's child screech about a spilled snack.

Some kind of artificial neon gummy thing falls between the seats and lands on the top of my hemp bag. Seriously? No wonder he's having a meltdown. What do people expect when they fill their kids with chemicals? He's probably a walking GMO billboard. That's right. The next generation of Americans, built with food "grown" in laboratories.

With the back of my hand I brush the junk away, then reach in and find my phone. Tucking the earbuds in tight, I pump up the volume of the Eagles and lie back, my head swaying with the rhythm of the music and the train.

Outside, we pass fields dotted with sagebrush. As we approach the

Cascades, the memory of the sweet, pure Northwest air expands my chest. On the other side of these mountains is a life I walked away from twenty-five years ago.

What a child I was. Oh yes. Back then I thought all our problems could be solved with recycling. And faith in God. What a joke. The Earth is ready to crumble. That beauty outside the window could almost make me forget the problems we're really facing.

Almost.

McCormick Wilson has chosen to destroy my life. Well, the joke is on him. My life exploded a long time ago. I killed my own happiness. All that's left is the burnt and broken pieces. He can't ruin something that's already obliterated.

I rip the headphones out of my ears. They may block the noise, but they let my thoughts loose.

Scrolling through email on my smartphone, I notice another from Professor Jensen. I'm due to arrive in six hours, and she's supposed to meet me at the train station. That will give me an hour to get ready for the first class of the day.

> Professor Jayne,
>
> Thank you again for coming to UNWO to speak with my environmental change classes. I noticed your name on the Emery House invitations list. You didn't tell me you were an Emery girl. I lived there from 1998–2001. I assume you'll be at the reunion on Saturday. It's such a shame about the closure.
>
> Sincerely,
>
> Sequoia Jensen
>
> Professor of Global Environmental Change – Ecology

Emery House . . . closing? My stomach sours. I may have been foolish back then, but it was a good time, probably the happiest time I'll have in this life. Closing my eyes, I see Hope, Vicky, and Jenna. My eyes snap open. I can't go there. Not now. It's futile. I can't bring the past back any more than I can restore the ozone layer.

Using my phone, I open an email account reserved for junk and type *Emery* into the search. Ten emails come up. The first five are pleas for alum to write the university. Then comes the final news.

My skin burns. Just like the money-hungry university to wipe out a house that doesn't give them the financial rewards of their sky-high hunk of metal dorms.

I open the last email. It's the invitation. It's such a coincidence. I have to consider it. I'm already on my way home, or whatever you want to call Carrington, Oregon. There's no way I would have made the trip for the reunion. And in all reality, I don't have the time to make it now. My train leaves again on Saturday afternoon.

But I have nowhere else to go. No family to visit. Dr. Doogan made it clear he'd prefer I didn't come back any time soon. This Mac kid could destroy the only good thing left in my life. He could crush my career.

The train jerks, sending my cell to the floor and my chia water pouring onto my lap. I grab the bottle and mop up the mess as we come to a stop.

In the middle of nowhere.

For two hours I sit in my assigned seat while the temperature climbs, transforming the train car into an oven. That GMO kid started wailing within minutes, but finally wore himself out and went to sleep. I think we're about to die a global-warming kind of death when they finally give the okay, letting us go outside into the fresh air.

Like a herd of enslaved sheep, we follow the line of people down the aisle and out the door. The air here is dry and hot, but it's not toxic like inside. Large rocks roll under my feet as I make my way as far as I can from the train while still ensuring that I won't miss the call to reboard.

My nerves remain unsettled since the Emery email. I have to get away for a moment. Take time to refocus. To find center. Balance.

Breathing clean air into my lungs through my nose, I count. One . . . Two . . . Three . . . Four. Then slowly blow out through my rounded lips.

The muscles in my neck and shoulders yawn as I roll my head in circles. My tension eases a fraction under the fingers of the penetrating sun.

If the universe is on my side, Mac will back down, and I'll soon return to my own little college, teaching a few young and enthusiastic students how to do what I hoped to do. Change the world. And I'll be comfortable again. Safe in the nest of the life I've built for myself.

Alone.

Shaking my hands out, I try to push those negative thoughts away. They have no place in my world. Neither does that girl I used to think I was. Emery House. It's Emery's fault.

Up ahead of me, a man and woman walk hand in hand. Her multicolored skirt brushes the ground, and she seems unaware that she's picking up twigs and fallen leaves with her hem. They stop. He turns her toward him, revealing the child bound to her chest, curly blond ringlets spilling over his eyes, his fist slurped into his mouth. The man takes her face in his hands, scooping his fingers into her dreadlocked hair. And I look away.

We must have looked so much like that family.

Why can't the past stay in the past?

Yesterday, I was fine. Now my peace is cracked and memories are flowing in through the holes.

Pain starts to claw at the left side of my head. Another migraine. I reach into my bag and pull out the brown dropper bottle. Unscrewing the cap, I inhale the scents of peppermint, eucalyptus, and valerian root from my self-made mixture. I release drops onto my finger tip. Rubbing the oils into my temples, I feel myself returning.

A fall chill rides on the gentle breeze. I turn toward the train. Back to my cave. It may be restrictive, but it's also safe.

Back at my seat, I pull my copy of *Silent Spring* from my bag. Without the squawking kid to distract me, I'm able to go deep into the words, making scribbles in my notebook. My issue becomes clear: I need to get free from the clutter of society. Maybe a retreat of some sort. A true sabbatical. I need to be in nature, and let it become a part of me.

❖　❖　❖

When the train finally rumbles into the station, I'm worn from traveling and my skin is sticky with dried perspiration. I need a long shower and a bed. The day is gone, and the classes I was to speak to, they're over. It fits. I'm sure my career is over too. And my job is all I had left.

To my surprise, Dr. Jensen is standing on the sidewalk outside my window. She's alone, the only figure in the dim light of a flickering safety lamp.

I heft my bag onto my shoulder and stand. Age cries from my joints, especially my hips. It tells me I'm too old to start over again. Too tired to form another new life in another new place with all new people.

Cold air floats over my skin as I step onto the platform. The sensation is both shocking and luxurious.

Jensen approaches me. She looks like her picture—young, her skin still taut and unblemished. Brown spiky hair is tipped with bleached ends and her deep blue eyes shine bright behind round glasses. The expression on her face, the way she bites at her bottom lip, gives away her anxiety.

Something's coming.

"Dr. Jayne. I'm glad you finally made it."

"I'm so sorry I missed the classes. It seems my trip has been all for naught." I brush at my wrinkled linen pants. At one time I chained myself to an old-growth tree not too far from here. I stayed there along with a dwindling crowd until the tear gas showed up. I don't think I felt as filthy then as I do at this moment.

She tugs at a hanging crystal earring. "I was wondering if you'd consider staying on through Monday." This woman gets right to business. "The university will pay for your hotel and travel. My students were so disappointed today. It's not often we have someone of your experience and expertise come to visit. And an alum even. What do you think?"

I think that she'll think very differently if the news of my impending scandal hits social media before I'm able to impart whatever knowledge I may have to her students.

My stomach growls. Roasted pumpkin seeds only last so long.

She smiles, like my discomfort may give her an edge. "We have a wonderful vegan restaurant near campus. Have you heard of Almost Normals?" Without waiting for my reply, she turns and starts walking toward a blue Prius, one of the few cars in the parking lot.

She's got me. I'm starved. "Let's talk through the details as we eat," I say.

I tag along like a hungry stray. The truth in the phrase is so real, so tangible. I should skip dinner and march down the street to the tattoo parlor. *Hungry Stray.* I can see it stamped across my flesh. Identification. It's freeing, the thought. The real truth of who I am out there for everyone to see. No more hiding, trying to be someone I can't. No more putting on a show as if I'm really to be listened to. It's just me. The hungry stray.

Whether it's the hunger or the familiarity of this town, somehow I'm so vulnerable the breeze on my skin stings. I'm raw and ragged, and I don't know if I can go another step without collapsing.

"Dr. Jayne?"

My chin snaps up. How long have I been standing in front of the open hatch of her car, my bag pulling down my right shoulder? "I'm sorry. The trip drained me."

"We'll get you dinner, then I'll take you to the hotel. I think you'll like it. It's right down the street from Emery House."

I nod. She's taking me home. The only home my life can claim. And though I didn't think I'd ever come back, I realize this is the one place for me right now. This is where I can find myself again. Where I can ask forgiveness for my life . . .

Before it's completely wiped away.

Chapter 2

JENNA SAVAGE

Every bite of my second cinnamon roll stretches my stomach, but I keep shoveling in one forkful after another. The sticky frosting I lick from my lips doesn't have the same sweet-as-heaven flavor as it did when I began this feast.

The fork clanks on the plate as I slide it onto the coffee table.

Andy Griffith plays on the television. His deep southern drawl washes over me like my father's once did. Maybe that's why I never miss this show. Or it could be the fact that everything works out in Mayberry. And it only takes thirty minutes. Less if you don't count the commercials. But Andy had more than Opie. He was the sheriff. When Opie left the show, life went on.

A door clicks at the end of the hall and footsteps approach. I fluff the knit blanket draped over my legs, sending crumbs flying through the air and landing in the carpet.

"Smells like the first day of school." Mark enters the kitchen. He stops at the counter and stares down at the pan of cinnamon rolls. "Couldn't you cut down this recipe? There's no way the two of us can eat the whole pan." He's smart enough not to mention the two missing rolls.

"I suppose I could have done that, but I don't even have a pan that small." There's a sharp edge to my voice I wish I could reach out and soften.

"It'll just take some adjustment. We'll figure it out."

We. From where I sit, I see a man who's moved on with life as though our triplets were never here. As though the last eighteen years were a dream, and he's awoken to just another day in his satisfying life.

He pulls a roll from the pan and drops it onto a plate. Melted frosting dives off the sides of the steaming bread. "What are your plans today?"

Right now, my plan is to have another cinnamon roll, but that's not the answer he's looking for, or the one I'm willing to give. "I'll take Scoop for his walk, then make cookies for the care packages."

"Didn't you just send them boxes last week? Calvin won't even get his until basic training is over." He pushes his plate aside, a chunk of roll still sitting in a puddle of goo. "We've got to be careful about the budget. Shipping is expensive."

"So were children, but you never complained about feeding and clothing them."

"You know what I mean. I'm trying to make sure we have enough to help out where we can."

"And making sure they remember that we're here and we love them is not help?"

He steps around the counter and walks the three strides into the family room to where I lay. "Maybe you should talk to someone about what you're going through."

I push myself off the couch. "What exactly am I going through?"

"You know." He has the decency to retreat two paces. "Empty-nest syndrome."

Is he kidding me? No way he just said that. Next he'll be attributing my moods to PMS or menopause. "I'm a mother, Mark, not some crazy plumbing problem. I'm not going to talk to a professional about the fact that I miss my children. They are my children. What kind of mother wouldn't?"

"I think maybe this has gone beyond the typical missing. You barely get out of bed."

"Do I look like I'm in bed right now?" I glance down at my pajama pants and nearly-worn-through slippers. Ugh. I've been bested.

"All right. Listen. Tomorrow is our anniversary. Let's take the chance to enjoy being just the two of us again." He steps closer and rubs the fabric of my worn t-shirt. "Please."

I nod, keeping my gaze on the carpet.

He hooks his fingers in mine and leads me to the front door.

What started as an act of love has become a twenty-year-old ritual.

I step outside with my husband and tip up on my toes to kiss his cheek. This has been my routine every day of the school year since he started teaching. I walk him out the door to his truck and wave as he leaves. It used to make me feel like Lucy Ricardo saying goodbye to Ricky. Now it's just habit. But this tradition is about the only thing in my life that hasn't left me in the last few weeks.

"I love you," he says.

Before I can tell him I really do love him too, he hops into his pickup and backs out of the driveway. His red and rust tailgate disappears around the corner, and he's gone. Today marks what will be his twentieth year teaching science at the high school in our small Northern California community. And one day away from our twenty-fourth anniversary.

Even after all this time, and even with my heart now splintered and cracked open, I still love him. And I think he loves me too. But I'm not really sure why. I don't bring much to our marriage.

Empty-nest syndrome. That shows just how little he really understands. My emptiness can't be mended with a diagnostic Band-Aid. The simple dismissal with those three words bring me further down until I plop onto the porch. The same porch where I posed my long-prayed-for triplets each fall from toddlerhood, through homeschool, and before each first day of high school.

Here, with the jasmine climbing up the trellis, the sweet scent floating over me, I can still see their matching smiles as they packed up the most essential of their belongings and, for the first time, moved to places other than this house. Three separate places. Calvin, the last to leave, started basic training for the Air Force only a couple weeks ago. Carrie's been gone for a month to college in Washington State, and Caroline, she left a week after her sister, but to school in Southern California.

Never has the length of our state seemed so unbearable. It would take me a full day to get to either one of my girls, and even longer to reach Calvin. What if they need me? What if one of them gets sick or injured? How can I stop being their mom in the way I have been since the day the doctor confirmed their beginnings? It's unnatural.

Behind our cherry-red front door, the kids' Airedale terrier whines. Scoop understands. He's the only other creature who seems to realize how vacant our home is without the triplets.

I pull myself up and open the door. At the same time, a gray squirrel darts across the lawn.

The Airedale's ears lift and his back straightens.

I loop my fingers into his collar as he lunges forward. For a few awkward strides, I stay with him, then it's too much for my stubby legs, and my knees collide with the freshly watered lawn.

Scoop runs free.

"Scoop. No. Scoop!" Water soaks into my pajama pants and slippers. My shoulders slump, and I give up, falling back onto the grass. The scent of earth and bark mulch rolls over me. A single cloud floats through the blue-as-the-ocean sky. "Scoop."

This time the plea comes out with no real urgency. He'll come when he's ready. And not a moment earlier. Ten years with this dog, I know the only thing to be gained by screaming his name are odd looks from people who wonder what kind of a person would name their dog Scoop.

The kids begged me to get the beast. And my response, for as long as I could hold out, was, "Who's going to scoop all that poop?" Maybe I'd said it too many times.

Closing my eyes, I let the fact that I'm lying in the front yard in full view of the neighborhood, with wetness seeping into my clothes and hair, while my dog runs free after an uncatchable squirrel, slip away. This is another type of Lucy moment. Not the kind I want to dwell on.

It's time to surrender. My life has become inconsequential and obsolete. I'm the outdated model of a mother with my only hope being the future possibility of revival as a grandmother.

A warm tongue slaps me across the mouth and I sit up, aware that my rounded middle makes bending less graceful than when I was young and active. I lift the neck of my shirt and wipe it across my face. "That's nasty, Scoop."

He flops down next to me and flings a mud-lined leg over my lap.

"Well, I hope you're happy. That was your walk for the morning."

He doesn't answer, and I'm struck by the fact that the majority of my conversations are with this overgrown, breathing teddy bear. But I'm fine. I've had friends. They were an expensive investment and the loss of them hurt too bad.

"Come on, dog. Let's get cleaned up." I roll to my knees and heft myself to standing. Chunks of grass clippings cling to my skin and clothes. The back of my head is soaked, and the hair sticks to my scalp.

In an oddly obedient manner, Scoop follows me into the house where I wipe him down with the dog towel then flip my slippers off and head through the silent hall. On the way to the small bedroom I share with Mark, I pass two closed doors. If only I could go back. I'd enjoy every moment of craziness. I'd hear their music booming from their rooms and recognize the noise as a beautiful sign that my children were happy in our nest.

In my room, I peel off my wet clothes, throw them along the edge of the hamper, then yank on a pair of sweatpants I have to roll up to fit my stubby legs. I finish my housewife-chic ensemble with one of Mark's t-shirts.

As I walk back through the hall, I touch Calvin's door, then Carrie and Caroline's. It's become another of my rituals, a way to wish them well and pray for them when words are too heavy to speak.

On the television screen, Barney Fife pulls his trusty bullet from his pocket as I drop onto the computer chair. None of my eighty-four

Facebook friends have updated their statuses since the last time I checked. I hit refresh again. Still nothing.

I lean back in my seat and twist around. This room is the reason we chose to buy the house. The family room is an extension of the kitchen. Here I was able to be part of my children's everyday lives while I cooked the endless meals that three growing people required.

I loved it then. Now, not so much.

Tears prick my eyes. I can't even think about the triplets without a waterfall of emotions flowing over my cheeks. What am I supposed to do with my life now? I scan their graduation pictures, hung evenly over the gas fireplace. Three individual shots of Carrie, Calvin, and Caroline, then under them a large print of the five of us together, the kids still in their black robes, gold tassels hanging to the side of stiff mortarboards and smiles stretched across our faces.

The photographs give no hint of what was to come when they went separate ways. There's not even the smallest clue on my face that soon that mother would be alone in a vacated home day after day, with nothing to show for her life. Nothing to give her days value.

Where did I go wrong? My friend, Laura, her kids have all gone to the local college. Her oldest daughter was married a year ago and is now expecting Laura and Dan's first grandbaby. They live less than a mile apart.

I can't breathe. The loss suffocates me. I gave everything to have those three precious children. How could I have missed the fact that someday, a day that would come too quickly, they would all three leave me at nearly the same moment. That's what people don't understand, the plight of the mother of multiples. They all leave at once.

❖ ❖ ❖

The light outside is dimming and the candle I've placed in the middle of the table has burned halfway down, but still no Mark. I scoot the chair back and sigh as it creaks with the relief of my weight. How could he be late on our anniversary?

I blow out the flame, leaving the room dark. In the silent house, the quiet tenses my muscles. Feeling my way to the couch, I let my body flop over the armrest and onto the cushions. My fingers graze the remote. Just as I'm about to click on some needed distraction, light cuts across the room.

The rumble of the engine dies and a door slams.

I roll off the sofa, my knees hitting the floor hard and the wind puffing from my lungs. With all I have, I scramble to my feet in a race to be upright before Mark switches on the hall light. The effort leaves me breathless and damp.

"Jenna? Are you here?" The light snaps on, and we're staring at each other.

I wipe my hand over my forehead. "Dinner is cold."

"I'm so sorry. I sent you a text. Didn't you get it?"

I roll my eyes. So what if this expression of my emotion makes him furious? I haven't even charged my cell phone since the last road trip. I use the land line. Why would I use my cell when I'm almost always right here, waiting?

"Listen. I told you I could be late. It was all I could do to get here this early. Tonight is the fall sports parents meetings. Ken was not thrilled I was having my assistant coach take over. I really thought he'd let me out of it."

My shoulders slump. Ken may be a friend, but he's still a harsh principal. Mark isn't making anything up here. It was my own fault for expecting him to be home at six. But still, I can't turn and let Mark off the hook. Something keeps my feet planted and my face turned away from him. I don't want to be wrong—again.

He makes the effort and walks around to face me. "I have something for you." His eyes twinkle as he reaches into his pocket and extracts a lavender envelope.

A card? He gets me a card every anniversary. Running my finger under the flap, I tear the top and pull out a Hallmark anniversary greeting. I think it's the same one I got last year. As I open it, a folded piece of paper slips onto my palm.

Electricity runs over my nerves. I look up into his gaze and see excitement in his features.

"Come on," he says.

Dropping the card and envelope onto the coffee table, I train my attention on the small print. It's an airline itinerary. For one person. To Carrington, Oregon. How did he know?

"I heard about Emery House closing and the reunion. I thought this could be a great chance for you to reconnect. What do you think?" His palm warms my shoulder, and tension melts away from me as I lean into him.

"I'm scared."

"Of what?" His arms encircle me, pinning my own to my sides.

"Of what everyone will think of me at the reunion. I'm not the same."

He lifts my chin. "No one is the same after this many years. No one. I'm sure they're all thinking similar things."

"They have careers, lives. I have—I have a spare tire around my middle and no idea what to do with my time." My forehead drops onto his chest.

"First of all, I think you look great. Secondly, it sounds like this is the perfect opportunity for you to take some time and find your path. Maybe being at the university will inspire you. You know, you could take classes here at the community college or online. Instead of thinking about how much you miss the kids, how about looking at the life you have left to live? You can do almost anything."

I've married a dreamer. In his mind, I still have time to do wild things like fly to the moon. But in reality, I'm a forty-six-year-old woman who hasn't used her degree in almost twenty years.

Doesn't he realize I still listen to eighties music? I have no idea what's playing on the radio, and I have no desire to find out. My main source of entertainment is the oldies television stations, the more black-and-white, the better. I'm not the kind of woman who's about to take a leap and do something new and unfamiliar. I love reruns. Even in my real life.

An overly dramatic moan weaves from my mouth. It's like it hangs there and no matter how much I cringe at the immaturity of it, I can't pull it back or make it drift way.

"I'm sorry. You're right. I'll give it a try." The lie in my words sickens me. But I can't have this talk again. Not tonight. It's our anniversary.

Chapter 3

Victoria Cambridge

"Cori. Are you out there?" I lean over the smooth wood of my polished desk and scan what I can see of the reception area.

Jennifer appears in my doorway. She's neatly groomed, but dressed like a woman of forty rather than a college intern. It's like she's mimicking me and mocking me all at once. Of course, fifty is closer to my age than forty, but no one needs to know that.

"Do you know where Cori is off to?" I tap one of my pink fingernails on the desktop.

"I'm not sure. She said she needed to step out for a minute. Should I be asking her where she's going?" Jennifer's eyelashes flutter. She's got to slow down the coffee consumption.

"No. I'll handle this. Could you get me a glass of iced tea?"

Jennifer clamps her hands together and nods, but it takes her a minute of wasted time before she turns away and gets to it.

My calendar is a mess of disorganization, and that problem falls cleanly on the lap of my assistant. I think I'm going to have to let Cori go. She's late, she doesn't listen, and I have to watch her all the time. There's just something not right about the girl.

I mentioned my issues with her to Daniel a couple days ago, and he nearly came unbuckled, accusing me of paranoia, selfishness, and jealousy. Who does he think he is? He's my husband, and he should be on my side.

Interlacing my fingers, I gaze at the formal wedding portrait on the wall across from me. I have the figure of a young woman and hair that glows with the naturalness of the blond. Now it's the shade my hairdresser concocts with her expertise in dye alchemy. A chemical illusion for the people who watch my show each week.

Daniel really hasn't changed much. At least not in appearance. His jaw is still square and strong. Gray hair now adds salt to his dark, but it only serves to make him more handsome and distinguished.

He's changed though. I married Daniel because we were a good match. My mother pushed us together soon after college. She was in a hurry for me to marry well, seeing her chance once my college boyfriend was out of the picture. And I understood. Marriage is a kind of business, in a way. Both partners bring something to the table. It was up to me to make a proper selection, and I thought I had.

Daniel came from a good family and was well-educated. His future in law and politics looked like mile after mile of unlimited potential. And that's what happened until our kids were born. Daniel kept taking more time away from the office, until one day he announced he was becoming a carpenter. It's been fifteen years since his proclamation, but I can still see the determined glare in his eyes. Though I didn't agree with him, there was something about his drive I admired. My heartrate speeds up at the memory. There's something about a man who knows what he wants . . .

Shaking off the past, I push back my chair and march into Cori's office. She's supposed to be at the photographer's in thirty minutes, setting up the final plan for our family holiday photo shoot. Moving a bag off her chair, I sit down and run my finger over her touchpad. The screen comes to life. She doesn't even have it set to need a password. She should. I send information to her that's not for public consumption.

There's an email account open. It's not the one I use to communicate with her, but I recognize the top address as Daniel's. Probably something to do with my birthday next month. No wonder he doesn't want me to fire her. He's using her to help him set up a surprise.

As much as I'd like to avoid growing a year older, making that public, and having to deal with the temptation of birthday cake, I'm touched that he cares. Lately, I've wondered. Before I can stop myself, I click the email, eager to see what my dear husband has planned.

I can't wait to see you again. That seems a bit personal for a greeting to my assistant. *You understand me in a way she hasn't for so long. I'm lonely.* My mouth hangs open as the blood retreats from my extremities, leaving my arms cold and weak. I select "mark as unread" and stumble back toward my office, my stomach pitching, my eyes blurred.

No.

This can't be happening. I've built my *ministry* on a happy marriage. The room swirls and twists with the agony in my chest. Fire lights across my skin. There is no way this can be happening. I won't let it. I won't.

"Mrs. Cambridge." Jennifer is at the door. She doesn't enter the room, but it's like she can read the email across my forehead. "Are you okay?"

I blow out a shaky breath. "Just a little headache." The lie burns behind my eyes, but it's necessary. "I need to leave town. It's sort of important. Cori will have to go to Idaho for me and make the arrangements for my video conference. Please get her a plane ticket to leave tonight, and get me on the next flight to Portland, Oregon." The only place I can think to go is back to Emery House. This will be my last chance to see my college home before it's destroyed.

"When do you want the return flights?" She sets the iced tea on my drink coaster.

"Let's leave Cori's open for now." Or maybe she can just stay there. "Actually, leave mine open too."

My stomach clenches as Cori, all smiles and secrets, comes up behind Jennifer. "I'll take care of the arrangements."

I want to scream. No, what I really want to do is far more violent.

I stand, stuffing my laptop into my bag, the spike heels of my shoes shaking in the plush carpet. "Let me know when it's done. I will be at *my* house with *my* family."

❖ ❖ ❖

"Why would he do this to me?" I ask the question to no one in particular as I pull my Lexus up to the gate that protects my home and family from unexpected or unwanted visitors.

I tap the security code into the pad and the ornate iron barricade slides open, and then I remember I've given Cori the access numbers. She has free rein in the one place that should be a sanctuary.

Has she been here when I've been out of town? Have they spent time together—with my children?

My mouth turns dry and my stomach wavers.

In the last ten years, I've taught thousands, maybe hundreds of thousands, of women the art of keeping a beautiful home, successful children, and a happy husband.

I'm a disappointing punchline to a very long joke.

I can't guess how much time has passed, but the gate is closing, its automatic response to being left open. I punch in the number again and drive through as soon as the opening is wide enough to accommodate my car.

Winding my way up the drive, I take in the sprawling house with its perfectly manicured lawn, gurgling fountain, and myriad of blooming end-of-summer flowers—none of which gives me the usual puff of satisfaction. Today, the picture looks cold, and I can no longer enjoy it now that I've discovered it's an illusion.

As the garage door drops into place, I consider letting the engine run. Just going to sleep and leaving my failure behind. Wouldn't that be a treat for my critics?

That last thought is just enough incentive to kill the engine.

My heels echo along the polished cement floor to the mud room. The walls are covered in a grid of bright white cubbies with sunshine yellow baskets slid into each opening. Along the counter are two fresh bouquets of wildflowers with wide green and purple ribbons tied in neat bows at the top of crystal vases. Between them, Georgia, our white fluff-ball of a cat, stretches in the line of sun shining in from the window.

I run my fingers through the cat's long hair. The sweetness of her brings tears close to the surface again.

She pushes into me, eager for more of my attention. When was the last time I just sat and held her? When was the last time Daniel and I were together without the distraction of my endless to-do list? We used to picnic by the pond at the end of our property, laughing and dreaming. That was before we built this house, when we still lived in the falling-down three-bedroom that originally claimed this land.

When was the last time we laughed?

The back of my nose tingles with the tears I will not shed. There's nothing productive about wallowing in emotion. No one is served, no forward motion, only puffy eyes and a runny nose result from such indulgences.

I pull the cat to my neck and nuzzle into her soft fur, blaming the watering of my eyes on her feline dander. If it were possible, I'd sink into her and disappear.

A claw closes through my thin blouse and into the flesh of my upper shoulder.

With care, I disengage the cat from my body and lay her back onto her square of sunshine. What a life.

The house is huge and empty. It didn't feel this way when I walked out this morning. Suddenly, the fact that the kids are away busy with school and sports, and Daniel is gone in every way but physical, strikes me as a cruel slap across the face.

I've created this home as a showpiece, an example of how to be the wife and mother God calls us women to be. I've done countless shows from my own kitchen, had promotional photographs done in the living room and the garden, hosted fundraisers and even taught Bible study right here. It's more than walls and plaster with fine décor. This place represents my ministry and my purpose.

I climb the stairs with legs almost too heavy to make the trip. At the top, I stare out over the vaulted living room, where the stone fireplace climbs the opposite wall. Much of the furniture and woodwork were handmade by Daniel, the would-be-governor turned carpenter. From the wall of windows, I can see the edge of his workshop. The main door stands open and his rusty old pickup is backed up to the opening.

We've had that truck since we were first married. It was newish then. I haven't ridden in it for many years, probably over a decade. I bought him a sparkly new Ford for our anniversary last year. His disappointment was so real, it was like another person standing in the room. That vehicle sits in our four-car garage. Our son drives it on occasion.

Turning away from my thoughts, I dive into the grand master bedroom I share with the man who's supposed to be faithful to me for the entirety of our lives. I pull my oversize Coach suitcase from the walk-in closet and toss it across our antique wedding-ring quilt. Yanking five or six items at a time, I have myself packed within minutes.

My phone buzzes. It's a text from Cori. She's made the arrangements and will personally pick me up in twenty minutes.

I'm dizzy with the horrifying thought that my assistant is coming to my home, where my husband works only fifty yards away. That I will witness them looking at each other. That though I've missed all the signs, suddenly the feelings between them will be blatant and if I see them, I will be ruined. The truth will become undeniable. My marriage will be over, and it will take my ministry and my career with it. I'm not ready.

Not now, and definitely not here.

I flip the lid over the suitcase and zip it tight, then grab my carryon bag, which I keep packed with all the necessities for quick travel.

The suitcase clunks down the stairs behind me. In the kitchen, I carefully craft a note to *my* husband and slide it into the communication center on the refrigerator. I should take the time to go to his shop and properly say goodbye, at least tell him I'm leaving, but I can't do it. I can't look into his green eyes. I can't see him now and remember him the way I want to.

I give the cat a final pat on the head and walk out the front door, pulling my suitcase across the asphalt, along the lane, and out the gate. Before I continue on this path, there's another task I must accomplish.

Opening the casing for the gate control, I type in the master code, wait for the blinking light, then press the function I desire. In a moment, the code is changed. Cori will never enter my property again as long as I have a say about it. And Daniel will struggle if he doesn't think to use our anniversary date.

❖ ❖ ❖

"Cori, did you get the itinerary worked out?" This commute will be business, and all business. But when I return . . .

Well, by then I'll have figured out how to get Daniel to fire her himself. "I can't make the women's breakfast on the eighteenth, but send my apologies. There's a list on the drive for you. Make sure the publicity is handled for the video seminar next month. That was a disaster last year, and I don't want a repeat."

This is just the tip of the tasks I've left for her. With the travel and the details, she'll be slammed with work until I can find the best route to be done with her.

She pulls the car up to the curb at the Dallas Fort Worth airport, but hasn't answered any of my requests since we left the freeway.

"Are you hearing me?" I'm all too eager to get out of this car and be done with this woman. I can't help hoping that she's delayed in the parking garage or security so I can get to my gate without seeing her smug expression again.

"Yes. I know what I need to do." Her mouth is shaped into a tight smile that makes me want to lunge across the gap and shake her.

But I manage my own smile and pop my door open. "You have to work hard for the kingdom. This isn't playtime."

I know she's young, not even thirty, but we have a responsibility to those my ministry touches. It's God's work. There are so many women who don't have a clue how to maintain a Christian marriage, family, or home. I'm not one of them. And Cori will soon see that.

"I'll pray for you." I put one foot carefully on the curb to avoid any street gunk. "And please, let me know what you've finished so I can mark the tasks off my list."

I climb out, brush my skirt flat, and use both hands to check the shape of my hair. From the trunk, I pull my large rolling suitcase, my over-the-shoulder carryon, and my purse. The street noise silences as I leave the Texas heat behind and make my way into the building.

Again I check my phone for important emails, then pull up my boarding pass before removing my driver's license from the pocket on the side of my bag. Everything is in order for now.

I'm pre-checked so I pass by the lines of people waiting for security to accost them and enter through the side with no delay. In a moment, I'm done and off to my gate.

When I stop, the shaking starts.

I'm fine.

Get control.

Pray.

Lord, help me. I don't know what I'm thinking. I have literature to finish, four major speaking engagements before Thanksgiving, and a home to decorate for the holidays. And Daniel's indiscretion.

But I can't think about Daniel right now.

Instead, I start forming the list for Christmas in my mind. I need to find the right gifts for my staff. They'll all be in attendance when we have our annual Christmas party, plus the television cameras. I still haven't written the dialogue for our family's Christmas greeting.

And we'll need new clothes that don't match but still complement each other. We'll shoot in front of the fireplace this year. Daniel will stand behind me with his palm covering my shoulder, just like every other year. Won't he?

I need coffee. Glancing at my phone, I see there's at least thirty minutes to spare before priority boarding. They'll have refreshments on the plane, but they're never able to make the needed adjustments, so I head toward the nearest barista.

With an upside-down skinny caramel macchiato warming my hand, I return to the gate.

A couple bump down the terminal, their fingers laced, her head on his shoulder. The need to hear Daniel's voice claims me. I line my bags up on the seat and order my phone to call my husband.

"Hello?" His voice is distant. I'll have to work to keep his attention.

"Daniel. It's Victoria."

"I know. Your picture is on my screen. I got the memo. Aren't you supposed to be on a plane?"

"We're close to boarding, but I wanted to check in with you." A good wife is organized and always has a meal available for her husband, even when she's out of town. "Did you see the list on the refrigerator? I emailed you a copy just in case."

"I got it."

"Your meals are stacked in order with the individual directions on the lids. Do you need anything else? I can have someone come by if you need."

"I'm sure you've handled everything. You know, I can think for myself."

"Of course you can. The housekeeper will be by Monday morning. Please stay out of her way. It just slows her down if you chat." I tap my toe.

"I'll try to stay in my office, dear." His tone is a touch higher than sarcastic. I do this all for him, to make his life as easy as possible. I have a flight, the reunion, and an appearance, then I can get back home and fix whatever is going on with Daniel.

They announce first class boarding. "I have to go. That's me."

He grunts something and the phone disconnects. What happened to our *I love yous*?

As I make my way down the ramp, my stomach twists. The few sips of coffee I've taken do not agree with the pain I swallowed for lunch.

I settle into the leather seat and lay my head back. I'd love to kick off these pinching heels, but this isn't the place. It's the drawback of living a public life. One of them. There's also the pressure, the fact that every other woman I speak to is judging me, and I haven't indulged in a good hot fudge sundae in over fifteen years. Just once I'd like to wear sweat-pants all day, go out with a friend, and feel like I could really share my life, or just get fast food for dinner.

I didn't even realize I'd closed my eyes until a man taps my shoulder. He's huge, at least six-three, and just as broad. He's wearing the biggest cowboy boots I've ever seen and a hat to match. There may not be room for him, even in first class.

"Ma'am, I think I'm in that seat there." He nods toward the window beside me.

"Of course." I force a pleasant smile and stand out of his way. "Wel-come." That's what I do. I make people feel welcome. My ministry is all about hospitality, serving our families, and our God. I want to scream at him to find another seat or take the train.

Once we're settled again, I start to run through next week's to-do list on my phone with that manufactured smile cemented on my face while coach passengers hit me with elbows, bags, and even the feet of their small children. Why does first class board before everyone else?

I send encouraging texts off to my children, Brooklyn and Cameron, just in time for the plane to move toward the runway and the announce-ment reminding passengers to turn off cell phones.

This is the part I can do without. I fly at least twice a month, and I still have to beg God for mercy with each takeoff and landing. The plane lines up on the runway, and I anchor my fingernails into the armrests. Swirling whines from the engine grow until I can't take anything but short puffs of air. Are we going faster than usual? What is that sound? There's a banging outside.

The plane lifts and the shaking settles. Another successful departure. I won't think about landing until we start our descent, then I'll let the internal panic run wild.

"Excuse me." The flight attendant leans down beside my seat, her silky blond hair tied back in a neat bun at the nape of her neck. She looks behind her as if checking to see if the coast is clear. "Aren't you Victoria Cambridge?"

I force my eyebrows into their most interested position and grin at the girl. "Yes. Have we met?"

"No. But my mother-in-law took me to one of your seminars. She says I'm a lost cause. I think you were her last hope."

I'm still sick to my stomach from the takeoff, but I keep smiling. "Was I able to help?"

Her features fall, tears touch her lashes, and her shoulders drop. "I'm supposed to host the family for Thanksgiving dinner this year. I don't know what I'm doing, and I know she'll be waiting for me to screw up. I fly in that morning at eight. Do you have any suggestions?"

"Can you hire help?"

She bites her bottom lip between her teeth until she's steadied her emotions. "We can't really afford that."

Behind her another flight attendant stands, her face grim. "Bridgett, it's time to be serving beverages." She looks to me. "I'm sorry, ma'am."

Bridgett's head bobbles with quick nods. "Please, excuse me."

"Ma'am." The older woman clasps her hands, tilts her head, and smiles so hard it squints her eyes. "Can I get you anything to drink?"

"Club soda with a slice of lime please. Is the lime freshly cut?"

"I'll make sure yours is." She straightens and walks away.

My stomach sways and I don't believe this time it's from the takeoff. I've given Bridgett nothing. Not a plan, an affirmation, or even a dose of hope. *Can you hire help?* Of course she can't. It wasn't long ago that I was a young wife, happy just to be with Daniel regardless of our finances, the size of our home, or the quality of our belongings. I was his, and he was mine.

And that was all that mattered.

Chapter 4

Jenna

The man who had the window seat throws another glare my way before exiting the airplane's jet bridge. I don't turn to see the woman who sat on my other side. I'm sure her expression isn't much kinder.

I fidget. I can't help it. Sitting still makes me nervous, and the extra ten pounds—okay, the extra fifty pounds—don't really help me fit comfortably into the three inches of seat space.

People mill around, waiting to board the plane we just left.

All these people, and I'm alone. I consider dropping the bag that's biting into my shoulder and sobbing in a corner. Then I spot a kid with a Happy Meal.

There's no one here to see me indulge in a greasy, salty dinner. No one to question the choices of the she'd-be-pretty-if-she-lost-the-weight woman. I head down the wide hallway until I spot the golden arches.

There isn't time to rethink my decision. This truly is fast food. Within moments I'm the owner of a double cheeseburger, large fry, chocolate milkshake, and, of course, a Diet Coke. I take a table near the window and go for it with enthusiasm. The warmth of the juicy meat is salve to my injured ego. It's all about the food now. I reach for the soda to wash down a bite before ripping into the next one, but my arm scrapes the lid of the shake and it tips toward me, the cold slush spilling onto my stomach and rolling into my lap.

Jumping up, I scoop the frozen goo off my clothing and wipe at my front with paper napkins that disintegrate on contact. *Great.*

Before I can get away, an employee is there with a giant yellow mop bucket and warning signs. I could just die. So I stuff the rest of the burger in my mouth and grab the box of fries. I'm already humiliated. I might as well be full.

"I'm sorry." My last bite is still wedged in my cheek like a squirrel hoarding nuts. I pitch my trash and head away from the scene as fast as my short, middle-aged legs will carry me.

Diving through the restroom door, I take the farthest stall and relish the fact that no one can see me as long as I stay in here behind the partial door with the flimsy lock. They can't judge me if they can't see me. Maybe I'll stay here forever. There's a toilet, and I could use less food in my life. Those are my doctor's words, not mine. But of course, he's right.

Maybe if I lost this baby weight, Mark would find me attractive again.

My right hand is sticky with milkshake, and I can't take the elastic feeling on my skin any longer. I only hear one sink in use. That's as good as I can hope for.

Opening the stall door a couple inches, I scan the room. My breath jams in my throat. I can't breathe. I can't even swallow. All I can do at this moment is ease back and relock the door.

Like a little kid, I spy through the crack at the meticulously put together woman. Yes, there's no doubt. The famous Victoria Cambridge picks at her already flawless hair. From her purse she pulls lipstick, the muted shade that's oh-so-perfect for her skin tone. She applies the makeup, then blots it with a flowered tissue.

I'm forty-six years old, and I still can't pick out my own lipstick.

Looking down, I evaluate my mess. Without full use of a washing machine and shower, I have no hope of being presentable. I'll stay in this prison as long as it takes. This is not the way I plan to greet my old roommate after all these years. I've seen Vicky's seminars online. She won't find me quirky, only see me for what I am—an empty, aging failure.

I look again. Now she's doing something with her eyes. Seriously, how long is this going to take? The bag falls from my shoulder, crashing to the floor. The book I brought along to read escapes on the way down and dives into the toilet with a loud splash.

Lord, are you kidding *me?*

Frustrated tears prickle my nose. I've made the biggest mistake. All I want is to be back home right now. I want to . . .

I don't *know* what I want. To turn back the clock. To have my babies back. To be needed. To be anywhere . . .

Anywhere but here.

❖   ❖   ❖

I wake up Saturday morning later than I'd planned. A night of black-and-white reruns and a vending machine right outside the door has left me with a unique kind of hangover. The three empty soda cans and colorful candy wrappers mock me now. But last night, I felt like I couldn't do without them.

I tug the curtain open with both hands. The morning welcomes me with the rumble of a garbage truck followed by a blaring car alarm. What was I thinking? I can't go to Emery House. Stepping in front of the mirror, I suck in a breath. Mascara is smeared across my cheek. My gray roots are starting to show at my temples. It seems the dye only holds for a couple weeks now. My belly hangs over the elastic waistband of my pajama shorts. I've aged more than twenty-five years since leaving here. The woman in the mirror, I don't know who she is. How can I take her to the reunion?

I fling myself onto the bed, which makes a hard boom as I hit. Reaching my cell phone, I call my husband.

He answers after five rings.

"Mark, I've made a mistake. I want to come home."

He clears his throat. "Take the next step. You're going to be fine."

I'm not getting through to him, and I don't have the words to express the depth of my desperation. "I think it was a nice gift, but could you get me a return flight for today? I'm homesick."

"You haven't even been gone twenty-four hours. Give it a chance. Have you seen any of your old roommates? What does campus look like? Any major changes? I wish I could be there with you, but I know you're going to have a great time. Call me tonight, okay?"

He's dismissing me like one of his students—forcing me toward independence, he'd say. The muscles in my jaw twitch. "Fine. I'll talk to you tonight, if I'm not too busy reclaiming my youth." I press the end button and immediately regret my words.

I text, "I'm sorry."

He texts back, "I know. Have a fun time."

Ugh.

After doing my best to turn back the clock on my appearance, I leave the hotel, determined to go to Emery if only to be able to tell my husband I did it.

Five minutes later I'm sitting in the economy-class tin can I rented from the airport. The seat belt digs into my neck as I take the familiar route toward campus. A right turn past the taco joint, and I'm nearly there. I can see Emery House halfway down the block. Nothing has changed.

When I graduated college, I was the president of Emery House. The leader. I'd been a cheerleader. I was the one people came to for guidance. I was important and needed. What will they expect me to be like today? Will they assume I've made something of my life? I don't regret a minute with my kids. Having three at one time quickly changed our family dynamic, but I jumped in and made them my world. The homeschool years are a time I will treasure forever. And the high school years, I was so busy helping with fundraisers for drama and sports activities, the time flew by.

But now a new school year has begun. And it's someone else's turn. I'm that mom whose kids graduated. If they remember me at all.

Two thirtysomething women walk past my car. Their voices are loud and every few steps they turn toward each other and giggle.

I want to go back. To be that girl again.

Pulling down the visor, I check my makeup. It's as good as it's going to get. Then I step out, paste on a smile, and try to revive the girl in this old woman's body. It's just acting.

But then, wasn't it always a bit that way?

At the walkway, I pause. The tree in the front yard towers strong, its broad leaves just starting to turn. They'll be scarlet. I know, because I picked that tree out myself. And together, we planted the little seedling, Vicky, Hope, Ireland, and me. It was our farewell of sorts.

And here comes the emotion. It's climbing up from my toes. How could the university close this house? This is more than college housing. We were family.

"Are you an alum?" A young woman with bouncy curls comes through the great double doors toward me.

"Yes. I was president." I straighten, trying to present myself with an air of authority. "Did you live here?"

"I did." Her eyes are sad. I can see the house has the same effect on her residents even now. "I was the final Emery House president. That's what they call me. I kind of hate it. It makes me feel like I failed Emery, and all of you. We did everything we could."

I think back over the emails. The students had organized a year-long campaign to change the college's mind. But it didn't work. From where I stand, I could have told them it wouldn't, but they're still young and hopeful.

"You all did a great job. Thank you for organizing this event. A lot of women will want to say goodbye." Oops. There are the tears again. I blink them back.

"Come on in." She ushers me through the doors to a desk set up in the foyer. I sign the guestbook, then start my own personal tour.

Climbing the front staircase, I'm touched by the notes taped to the walls. Farewells. Thank-yous. Memories. It feels . . .

Like a part of me I'd forgotten is being permanently ripped away.

At the top of the stairs a door opens into the side of a long hallway.

I know every room, every door. I turn to the right and take the first entrance on my left. Row after row of three-high bunk beds line the room, but they've been stripped bare. I close my eyes and can see the bedding pouring over mattresses, the fans in the windows. I can hear the hum and the soft snores.

"It's like we never left, isn't it?"

I swing around. Vicky has one hand on her hip and the other holding a leather handbag embellished with gold that perfectly matches her unblemished pumps. She tilts her head, revealing the young girl in her eyes. Standing here, together, it wipes away years of missing her. Now I really do feel like I'm home.

"It sure is."

She reaches her arms out and I'm there, squeezing a bit too tight and holding on a bit too long.

We step back, and I take her hand. "Let's go to our room."

Weaving through the maze of beds, we exit the sleeping porch and head down the hall. At the corner door, we turn to each other, exchanging smiles like the years are gone. When we enter, it looks so much like it did the day we came back from summer break, ready to be decorated and made into our own space. This is one of the bigger rooms, a four-student room.

I walk to the window and touch my hand to the closet door. "Do you remember Ireland's gigantic Recycle, Reduce, Reuse poster?"

"How could I forget?" Vicky drops her purse on a desk near the door. "She was something else back then. All passion and spirit. I imagine she still is."

"Imagine all you want, but you're wrong."

I turn to the door, my heart beating just below my collarbone. Ireland is an older version of her naturally beautiful self. She always has been lovely, but now, there's sadness in her big brown eyes. Something about the way her smile only lifts one side of her mouth brings out the mother in me. Without hesitation or even a thought, I close the space between us and wrap my arms around her.

She stiffens, so much like she did in the beginning. The untold brokenness has returned. Where did the years of healing go? I step back, giving her space, and giving me a chance to look at who she's become.

IRELAND

Jenna and Vicky stare, their mouths hanging. It's the expression I expected. Gaping. Like they've seen a ghost. That could be right. I'm sure I look like an apparition to them.

"Ireland?" Jenna moves forward. She's reaching out, and I can see where this is going. Her arms encircle me while mine remain raised as if I'm dealing with the cops. Her shampoo is familiar, chemically floral, laced with memories.

When Jenna finally lets me go, she steps away and joins Vicky.

One of Vicky's eyebrows cocks up. Gag. Judgment. I don't need this. I harden my jaw.

She makes a move at me, but must think better of it and stops a few feet away. "I didn't expect to see you here."

"Actually, I'm here for a speaking engagement. It's a coincidence."

"There's no such thing." Vicky eyes me. "I'm sure God has a purpose."

I grind my molars together. Is this how it's going to be? If so, I have no issue spending the rest of the weekend in my hotel room. "Maybe."

"How is Skye?" Jenna tugs at the hem of her shirt.

"I'm sure he's fine. We haven't spoken in years."

Shock registers on their faces and a small gasp puffs from Vicky's mouth.

"We're divorced." As if that needs to be said.

Vicky's eyes are still as round as platters. "I'm so sorry. Is there any chance you can work it out?"

Is she *kidding*? Instead of answering, I step around them and over to my window that looks out on the field where we played Ultimate Frisbee with the guys' house on the next block.

"It was for the best. I'm happy." Even I hear the loss in my words. Great. I've set myself up. I know what Vicky is thinking. Please. If there is a God somewhere, don't let her say it. I will not be able to handle that question.

"Has anyone seen Hope?" Jenna sounds as perky as ever. "She's all we're missing now."

Really? Do we owe each other something? We were college roommates, not sisters. I can't look them in the eyes. It's too hard to keep the memories back when I see Vicky and Jenna here in this room. Like we used to be. But I can't deny my desire to see Hope.

"I checked. She still owns the coffee shop around the corner. She'll be here." I want her to be here. Hope never made me feel like the odd one. She's the roommate I stayed in touch with the longest. But she's also the one who knows my secrets.

Loud voices boom down the hall. A moment later four women, probably somewhere in their thirties, bust into our room. One has a toddler on her hip and another is so pregnant I want to stand way back.

"Sorry," the pregnant one says. "Was this your room too?"

Jenna nods and starts to speak, but the one holding the toddler squeals, cutting us all off.

"You're Victoria Cambridge." She covers her mouth with her hand.

Oh brother. *Victoria*. Now would be a great time to tell everyone about when Vicky got locked out of the house one night, climbed the drainpipe, and tumbled over the balcony outside the sleeping porch just to come face-to-face with an opossum.

Yeah, she's classy.

Vicky shifts to plastic mode and extends her hand. "It's so nice to meet another Emery girl. I hope y'all enjoy your time together." Then she steps out of the room. What, are we supposed to follow like her roadies? But we do.

I glance at Vicky. "What's with that accent?"

"What accent?" she drawls. "I guess I've been living in the South long enough to pick up the culture."

Culture? All I see is the fakeness of a Stepford wife. I shake my head. That's not fair. This reunion is bringing out the judgmental kid in me. I've come too far to go back now. Center. I breathe in slow, out slow.

"What are you doing?" Vicky studies me.

"Meditating."

"Why?"

"Why not?"

She dips her chin. "Because praying would be a better use of your time."

"How would you know what would be a good use of my time? If I recall, we haven't been in the same room for years. Years."

Jenna weaves between us. "I'm starved. How about we check out the buffet?"

Vicky keeps looking at me as if I've grown a second nose right next to the old one, then her eyes shift toward the ceiling.

I know exactly what she's thinking. It's the same thought that's been on my mind all morning. Our letters. "Let's just get them, burn them, and move on, okay?"

"Why would we destroy them?" Jenna asks.

Vicky shakes her head. "I'm with Ireland. Jenna, you stay down here and watch for anyone coming down the hall."

I look Vicky over. She's wearing a snug skirt and spiked heels. "Why don't you stay down here? You're not really dressed for espionage."

She unthreads her arm from an overdone purse and hands it to Jenna. "I'm as capable as you are."

Looking to check that no one else is around, I reach up and grab hold of an antique doorknob dangling on the end of a long rope. The hinges squeal as I pull down the attic door and the stairs uncurl. Before I can release the knob, Vicky is climbing the steps.

The air is hot in the attic and dust swirls in the lines of light coming from unsealed cracks. I pull the stairs up so no one can see where we've gone, and then feel around over my head until my fingers graze the pull string for the one hanging bulb. It clicks on, and we're surrounded by insulation and forgotten treasures.

Vicky coughs. "They haven't cleared this stuff out yet. That's good for us."

Lifting my shirt collar over my nose I follow her to the far side. I can't imagine the chemicals this air is laced with. It's a cancer factory, and I'm up here voluntarily.

Along one wall is an opening where there once was a pocket door. Why this was ever built is a mystery that long ago died with the designer, but it provided a secret place to store our letters. No one would ever think to stick their hands into this dark hole.

Clasping her palms together, Vicky stares at the wall. Her nose is twisted and wrinkled.

"I'll do it." I step forward, but her arm extends, blocking me.

"No. I'll get it."

Looks like the queen has something in her letter she doesn't want the world to see. But who am I to judge? My letter will be ripped up before I get two steps down the ladder.

Vicky kneels on a beam and reaches her hand into the hole. She leans farther, her arm disappearing to the shoulder. Okay, she has more to her than I gave her credit for.

Finally, she sits back, her shoulders drooping. "They're gone."

Chapter 5

The battle has only just begun, but I'm not in the lead and that claws at my nerves.

Jenna answers with a shrug when I explain the letters are missing, stolen from our very secure hiding place. I shouldn't be surprised by this nonchalant attitude. What would she have to hide? For that matter, what would she have to lose?

We were so young and foolish with our silly games and sentimental choices. My thoughts shift to my daughter. Will she be so frivolous with her life? These are the kinds of things my mother was always trying to warn me of, but I wouldn't listen. I couldn't see past the coldness of her presentation to the wisdom of her advice. Brooklyn doesn't listen any better.

Those letters didn't disappear on their own. Somewhere out there, a stranger has read my deepest thoughts, my flaws, my mistakes. Somewhere in the world there's a person who could embarrass me and my family. It doesn't matter that the letter was written by a young woman who hadn't yet found herself. And it won't matter that the words scrawled on that page were only what I thought I felt at the time. Perspiration prickles at the back of my neck. My world has never been so out of my control.

As I run my fingers along my hair, they come away with clingy strands of spider web. My stomach clenches and a shiver slides across my skin. I shake my hands as my feet do an Irish jig, but the offensive strings won't fall free.

Ireland snatches the web and wipes it across the side of her loose-woven hippie pants. "You've got more on your shoulder."

I slap my hand across both sides but find nothing. When I look back at her, she's grinning. And I've fallen for it. "Very funny."

One natural, but oddly perfect, eyebrow lifts. "I thought so."

My breathing grows short as my face warms. I'm no one's joke. Especially not to someone who doesn't value me enough to stay in touch. I can't believe the gall of this woman. I step toward her, not really thinking what's coming next, but I don't care. I just need to let off some of the stifling tension that's binding so tight across my chest it's strangling my lungs.

Jenna slides between us. "Seriously. The buffet?" She rubs her palm over her round stomach. She was never one of those stick-thin type of cheerleaders. Jenna was built like a gymnast, short and teaming with muscles. It's like she gave up on herself, and it looks like it was quite a while ago. Has she ever seen any of my teachings? Could I have helped her? Or would I have been as useless to Jenna as I was to the flight attendant?

IRELAND

In the dining room the food table is dressed up with balloons and ribbons, items that will surely find their way to the landfill by next week. The food looks much like it did in college. We walk down the line with plates in our hands. Jenna scoops a bit of everything, Vicky takes tiny servings, and I search for just one thing that I'm willing to put into my body.

This is not a vegan wonderland. The smell of cooked animal flesh makes my stomach shift. There are hotdogs and hamburgers, obvious nos. There's pasta, but it's drowning in some sort of cream sauce. The bread has a layer of garlic butter so thick it should be called frosting. The green beans are in a casserole with a slimy, dairy-based topping. Even the fruit salad has been assaulted with whipped cream.

"Aren't you hungry?" Jenna stares at my empty plate.

"I'm hungry." I can't believe she didn't hear my belly growl. "I'm also vegan."

"There's no meat in the pasta."

"Vegan. Not vegetarian. I don't eat anything that has animal products in it."

Vicky huffs. I imagine her Texan diet includes a plateful of dead calf every night.

Jenna inspects her plate, then looks at my empty one. "How do you survive?"

It's ignorant, but I can't help smiling. Jenna is hard not to love. "It's easy at home. Just a struggle when I'm in a place out of my control."

A girl walks in the back door with a tray of vegetables roasted on the barbeque I can see through the window. The smell is rich and herby and wonderful. "Excuse me."

She smiles and sets the tray down.

"Were these with the meat at any time?"

From the corner of my vision I see Vicky's mouth twitch. I'm sure she'd love to tell me how to be a good guest about now.

"No. We had them on a disposable tin tray."

I scoop a few. "Do you realize what an impact that choice will have on the environment?"

Her face is blank. "What?"

Jenna cuts in. "Please be sure to recycle the tin."

If only that were enough, but it's as far as we'll get today.

I stab my fork into a chunk of cauliflower, browned on the edges and sprinkled with green herbs. Before I even find a seat, the veggie is in my mouth, and the flavor is bursting to life on my tongue.

Vicky waves us to a table near a full-length window. It's the same place we sat in college. We were stuck in our habits back then. Or maybe it was Vicky all along. She liked to do everything the same every day, and we just went along with her. I'm not that girl anymore, but a savory scent is floating up to my nose from my plate, so this time I won't argue.

As we sit, Vicky reaches out her hands to both of us. Jenna tucks her napkin onto her lap then connects her fingers with Vicky's.

"Really?" The muscles in my forehead squeeze.

"Yes, really." Vicky looks more like a disappointed teacher than any kind of friend.

I tuck my hands beneath the table where I claw at my legs. The pinch of my fingernails bites through the fabric and gives me enough distraction to keep my mouth from running out of control.

After another look of disgust thrown my way, Vicky bows her head and proceeds with a blessing over the food that sounds like it's come from the very mouth of the pope.

By the time she says amen, I've stuffed my face with two more bites, and I'm too busy chewing to care what she has to say about my heathen lifestyle.

The tension is more than I can breathe away, more than can be remedied with the refreshment of lavender oil. We need Hope. She was always our glue, the one that connected us regardless of how clearly different we all were. I don't know why it matters to me, but it does. I want to feel for a moment that the four of us really existed. That the memories are true, not something devised by need.

Because without that, we are truly lost.

VICKY

I haven't been called Vicky by anyone but Daniel since I started my ministry. It's a strange sensation, being her, being called by that old name, seeing these two.

Jenna is still the same on the inside. She's as perky as ever, but sometimes her eyes seem to cloud. When she talks about her children, the glow returns. I love my kids, but there's always a distance when we're together. A teenage void I don't know how to cross.

"So, Carrie is studying to be a teacher." Jenna barely breathes before taking on the next sentence. "She's at school in Eastern Washington, so she could come home on long weekends. Maybe she will. I talk to her every Wednesday. On Thursdays I Skype with Caroline. She's very busy with starting pre-law in Southern California. I worry about her there. It's so far away, and you know what they say about that area of the state. And Calvin, I can only talk to him when he calls. He won't be able to do that for a few more weeks. He's at basic training. It sounds like his commanding officer is a major pain. I'd love to get my hands on him. Maybe I'll be able to next month at Calvin's graduation. We'll all be there. I can't wait, except I don't know what will happen to my son next. I worry about him."

Ireland sets her fork down on the edge of her plate. She's as earthy as ever. Tucked in a drawer in my office is a copy of one of Ireland's crazy-about-the-environment articles. I don't agree with much of what she pronounces, but I couldn't discard it. In the picture, she's covered in piercings and her hair is long with clumps of dreadlocks. The piercings and the dreads are gone now. I want to look more closely, but I know I'll just offend her. Her hair is cut short and the tresses are a beautiful chestnut brown, with silver threads creating a brilliant highlight rather than giving her an aged appearance. There's not a bit of makeup on her face. She's gorgeous, and angry. She didn't even pray before diving into those veggies.

"Let's go to her." Ireland stands as if it's been decided.

"What?" I ask. "Go to whom?"

"She's talking about Hope, right?" Jenna gets up too, but her gaze takes a turn, and for a moment she's staring at the cake like it's gold.

Ireland nods, and for the first time in years, I feel like the next move isn't up to me. I'm riding on their wave.

I run my fingers across the smooth beads that hang at my collarbone. Ireland is still powerful. She was the one I clashed with, the one I couldn't control, the one I've missed so very much.

She's also the one I've let down the most. No longer. Ireland is my new project. I'm going to bring her back into the fold, even if it means driving myself into a straitjacket from dealing with her nonsense.

I collect my plate, my napkin, and my empty water glass, then take them to the kitchen like we did when we lived here.

Former students weave in and out of every room, too many staring at me to see if I'm really who they think I am. I despise that. I'm a person. Believe it or not, I still have a feeling or two.

"I'll drive." Who knows what these two have rented.

Ireland curves her finger into one of her short curls. "It's only a few blocks. I'm sure we can still make the walk. Unless you two have gotten old." Her lips bend up, lines etching into her temples, her cheeks lifting her thin glasses higher.

"Okay, I'm in." Jenna's face is as round as a basketball. She's still so cute, innocent, even childlike, but she doesn't look like exercise is common-place in her life.

I look down at my own feet. I love these shoes, the look of them any-way. But the pointed toes, high lift, and spiked heel are not exactly walk-friendly.

Ireland's head cocks, a challenge.

"Let's go then." Challenge met.

JENNA

At Ireland's suggestion, we walk the half mile to the coffee shop. We used to make this trek all the time in college. We're not twenty any-more. At least I'm not. Even then I struggled to keep up, my legs signifi-cantly shorter than my roommates'. Now I'm carrying along the weight of twenty-five years spent perfecting my chocolate chip cookie recipe. And it's heavy.

Vicky's fancy shoes, which probably came from a store I can't even afford to walk past, click along the sidewalk like the giggling of judgmen-tal middle schoolers. Why am I here? I can only pray that seeing Hope will put everything back in perspective. She was always a star in that way, but still so quiet, behind the scenes.

As we cross the street and make our way through the small parking area, I run my sleeve over my forehead and fan my hand in front of my face. But I'm sure I still look like the average American woman if she were forced to climb Mount Everest.

There's a new sign over the door: House of Hope. A ladder rests on the siding and a hammer lies in the bark mulch. Maybe the job of running this place is what kept Hope away from Emery this morning. Maybe it wasn't that she doesn't want to see us, or me.

Vicky gives the door a tug and it pops, rather than slides, open. But she doesn't even stumble. She's all grace, all confidence, all perfection. My kids might say that she's "all that." I'm the bag of chips.

Even with this many years and the change in ownership, the scent of spicy and earthy mix together here and bring me back even more than being in Emery. We had so much to look forward to. It's like our fearless enthusiasm was bottled up and stored, but when we stepped through the door, someone unscrewed the lid.

We approach the counter. Emotion bubbles in my chest. I'm afraid to speak. I only bite at my lower lip.

A woman walks through the swinging half door that separates the kitchen from the counter where the baristas mix up sweet, rich coffee drinks. I put my hand to my chest and feel the thump of my overworked, under-cared-for heart. She's the image of Hope. Dark blond waves trace her face, the longer ones pulled back and held in place by a red hand-kerchief. Freckles are sprayed across her nose, and her eyes are the same crystal blue that had all the young men staring at Hope.

For the first time since we met up in our old room, maybe the first time since we met, the three of us stand silent, shoulder to shoulder. It's crazy, but we've gone back in time. I run my hand over my middle. No, I haven't. In my mind I know this must be her daughter, but I don't really want her to say that yet. Any moment Hope will walk out here and the beauty of being young again will be gone as we see the wrinkles and lines on her aged face.

"What can I get you?" The spell is broken.

"We're looking for Hope. We lived with her in college." I look from Ireland to Vicky, ready for one of them to take the lead.

"I was wondering if you'd make it." She dries her hands on a bar rag and hangs it on the handle of a cupboard. "I really didn't think you'd all three be here at once. Although I prayed you would."

The girl positions her hands on her hips. "I'm Em, Emery Blue James. Hope's daughter."

Vicky nods. "I have your birth announcement framed in my office. You've grown."

The sentimentality of that statement makes me tilt my head and give Vicky a good long look. That's the kind of thing I would do. But I don't remember what happened to Emery's announcement. I do remember the tears I shed looking at her precious face in the photograph. We'd been trying to have a baby, and I'd just had another month of failure to conceive verified. I don't even think I sent a congratulatory card.

I cover my face with my palms. That's when it had started for me. That's when I began to pull away. For almost twenty years I've blamed circumstances, but it was deeper. I was jealous.

My first apology will be to Hope. "Is your mom around?"

Em's eyes shine. She blinks hard and blows out a breath.

And in that instant before she can speak, when the coffee shop seems to go silent, I see it. Behind the double-wide espresso machine, in a frame with Scripture burned into the wood, is a photograph of Hope. It hardly looks like her with the bright pink shirt, the purple scarf tied tight around her head, and the ashen hue of her once rosy complexion, but the eyes give her away. And I know what's coming next.

If I could run, if my feet would only move from the place they're glued to the floor, I'd be out of here before I had to hear the words. But I'm stuck.

"Mom passed away last February." Em fidgets with a strand of her hair. "She fought hard. For a while we really thought she was going to beat it, but then there were more complications."

A tear spills over my lashes, runs down my cheek, and wets the crease of my neck. Before I can even manage to look for a napkin, Vicky is pressing one into my palm. She's stoic, solid. It's Ireland who's really hit. She doesn't cry. Her arms are tight across her chest, and her jaw is so taut that it quivers under the muscle strain. The way her eyes glare at the picture of Hope, if I didn't know her like I did, I would think she was angry. But she's only trying to hold it together. Some things don't change.

VICKY

Hope is gone. The friend and the feeling. Above the music floating down from speakers attached to the coffee shop ceiling, the hum and the buzz of conversation fills the gaps. And I don't fit. Not anymore. Was I myself when I shared this wobbly table with my roommates all those years ago, or am I me now?

Please don't let it be now.

A burst of cold air rushes us as the door swings open, banging against the wall.

And with it comes a mountain man—no, woman. She yanks off her knit cap and two silver braids fall over her shoulders.

"Glenda." Em is around the counter and to the woman in an instant. "I was hoping you'd be in today."

I dredge my memory for a picture of Hope's mother, but then remember that she died young, of breast cancer. My hand covers my heart, the pounding like a kettle drum beating with worry. Will this be what happens to Em too? When was my last mammogram?

Em threads her fingers into those of this character of a woman and pulls her toward our table. A sparkle has ignited in Em's eyes. The stranger has done something to revive the Hope-like joy in her. There must be a special quality under that sun-leathered skin.

"What brings you down from the hills?" Em asks her as they near us.

"I like to come pay my respects to your Ma when I'm in town, and I have a few flyers to hang. I decided to take one last trip up the mountain in a few days. Thought I'd try to pull together a group."

"I'd like you to meet my mom's old friends." Em introduces us.

"I remember Hope talking about you three. You're the ones she said were in need of prayer. I see what she meant."

The implication stiffens my spine. I reach my hand out to shake Glenda's, momentarily startled by the way her palm scratches mine, then change the course of this conversation. "Have you known Em long?"

"Since she was a little tot." Glenda indicates knee-high. "Her mama helped me out of a tough spot once upon a time."

Hope helped Glenda? The woman standing next to our table looks like she could push a mountain into a valley if dared. But there's the tiniest glimmer of emotion on her face when she mentions Hope. She knew the same girl I knew. My bones ache to have been here with Hope as she battled. But I've never been brave. Not really.

"Glenda takes groups into the Cascades on survival trips. Mom always wanted to go, but I was too young, then she was too sick. I wish she would have had the chance." She turns a quirky smile toward Glenda. "I thought you said the group last spring was the last."

"I mean it this time. I'm growing old. Can't be responsible for taming the crazy out of people no more." She scratches at her jawbone as if she's got stubble. She doesn't. "You folks be interested in climbing into the Cascades and learning a thing or two about life and survival?"

Before I can stop myself, I gasp. It isn't very ladylike.

"Tell us more," Jenna says.

With the tip of my shoe, I attempt contact with Jenna's shin to shut her up.

Ireland lets out a startled cry. Scrunching her mouth tight, she levels a glare in my direction.

"I teach women the skills they need to survive and thrive. What better way to do that than to be out in God's country? Out in the crisp, clean air, a woman can find the person she was meant to be. It's God's way of granting empowerment." She claws at the side of her head with chipped fingernails brown around the cuticles.

"I think we're good." I uncross my ankles. This description sounds kind of like what I do, minus the dirt. "We're just here for a short visit." My stomach wobbles like the table when I hear myself talk about going home. I'm not ready.

"Don't speak for all of us." Ireland tips back in her chair. "You may not be up for the challenge, but maybe Jenna and I are."

"You have a lot of nerve." I lean across the table. "For your information, I have a life. And it doesn't include traipsing around in the woods to prove to you that I can." I glance at Glenda. "I'm sorry."

"No apologies needed. Some can hack it, some can't."

I'm about to put this woman and Ireland back on the straight path when Jenna's chair screeches back and she stands.

"I want to try."

She's got to be kidding. I mean, really. Jenna is five foot nothing and built like a marshmallow.

Glenda pulls a piece of paper out of her leather satchel.

Ireland eyes the bag in the same way she did the meat back at Emery.

"Here you go, girl. Give me a call when you're sure. I'm headed up on Monday with or without a group. Number's on the bottom."

"I'd like one too." Ireland holds out her hand. For the first time since graduation, I see the smile I remember spread across her face. "Come on, Vick. Don't be the girl who's afraid to get a little dirty."

She ruins my sweet memory.

I hold out my hand. "This doesn't mean I'm going," I say as Glenda presses the flyer into my palm. We're all just being polite.

Chapter 6

Jenna

I've missed Burgerville. They don't have this drive-through in California. It's an Oregon specialty, a staple in college. Even Mark would understand the necessity of a stop here. And, it's not an excuse, but I *am* hungry. Vicky watching me all afternoon not only ruined my appetite, but I think the anxiety burned off more calories than an hour at the gym.

The blue Volvo in front of me edges forward. I unroll my window in preparation for my turn. Blue Volvo orders a salad and water. Why come to Burgerville for bunny food?

This is not the kind of drive-through that means fast food. I could read a chapter while waiting, but the cars finally move another length, and it's my turn.

"What can I get for you?" a woman's voice crackles over the speaker.

Years will probably pass before I get another chance at Burgerville. "I'll have the Tillamook cheeseburger, fries, an order of the green beans, and a chocolate monkey shake."

I'll count those green beans as veggies even though they're fried. Heck, potatoes are a plant. I'm good.

She spits back my total which sends a shiver of regret through my middle. But I don't change my order. This is my time. Didn't Mark say I'm supposed to enjoy this trip? Find myself or something like that?

As if on cue, my phone starts to sing the eighties love song that means my husband is calling. I grab it, and hit the answer button before really thinking about the consequences. "Hello."

"Hey, there. How's the trip going?"

The Volvo pulls forward another car length. I roll up my window, cutting the outside noises. "It's good. I've seen Vicky and Ireland. The house looks the same. But it's sad."

"What about Hope?"

I know his question is innocent, but I want to scream at him for mentioning her name. Emotion makes my lips tremble. I hate technology. It's forcing me to spill horrible news and hear his reaction without being able to feel the warmth of his protective hug. Why did we ever leave the era of letter writing and telegrams?

"Jenna?"

"I'm here. Hope died."

There's only silence on the other end. Does he expect me to say more? Am I obligated to relate to him the horrifying picture of Hope when she'd already shrunk under the influence of chemotherapy?

"I'm so sorry. I wouldn't have sent you if I'd have even thought for a moment this could be the outcome. I'll make arrangements for your flight tomorrow."

Suddenly, I'm not ready.

A car horn sounds behind me. Looking forward, I see the Volvo is gone. I pull up to the window. A woman holds a brown paper bag in one hand and leans toward my car. I just stare. Frozen.

"Mark, can you hold on for a minute?"

"Sure."

I cover the mouth end of the phone with my palm and push the button to open the window with the other hand.

The woman rattles off my total, passes me the bag and extends her hand for payment.

With only my left hand to work with, I set the bag on the passenger seat and retrieve the cash from my purse. When I finally have everything, I ease forward and park in the nearest space.

"Okay, sorry."

"Burgerville, huh?"

My stomach wobbles. "What?"

"I heard most of that. Enjoy your burger. That's a delicacy."

Tears prickle my eyes. "I met a lady today who leads survival weeks. Hope wanted to go. I was thinking . . ."

"What?"

"Maybe I'd go."

"On a survival week?"

"Yes. Of course."

"That sounds like an interesting plan. We should talk about that. Maybe we could do it next summer. I wonder if the kids would be interested."

I'm struck by how he's stepping into something that feels oddly too personal to share with my family. It's about me. About Hope. About the four of us. "I need to do this on my own."

"Jenna? Are you serious?"

"Of course I am." The shaking in my arms is screaming another answer. I snag a handful of fries and stuff them into my mouth. Even the salty, fat-laced wedges lack flavor next to my words.

He chuckles. "I don't think that's the best idea."

And there it is. The words that cut me open and let the anger spill out. "You don't think I can do this? Well, I can. I'm not the helpless, middle-aged woman you've been living with. There's a whole lot more to me, and I very much intend to prove that to you and anyone else who thinks they can tell me what to do."

"Whoa. I'm not saying you can't. I'm just saying it's not a good idea." I can picture the way he's probably holding a hand up like I'm a horse requiring an order and he's the horse whisperer. "Come home tomorrow. We'll talk this through."

"No. Reschedule my flight for a week from Tuesday. That's when I'll be coming home. Not a day earlier. And when you see me, you can apologize for doubting me."

"Come on, Jenna. You're being ridiculous."

"Goodbye, Mark. I have important preparations to attend to. I'll see you a week from Tuesday." I press the end button and throw the phone onto the back seat.

What have I done?

IRELAND

The air outside is fresh and crisp, with just the smallest hint of winter. I usually love this time of year—the feeling of school starting and new beginnings—but not now. It's the start of something all right. However, there may never be another first day of college for this professor.

The survival week may be the opportunity I've been asking the universe to provide. A way to get into nature and be empowered by distancing myself from human interference. I'll plant my bare feet in the earth and grow back into the woman I dreamed I'd someday be. Or, at the very least, I'll be unreachable when the news of my disgrace hits the media.

I emailed Professor Jensen my apologies, a promise to reimburse the university for my hotel stay, and an assurance that I'd come back on my own dime to speak with her students. This opportunity is too big to let anything get in the way.

After Glenda left, our sad excuse for a reunion started to crumble. When I suggested we all go back to our own hotel rooms, there was not a single argument. Jenna requested we get together for breakfast in the morning, but Victoria had a prearranged church thing. I left before she could insist we join her. Or would she be too embarrassed to be seen with me?

So I have the morning to prepare for the trip. It's hard to be in Carrington, hard to be with them, hard to know how close my son is. I can't connect with anything while all these people are pulling me into the vacuum of the past. But I'm not ready to say goodbye either. The reality that this could be the last time Jenna, Vicky, and I are together hangs in the air. No Hope makes life's vulnerability real.

I continue to walk down a side road, seeing the sign for the secondhand store a block in front of me.

No Hope. It's a crazy play on words, but there's some truth there. She was the embodiment of her name. And even though I haven't seen her in years, since my River was a baby, knowing she's gone darkens my world.

A tremble spreads over my body. I slow my pace and take a moment to lean into the cool cement of a building. I'm no crier, but tears pound behind my eyes, wanting to change that truth. Easing my glasses from my nose, I rub them shiny on my cotton shirt. There's no going back, only moving forward.

With a shove of my palm against the wall, I force myself to keep going. Keep breathing.

The door jingles as I push it open. Musty scents mixed with incense that's been burned in a confined space hit me as I step in. Behind a counter piled high with clothes, a girl leans back on a stool, her feet crossed on top of the mound, her fingers busy with her phone.

"Welcome," she says without looking up. The piercing in her tongue is so large it slurs her speech. What have we come to? The save-the-earth movement is more of a fashion statement for lazy teenagers than a symbol of social and environmental activism.

I'm old enough to be her mother. There's a thought that needs to be shoved down hard and quick.

"I'm looking for hiking supplies. I was told this is the place."

She holds a palm up to me. "Just a sec." A minute later she kicks her feet down from the mountain of clothes and, for the first time, looks at me. "There's a room in the back. It's all that kind of thing. Don't steal. We have a camera back there." She tips her head toward a monitor I doubt she ever checks.

"No problem. Thanks for all your help." I roll my eyes.

The room she referred me to is small, stuffed with backpacks, coats, boots, and all other forms of material goods would-be hikers purchased then decided they had no use for. I guess that's good for me. I'm really going.

I drop my hemp pack on the floor and then start to dig through the merchandise. Who am I kidding? I have no idea what I'm going to need. Sure, I've camped. I've chained myself to old growth. I even lived briefly in a naturalist commune. But I've never hiked through the mountains, and I've never had any reason to know how to survive in nature.

Unfolding the flyer I took from Glenda, I look over the very short list of items she recommends. The column of belongings not to bring is much longer. But there's nothing I can't do without. I've already turned my cell off and buried it in the bottom of the bag that will stay in some back closet at the coffee shop.

After pulling seven packs off the shelves, trying each one on for size, I spot a green canvas backpack with patches covering most of the fabric. Someone took this with them all across Europe. They hiked the Pacific Crest Trail and the Appalachian Trail. Each patch has a date scrawled in black permanent marker below it. I thread my arms into the straps and hoist it onto my back.

This one is heavier than the others and the weight pulls my shoulders down ever so much, but it comes with history. There's the story of a life filled with adventure memorialized on its surface. This is the one for me. If I can't have my own history, I'll take someone else's.

As I choose the other supplies, I stuff them into the pack then take the whole thing to the counter. "This should do it." I drop the heavy load in front of the girl who's resumed her lightning-fast texting.

"K. Take the stuff out so I can add it up."

Isn't that her job? But I do it more to get away from her faster than to comply with her request.

She sets the phone aside, grumbles something under her breath, then starts to calculate the prices on the tags. "Big day for hikers. You're the second one this morning."

Alarms go off in my head. I quickly quench them with reality. Jenna's physical shape is enough to keep her away from the trail, and Vicky, well there's just no way she'd take the chance of chipping a nail in the wilderness. This will be my trip, and my trip alone. Glenda and whoever else is signed up are strangers and they will remain strangers if I have my way.

She finally rips the receipt from the register. "If you want a bag, it's five cents."

"Why would I want a bag? I just bought one."

She shrugs her shoulders. "Whatever." Before she finishes her one-word sentence, her attention is back on the black hole of technology.

I reload my purchases into the pack and strap it on. Leaving the store, I manage to knock a row of purses to the floor. For a second I stare at them, thinking how hard it will be to squat down with this weight on my back, then I look at the clerk glaring my way. Nah, she can handle this. It may be the only time she gets off that chair.

VICKY

The Lexus tires crunch over the gravel as I climb the hill to the cemetery. It's outside of town, one of the smaller locations, nothing like the finely manicured lawns of the memorial parks inside the city limits where the headstones set with precise spacing. Randomness and fir trees rule here.

Only one other car is parked in the tiny, oddly shaped lot. It's a miniature thing. A deathtrap. I sling my purse over my shoulder and open the door. The gravel is blanketed with fir needles. Swinging my legs out, I place my taupe pumps on the ground, wishing I'd thought ahead and brought more appropriate shoes for this occasion. Of course, how would I have anticipated *this* situation?

I could have stayed in touch with Hope.

I could have set my schedule aside and remembered the woman who never let me down.

I could have cared about something other than my own job.

There's no use dwelling on could haves and should haves. I've done the best I was able to with what I knew at the time. And I've done a lot of good for a lot of people. Something about being here makes me doubt myself, my life, and my ministry. Everything that consumes my days at home seems futile since I've been here. It's a perspective that's unhealthy and unproductive.

This morning I spoke to a women's Sunday school group at one of the large churches in town. There was a moment when I lost my words. My brain completely stalled. That never happens to me now. It hasn't happened since I was a twentysomething. This place is attacking me deep in my soul. I need to get back to my work and my life plans as soon as possible.

But returning home means returning to Daniel. It means learning the truth, and it means dealing with the fallout. This could be the beginning of the end for everything I know. If Daniel is truly having an affair, how will I respond? How can I forgive him? Does he even want my forgiveness?

My stomach clenches as if I've been punched, hard.

All my thoughts until now have been about how I would remake our marriage and family and my ministry in the light of his indiscretions. What if he just wants out? My hands are shaking. The skin seems to have aged since the last time I looked. My ankles are sharp and boney. I'm not the beautiful young woman I was when we married. I'm a fraud.

Without the ministry, I can't support myself or my children. Without Daniel, the ministry will crumble. Who wants marriage advice from a divorcée?

It's like someone has begun to pull the thread that will completely unravel my life. And I'm begging for them to stop. Tie it off. Weave the end back into the fabric. Let me be.

For the first time in years, I need to be comforted, but the only people who have ever done that for me are gone. Hope is buried somewhere over the hill beside me. I know she's not really there, but as far as my needs go, she might as well be.

And Daniel . . . How long has my husband been gone?

Ireland and Jenna are all I have left. But twenty-five years on pause has done irreversible damage to our friendships.

I'm alone in a cemetery. God, help me.

When I stand, I have to use the car to gain balance. My legs shake and my muscles have gone weak. I ease my way to the trunk, pop it open, and deposit my purse. The elegant arrangement of stargazer lilies, roses, and carnations fill the air with their sweet scents. I pull the flowers to my chest, inhaling. This is all I have to offer, and it's too late for Hope to enjoy them.

Keeping my weight balanced on the balls of my feet so my heels won't sink, I make my way up the path covered with damp wood chips. The air is fresh, the ground moist with the rain from last night. At the top, I see one other person. She's near the location I've been told is Hope's.

When the figure shifts, I see it's Jenna. Instinct has me taking a few steps in reverse. I come around the back of a wide fir tree, blocking most of my body from her view if she turns around.

Jenna kneels on the ground. Her knees must be wet. In her hands she holds an uneven bouquet of wildflowers. I look down at my own offering. It's a floral masterpiece. Hope would have hated it. Jenna took the time and energy to pick her flowers by hand. And she probably took the time to remember moments with Hope while she collected the blooms. She's here as an act of selflessness.

I'm here out of desperation.

The scent of my flowers has turned sickly sweet. It makes my head spin and my stomach waver. I don't belong here. And I don't belong where I've come from either.

Where do old Bible-teaching women who've lost themselves in well-meaning but pointless lives go to die?

I drop the flowers on a grave near my feet, wipe my damp eyes, and sneak away before Jenna sees me. At the car, I open the trunk and retrieve my purse. Before I get behind the wheel, I check my phone for any messages. There's a text from Daniel.

"I can't get the gate open."

I think I hear my heart crack open.

Chapter 7

VICKY

Rich coffee scents welcome me to the next step of my adventure, but I don't think any amount of caffeine will be enough to wake me from the nightmare I'm in.

I've lost my mind, pure and simple. There's no other explanation for my being here at Hope's. I'm completely fatigued in a way I've never experienced. All the years of raising my children, directing our home, trying to encourage Daniel to make his business grow, and running a giant ministry didn't create even a fraction of the kind of exhaustion that's now invading my bones like a vicious cancer. I'll never survive the task of survival. In the woods or at home.

For the first time in my life, I think failure is a genuine possibility. But failing in the wilderness is a great way to put off the disaster awaiting me in Texas. Public humiliation and abandonment trumps dirt and crawly critters. Not by much, but still, if I'm eaten by a bear it will be quicker and less painful than the slow demise I'll face at the hands of the media.

I just can't be me right now. What better way to avoid myself than to climb into the mountains? Victoria Cambridge would never do that.

"Which one are you?" Glenda leans on the edge of the coffee shop's counter. In one hand she holds a beat-up notepad. In the other, a pencil that looks like it was sharpened by beavers.

"Vicky Stevens." I gave her my maiden name when I made the reservations. No sense calling attention to my craziness. And I don't want anyone to know where I am. I want to disappear for a while.

She eyes me up and down, her eyebrows tight, like she sees the lie printed on my forehead. Am I that obvious?

"You're early. I like that." She scratches her scalp with the lead end of the pencil. "We'll have to wait on the others."

When I registered, there were no others signed up. That's how I hoped it would remain. Now, all I can wish for is a heathen or two. People who won't know me from Adam. "How many?"

"I had two of you, then yesterday, that bumped to three. A decent group, and not one with a lick of experience." She shrugs. "Just how I like it. Makes for a lot of fun."

My skin crawls. I'm not here for fun. I need a place to hide until my husband comes to his senses. Until I can find a way to fix my life.

Em glides through the kitchen's swinging door. Her eyes are big when she sees me. For a moment, her mouth hangs open. "Victoria?"

I look around making sure no other attention has been drawn our way. "I thought I could use an adventure."

She nods, but too slowly like she's trying to trick me into buying her belief in my words. "Are you ready, Glenda?" Em wipes her hands on a black apron.

"Still waiting on two more. We'll give them five more minutes to show, then we'll leave them behind. Failure before we even leave Crazyville." Her face doesn't resemble a woman confronted with a great disappointment. Instead she stands, works her lips around and yawns. I doubt she even wears a watch.

I glance at mine and make a mental note of the time then resume the door watch, tapping the toe of my sneaker. They've never touched the ground outside the gym until today. Already, I can see brown lines along the sides of the soles. It's easy to forget Oregon's mud after living in Texas so long.

The door bangs open, and Ireland and Jenna walk toward me.

My mouth gapes enough to catch a whole swarm of bees. Ireland looks like she's already climbed Mount Kilimanjaro. Her feet are tied up in hiking boots with army green denim pants tucked into thick wool socks. Her t-shirt over the top of another long-sleeved shirt, has a worn logo from some environmental cause. A purple bandana is tied around her short curly hair, the only source of real color in this ensemble.

The well-worn backpack she's wearing tells me I'm really in trouble here. Ireland has clearly hiked halfway around the world in the twenty-something years we've been apart. I've only climbed the ladder of success. A lot of good that will do me now.

"Close your mouth," Ireland orders. "We're here. Let's go."

I press my lips together and nod toward Jenna. She's ready to watch a soccer game, not hike in the woods. Both women wear a backpack and don't seem to have anything else. I've already dropped a load of my supplies in the bed of Glenda's truck.

"Glenda." Jenna squeezes around Ireland. "Are you sure we didn't need to provide anything else? I'd love to help out."

Glenda snorts. "There's always one." She turns her gaze to me. "Looks like there's two in this crew."

I splay my fingers across my chest. This woman is so full of herself. She'll see. I'm very capable. I'll show all of them. I can do whatever I set my mind to, and that means manage my marriage too. Daniel will have a change of heart quite soon. We don't miss what we have until it's gone.

IRELAND

The seams on these jeans pinch at my inner thighs. Now I remember why I banished denim for the more comforting feel of linen. And we haven't even begun to hike.

Glenda drives like a madwoman. I thought we'd surely die on the highway, but now that we've taken off on a dirt logging road, I'm positive we'll perish soon. The truck thunks and jerks each time a tire hits a pothole.

Beside me in the back seat of this gas-guzzling monster, Jenna tips her head up. She's been asleep on Vicky's shoulder for the last hour. A stream of slobber still connects them until Jenna realizes and slaps it away, her eyes wide open now.

Vicky keeps her gaze on the road, her jaw set. I guess motion sickness isn't something you outgrow. But the ability to admit weakness, that's something she's left in the past. I pull my pumpkins seeds from the outside pocket of my bag. The scent of chili and lime burst into the air when I pull open the seal, vanquishing the acrid exhaust for a moment. Vicky covers her mouth with two fingers, but doesn't look my way. She doesn't dare.

"You want one?" I hold the seeds close to Vicky. The muscles in my jaw actually twitch with held-back laughter.

The truck lurches to the side, slamming Jenna's body into Vicky's, and Vicky's into mine. Pain pinches my hip as the seat-belt buckle smashes into my flesh. We right ourselves, but now there's a glimmer in Vicky's eye. I should be mad, but I can't help it, I give in and laugh.

It's an unfamiliar feel in my mouth and the sound is odd to my ears. When did I stop laughing? Jenna joins in and Vicky inserts a snicker. Then the truck tosses the other way and we're all grasping for anything to sink our nails into.

"How much longer?" Vicky's voice is barely above a whisper. Glenda doesn't answer.

"Excuse me," I say. "How much longer until we stop?"

Glenda's shoulders shrug. "Don't know really. I've never been here."

"What?" Vicky yanks her body up against the front seat. "I thought you've done this hundreds of times."

"Sure. Just not here."

Jenna and I exchange questioning looks.

"I'm going to need further information." Vicky seems to have cured her stomach with a good dose of venom. "What do you mean you've never been here before?"

Glenda looks back over her shoulder. "Just what I said. I ain't been this way before. I'll let you know when I feel we're—"

"Watch out!" Jenna screams as she lunges onto the front seat back, grabbing for the steering wheel.

Glenda slams on the brake and the truck skids to a stop. A tree lays over the road and, to our left, the side drops off into a canyon. "Well, miss-needs-to-know-all, we're here." She cuts the engine and throws the keys under the seat. "Grab your gear. We can get a few hours in before the light gives up on us."

My legs ache from the hours crammed into the narrow backseat. Outside the air is fresh. It's cleaner than anything I've smelled in a long time. There's a possibility I'm even more appreciative after being confined in a cab that must have gotten wet at some point and never allowed to fully dry.

I fling my pack onto the soft ground near my feet. There's been rain recently. I wonder if Glenda checked the forecast, but I won't be the one to ask the question. Vicky can be that girl. Lifting my right hand to the sky, I see myself as a tree, growing toward the sun. Then I allow my body to sway with the imaginary breeze, stretching, extending, communing with nature all around us.

"What the heck is she doing?" Glenda's voice breaks into my peace.

I open one eye. She's squinting at me as if I'm a bug she's never seen before. One more breath, and I bring my arms down. So much for centering body and mind.

My attention is drawn to a moan behind me. Turning, it's all I can do not to be as rude as Glenda. Vicky has some sort of dead-animal-skin pack hanging from one arm. On her back is a brand new, tags still hanging from the straps, biggest I've ever seen, hiking pack. She's got pots and pans attached to the strap below a sleeping bag and cushion. The top extends far over her head and the cooking supplies will surely hit her legs as she walks. I kinda doubt that will be a problem, 'cause there's no way that waif of a woman will be able to take more than ten steps without a full-on face-plant.

She wobbles forward. The pack sways one way, then the other. It may only take five steps.

"Thirty years of survival training, and this is what you hand me for my final trip?" Glenda looks up at the clouds. "Nice sense of humor you got there."

Great, another believer. I may still be all alone on this adventure.

VICKY

There's no need for the critical stares. I've planned out this journey as well as anyone can when they leave with only twenty-four hours of preparation time.

"No way," Glenda says. "You're going to have to leave most of that junk here."

"I did my research. These are necessary supplies."

"Drop the pack." Glenda struts over to me.

I try to do as ordered, but the weight shifts and I start to go over sideways. Just as I'm sure my body is destined for a tumble through the dirt, rocks, and leaves, I'm stopped mid fall and righted. Ireland unstraps me and sets the backpack on the ground with the kickstand extended and holding it upright. I didn't notice that feature before.

Glenda loosens the top and starts dropping my carefully planned out items on the ground.

My inflatable pillow is tossed into the back seat of the truck without so much as a decent amount of consideration. She dumps my clothes in a stack right there on the filthy ground. I cringe and start to pick them up.

"What is this thing?" She holds my butane curling iron over her head.

"It's for my hair." My voice is small. This must be what persecuted missionary wives feel like. "I need it."

"Not a chance." She chucks it into the truck.

My makeup bag is shown no mercy. I'm allowed to keep my toothbrush, moisturizer, and toothpaste. No mascara, foundation, not even a tiny tube of lipstick. "Wait." I hold up a hand. "Lipstick is survival equipment."

She stops for a moment, looking up at me, one eyebrow higher than the other. "I think you're talking about Chap Stick. You don't have any of that."

I reach toward Jenna, but she takes a step back, abandoning me in my time of great need. When Glenda finishes, two-thirds of my needed belongings, including *The Dummies Guide to Wilderness Survival*, is piled on the back seat for anyone to steal while we're off in the woods dying a horrible-looking death.

"Well, you can count me out. I'm not going another step without my supplies." I tap my toe and cross my arms tight across my chest. The air is starting to chill, but I don't want to admit I need a sweater.

Glenda smirks. "Suit yourself, city-girl. You can stay with the truck until we come back next week." She turns to the others, the people who were supposed to be my friends. "We need to get going. Irish, you bring up the back. Holler if we start to lose the short one. I'll be in the front."

That should push the girls back to my side. But when I look to them for any signs of offense, I see only concern.

Jenna's eyes plead with me to come, but I know I've made a great mistake. This isn't my place, and I'm beginning to wonder if these are still my people. It only takes seconds for the group to disappear through the trees.

I pull my cell phone from my pocket. I may have to eat some crow and call for help. But there's no service here, and I've never had much of an appetite for crow. I turn it off and put it in the bottom of my pack. There's no way I'm leaving the road without any hope of contacting help. Reaching into the truck, I grab a roll of toilet paper that Glenda doesn't see as important. How can toilet paper not be important? For a week?

Taking a deep breath, I start after them, then turn again. I'm taking the book. Our guide looks more like a raging lunatic than a seasoned survivalist. I'll take my chance with the extra weight. And what Glenda Falls doesn't know may be the thing that saves her and all of us.

I pocket my lipstick. There's more to survival than sleeping on the ground.

It takes me ten minutes to gain enough ground to be in talking distance of Ireland. If I had the breath to speak, I'd call her Irish and see if it lit a fire in her. The ground squishes beneath my feet with every step that doesn't land on crackling sticks. Damp is already working through the seams of my shoes and the layer of cotton socks. I'll need to stop and put on a different pair soon. Then I remember, Glenda only left me one other pair. At least those are the wool-lined polar fleece. I thought they would come in handy at night.

When the great mountain mama isn't looking, I'll check the guidebook for what it says about socks.

Up ahead, Glenda's slashing of brush slows. I peek around the others to see if she's stopped, but her braids continue to swing as she struts forward on what appears to be an actual path. Maybe she has a plan after all.

Chapter 8

JENNA

There's a gap forming between me and Glenda. I realize when I've made a mistake. This is one of those times, but I'm kind of in over my head now. We've barely started and already my skin is damp with sweat. My chest burns with the anger of my previously unexercised lungs. The muscles in my calves are screaming to be elevated on couch cushions. And there's no way to disengage from the situation I've dropped myself into.

I pull at the collar of Mark's wool sweater, the scent of him rising to my nose. Tears prickle behind my eyes. If I give a moment to the fact that I've lost my children, and now I'm managing to drive my own husband away, I'll never be able to keep up. The path turns, and I watch the odd woman ahead of me start the climb uphill.

Twenty steps up and my thighs spontaneously combust. I'm sucking air and there's a pain stabbing at my side. I'm going to die on the first day, in the first hour. That's not the message I hoped to send to my family. Not the legacy I'd like to leave. Not the vacation I should have taken.

Branches crash behind us. I swing around ready to be mauled by a bear. Oh my, why didn't I think about bears when I signed up for this? Or cougars? Or wolves? This is nothing like riding around the Ponderosa with Hoss and Little Joe.

The flash of Vicky's raspberry pink coat is like seeing a savior in the distance. She's not a wild animal, and I'll get a minute to catch my breath while she makes her way to us.

"I'm so glad you changed your mind," I say when she's within earshot.

Ireland passes me, but I catch her smile before she tucks it away again.

Glenda nods her head, slowly. I haven't completely figured out how to read her yet, but I think she may be a touch relieved. Maybe she does care, or maybe she doesn't want to get sued. Whatever. As long as she keeps us alive until we find something to live for. At least me. Everyone else seems to have purpose and healthy legs.

Vicky squeezes me in a side hug. "I figured you might end up needing me somewhere down the line." Her words are so confident, but her eyes remind me of the ones I see in the mirror. Doubtful. Scared. There's something different about the Vicky that chased us up this deer trail in the woods. She's not the girl I roomed with at Emery anymore, and she's not the woman I've seen on television.

"Now that we've got that worked out," Glenda says, "let's get moving. We need to find a place to camp before the sun dips."

We trudge on, my own imagination my only respite from the pain. I try to replay an episode of *I Love Lucy*, but the pictures won't come. Not even Andy Griffith will step foot in these woods to save me. The only thing that comes to mind is a memory from Emery House.

It was spring term, and I was in the tiny room that held the only private phone, like an indoor phone booth. Through the long windows in the accordion-style door, I could see Hope, Ireland, and Vicky, their arms linked, Ireland's eyes closed as she silently prayed.

I lifted the phone to my ear and dialed my dad's number. When he answered, my breath caught. In the months since I'd left home, he'd become harder and harder to reach.

But getting him on the phone turned out to be the least of my problems. By the time I hung up, my spirit was broken. I'd never be carefree again. No amount of cheerleader spunk could ever erase the words I'd just heard.

I stood there with only a thin layer of glass and wood separating me from my crumbling future. Hope was the one to push it open. She didn't wait for me to step out into the hall. Instead, she reached in and pulled me into her arms where I broke down and sobbed.

We were back in our room before I could calm myself enough to speak.

"What did he say?" Vicky gripped my hand. "Why hasn't he paid your tuition bill?"

I shook my head. "I don't understand what's happening. It's not fair." Sliding onto the floor, I sat with my best friends in the whole world flanking me. "He spent my college money on a trip to Belize."

"He's going on a mission trip with your college money?" Ireland squeezed my knee.

"Nope." I tipped my head up and made eye contact with Ireland. "He's been writing to a woman down there. I don't know how they got connected, but he's decided to move there and live with her."

"Marry her?" Vicky asked.

"Just move in. That's that. He says it's his life, and I have no business telling him what to do with it. He's got to put himself first."

Hope's body deflated. "You're kidding."

"It's not April Fool's Day, and my father is not funny. I'll have to leave college."

Tears sting my eyes now just like they did that day. Even the memory is hard to take. I had nowhere to go. No home. No family. My mother had died during my senior year of high school. And I had no idea her death would take my father too.

When I voiced my grief at this realization it was Vicky who leapt up. "That's a bunch of garbage. You have a family. You have us. And there's no way in this world I'm going to let you leave here. Do you understand me?" Her words were like commands, and I nodded, still knowing there was really no hope.

Two days later, I put my last sweater in a box and sealed it with packing tape. My car was parked in the loading zone in front of the house, half-packed. My future was a job in a diner back home, a guilt offering from one of my mother's old friends. And all I could think of was how could I possibly return to the place my father, *the good pastor*, had left behind. And the humiliation that waited for me there.

That's when Vicky threw the door open, making my heart leap into my throat. "This just came for you." She slid a thick letter across the desk. "Open it."

"It's probably a bill."

"You haven't even looked at the return address."

"Connecticut? I don't know anyone in Connecticut."

"You don't, but I do."

I pulled my finger through the seal, slicing into my flesh. It was that kind of day, week. Sucking my stinging finger, I poured the papers out of the envelope with the other hand and unfolded them.

The pain vanished with the surge of adrenaline. "How did you do this?"

"That's not important. You'll have to work to pay for housing and books, but you can do that. You're paid up for the school year already, and we have a lot of the same classes. We can share books until you have funds available. What do you think?"

"I think a company I've never heard of is offering me tuition after my father took off with my college savings. I think the world is tipped upside down. And I think I love you so much." I stepped around the desk and grabbed Vicky in a hug. "Thank you."

"You're worth it."

For a little while, I marched on in the haze of things long forgotten, times that should have remained fresh. I take another puff on my inhaler and blink at the emotion that blurs my vision.

After another hour, we come out of the woods into a clearing where the sun beats down on us and makes me feel like a loaf of over-kneaded bread in the oven.

The back of my right heel has hurt since the first hill. Now the pain is stabbing and my sock feels wet. I'm afraid to stop. Afraid to look. My stomach sways with the thought of what I'll find there. This is a great diet plan.

When Vicky steps up beside me, I look at her eyes. She catches me and throws back an icy glare.

Glenda tosses her pack at her feet and starts to pull out a canvas tarp. "You all look pretty done in. We'll set up here for the night then take off again at first light. This will serve as our shelter. Anyone want to take a stab at setting it up?" Her eyes are hard on Vicky, who doesn't even blink in response.

"I've got it." Vicky throws her bag to the ground beside Glenda's.

"I'm sure you do. Here's what you have to work with." Glenda's grin is a little too cat-like for my comfort, but all I want is a shelter and somewhere to lay my head. After that hike, I'm not picky.

"You're kidding, right?" Vicky cocks her hip. "You expect me to produce a tent with a tarp, a hatchet, and a bit of twine?" She holds the rope out like a snake for added emphasis.

"Can't you do it?" Glenda crosses her arms.

Oh, a challenge. Ireland stands beside me. I think we're both eager to see how this episode plays out.

Vicky lifts her chin. There's no super-sweet Texas Christian smile on her lips now. "I most certainly can." She turns her back to Glenda and stares down at her supplies.

Easing myself onto a rock, I start to unlace my shoes and take a deep breath. Vicky's stubbornness has saved me again.

IRELAND

I need to keep moving, keep busy. My mind goes to broken places whenever I stop. It's a product of the fatigue. But when I move, my thighs burn with skin long past the point of blisters.

At the edge of the field I find a clump of mushrooms. Their tops flair out. Chanterelles. I've had them before. I'm not a huge mushroom fan, but this trip isn't about feeding my desires, it's about, I don't know. I need to find my meaning, purpose. A reason the universe keeps me alive.

I try to breathe in nature like I used to, but as my lungs fill I hear Vicky's frustrated howl behind me. I'm more shaken up now than ever.

When we were all together at Emery House, it was the best time of my life. I never felt off-balance. Scared of the future maybe, but never hopeless.

Without hope. How ironic is that? It would almost make me laugh, but Hope's daughter comes to mind and instead, I feel the grief in her. My arms are heavy as I pick the mushrooms Hope is gone, and so is the life I dreamed of.

I can still feel his arm around my waist, his wide palm pulling me closer. For most of my adult life, between earning advanced degrees, publishing articles, and lecturing, I gave Skye my entire heart. We were a perfect pair, not designed to grow in one place but to move around, making a difference, exploring cooperative communities, and learning from the people we met along the way. Skye and I always found each other on the path of life, until that final fork when I left the trail to travel on alone. Is that when I started to change? If we'd worked out our issues, could my life be whole and complete? Would I be like Jenna, with a family who loves her and a marriage that will last forever?

Gathering the mushrooms, I head back to the others, passing Vicky. I duck my head to the side, keeping my voice soft. "You need to cut longer poles and knock some sticks into the ground with the back of the hatchet to tie the rope to. It will hold the tarp tight that way."

She looks up at me, a thankful smile on her face. See, even the earthy heathen can be useful in some circumstances.

Glenda scratches at the skin on the back of her neck. "One of you is going to need to get that hatchet from city-girl and chop up some wood. We'll get to making a fire and start some grub."

Jenna sets her bare foot down on the ground and rubs her stomach. I wonder what she's been putting into her body for the last twenty-some years. Her complexion is sallow, and she's rounder than a beach ball. What if she has a heart attack up here?

Vicky joins the group, a look of superiority on her face. "There you go." She looks down at Glenda then tosses her head the way of our shelter for the night. It's sloped to the side and the top sinks in. And there's a root right through the middle of our sleeping area, but she presents it like she just invented the Internet.

Glenda saunters over. "Don't take this the wrong way, girlie. You did better than I thought you would." Then she taps the bottom of one of the poles with her boot, and the structure tumbles down in front of Vicky. "Try over there, close to the fire. We don't need to make ourselves dinner for the wildlife on our first night. And I'm too old to sleep on a root."

Glenda walks away from the mess, leaving Vicky with an open mouth that looks ready to spill a few words that would ruin her picture-perfect career.

"Now, ladies," Glenda hollers. "We need to get a move on if you're going to learn anything and be able to make a decent meal out here. Tonight, and tomorrow morning, we have some nourishment I've brought in, but it won't last long, and you'll need to be able to provide your own grub within twenty-four hours. More importantly, you'll need to be able to boil water—or you could die."

Jenna grins. "You wouldn't let that happen, though."

"Huh. You signed a waiver, kid." Glenda's eyes twinkle as Jenna's grin slides down.

I set the mushrooms next to the area where Jenna is piling wood.

Glenda nods, but doesn't give me a compliment outright. I already got the crazy-vegan lecture from her when I made the call to register and told her my needs. But I can show her. Mother Earth will feed us with her natural bounty as long as we do our part to protect her. I intend to hold to my values.

This time Vicky has the shelter righted in minutes, and while it's still not straight, as tired as my aching body is, I think it will serve its purpose just fine.

"Gather over here and I'll give you the fire lesson. This is an important one, and if you don't get it, you could die."

Again with the threat of death.

Vicky pulls a lighter from her back pocket. "Or we could use one of these."

Glenda holds her hand out and Vicky drops the blue Zippo into her palm. "No need to depend on things that can be lost or broken. You have to be able to take care of yourself out here. It's just you, God, and nature. Forget all these man-made trappings that make you feel like you're safe. It's a sham." She presses the lighter into her own back pocket. "Okay, gather close. I'll do this for you only once. After tonight, you make your fire, or you freeze."

"Wouldn't that mean you'd freeze right along with us?" Vicky's words are as sassy as a teenage girl's.

"Nothing doing, city-girl. I've got enough calluses on this old body to protect me in subzero weather. You keep to worrying about your hairdo."

Vicky

I want to scream, cry, kick, and just throw this woman over the nearest cliff. It's not like I couldn't turn myself around and march right back down this hill. The truck is waiting. I could leave her up here to live out old age in her precious wilderness.

"You paying attention, city-girl?"

If she calls me that one more time . . . My face is hot enough to light our fire right up. I can't imagine any chance of my freezing to death. "Yes, but my book had some different instructions."

"That book of yours is good for only a couple things: fire starter and toilet paper. Here's the way I prefer." She pulls a wad from the leather pouch that hangs from her belt. Dried pine needles and moss she'd collected on the walk in. She forms a ball with them, then sets it aside and pulls a pocket knife from another pouch.

I sneer. "Isn't that cheating, using a knife?"

Ireland slaps a hand over her mouth and Jenna's eyes go wild.

But Glenda doesn't even flinch. She carves a notch out of a flat piece of wood and stacks it on top of a hunk of bark, then puts the needle moss clump over the hole she's made. We watch her organize the fire pit with rocks around in a circle and a teepee of cut branches in its center. So much time has gone by, I wonder if it will be dark before the fire gets started, if it does.

With both palms, Glenda twirls another stick back and forth, the end pressed into the nest of needles. I lean closer. Smoke is starting to drift up from the clump. She blows gently, cupping her hands around the bundle, then holds it out like one would a baby bird. Orange embers glow within the fuel. She blows again, and there's a tiny flame. Glenda, knees settled into the ground, places the precious heat into the teepee and blows again. Within moments we're all staring at a crackling fire, and I'm stunned silent.

"Okay. Get your canteens out. Anyone have water left?"

Only Ireland nods, but she's got tight eyebrows. I'm guessing she doesn't have much.

"I've got a gallon in my bag." Glenda says. "We'll use this to soak the beans and jerky tonight so we can cook them for breakfast tomorrow."

My stomach sours. "We're having beans and jerky . . . for breakfast. What about eggs or something?"

"This isn't the Hilton—"

I hold a hand up and stop her flow of words. "The name's Victoria."

She laughs. "I'll hand it to you, you got spunk. That surprises me. I've seen you on the tube. It doesn't show much there. But that's one of the reasons people come up here with me. They've lost their spunk. It'd be a good idea if you all figured out why you're here. It'll help you when it gets tough."

Jenna holds her head in her hands. "This isn't the tough part?"

"No, ma'am." Glenda ruffles Jenna's hair. She pulls out a tin pan and pours in beans, then covers them with water. Opening a cloth bag, she produces some kind of homemade jerky.

"Wait." Ireland points at the meat. "I can't eat that."

"So, you'll pick it out."

"No, I don't think you understand about being vegan. If you put the meat into the same water as the beans, I won't be able to eat any of it."

"You've got to be kidding me."

"No. No kidding here. I really won't be able to eat it."

Glenda rolls her eyes. "How the three of you ever got in the same place, I'll never understand. You all figure it out. I'm headed to the john." She tosses Jenna the sack, grabs a small shovel, and walks into the woods.

The other two start to talk, but I'm sick with the reality of what Glenda is doing and where.

"Vicky?" Ireland nudges my shoulder. "Is that all right with you?"

"Sure," I say. "What?"

"If we don't add the jerky and just eat it like it is tomorrow." Jenna tears off a piece and bites it with her back molars. "There's only one pot," she says through the food.

"Whatever. It all looks disgusting anyway. We could leave. Right now, we could climb back down and head to town. I'll pay for a resort."

Jenna starts to laugh and Ireland joins her.

"I feel better," Jenna says. "It's been all I could do not to be the first one to crack."

"I'm not cracking. I just didn't think it would be like this."

"Take a deep breath." Ireland closes her eyes and lifts her hands up. The sky is darkening around us, and the air is cooling. "There's a peace here. I don't want to give up yet."

"Me neither," says Jenna.

And I will not be the weak link. Anyway, they need me. God bless them. I couldn't live with myself if I went home and then found out one of them had died up here.

Glenda emerges from the trees, still buttoning her pants. "Did I tell you all why I picked this new location?"

Jenna shakes her head. "Why?"

"The legend of the wild man livin' out here. It's a whopper."

I roll my eyes. Seriously? A ghost story. We're stuck in a bad cliché.

Chapter 9

JENNA

The wilderness isn't silent at night like I thought it'd be. In fact, it's downright loud. Not the noise you hear on television, the crickets and whatnot. The wind tosses the treetops and their branches hit together like drumsticks. Sometimes I hear something moving, but I'm too afraid to ask what it is or even to speak. The fire crackles and pops. And off in the distance there's the sound of coyotes crying in a way that makes me wonder if their hearts are broken. Maybe that's the sound of my own heart. And I'm starving. I wonder if the coyotes and I have that in common too. I'd make a great meal.

Next to me, Glenda grunts, rolls over, and makes a noise I don't want to consider. Then she starts up a snore that's like a train barreling toward me down a long tunnel. Or like she's bait for a hungry animal. But they'll surely choose me first. I think that might be a blessing.

Ireland giggles. It's a sound I haven't heard from her since college.

"You're awake too?" I say as quietly as I can, while still being loud enough to be heard over the racket.

"I am, but I don't know how. Every part of my body is exhausted, except my brain."

"We made a mistake, didn't we?"

"No. We've gone on an adventure. Every journey holds pain. From pain comes healing."

"From God . . . comes healing." Vicky's voice is so sticky I wonder if she's still asleep and controlling the situation from her dreams.

"That's fine for you, Vicky. It's just not what works for me." Ireland clears her throat.

I bite at the fingernail on my pinky, already down to the quick. "Don't say that, Ireland."

"Why not? It's the truth. God didn't do me any favors. I'm not tied down by religion. God is not one big thing with a hand on all the little happenings of the world. That's just something we say to ourselves when we need to feel better. I don't need to feel better."

"What happened?" I ask.

"Nothing. I just grew up, is all."

Vicky props herself up on one elbow, her pale face visible in the moonlight. "You shouldn't talk like that."

"Why in the world not? Listen, I don't tell you not to believe in God. How about you don't tell me that I *have* to believe?"

"You always believed." Vicky wipes a hand over her eyes. "You were the one who had the genuine faith. I saw it. You can't deny what truly was."

Ireland doesn't respond, but I can tell by her breathing that she hasn't gone to sleep. It's ragged, like the girl I once knew. The girl who never wanted anyone to know when she cried.

The tears flow from my eyes. I swallow. Suddenly, there are bigger fears out here in the dark than woman-hungry cougars. We're twenty-five years older. With twenty-five years of hurt and disappointments, twenty-five years of joys and celebrations, grief and sorrow. All I know is my own jagged wounds. I have no idea where life has taken my friends.

✧ ✧ ✧

I'm awake to see the pink hues grow as the sun rises. It's like the light is pressing up into our camp, forcing a new day on us. Or maybe like God himself is waking the earth. I'm stunned as I push the bedroll back and climb to my knees.

Glenda is up, stirring the fire and the beans. Her hair hangs in newly braided ropes that trail down her back. She seems comfortable in her element, so much different than when we met at the coffee shop.

I lean forward, getting my feet beneath me, and stand. Every single muscle in my body screams and throbs. Looking at the boots I once again have to stuff my feet into, I can already feel the agony of my broken and bloody blister. If the sky weren't transforming into a brilliant painting right before my eyes, I'd snuggle back into the shelter and have a good long cry.

Glenda picks up a stick and clanks it on the side of the bean pan. The noise echoes in my head. "Rise and shine. Survival requires action."

Vicky moans and rolls over, taking Ireland's covers with her.

One eye opens and Ireland sweeps her hand behind her head until her fingers find her glasses. She crams them on her face and sits up, yawning. Somehow, I expected she'd be up and taking in the beauty of nature, but she doesn't seem to notice as she staggers to the fire.

"You put the jerky in the beans?" She's awake now and her voice hits an octave that brings even Vicky around.

"Relax, Granola. I put your precious and pure breakfast in your bowl before I added any flesh." Glenda shakes her head. "You're not going to keep this up. I guarantee it. But if you want to try, be my guest."

Ireland's chest rises and falls. She presses her palms together and breathes in and out again. "Thank you. I appreciate your consideration." The words hold about as much emphasis as a robot's. Picking up the bowl of beans Glenda is pointing to, Ireland walks to the edge of the clearing, visibly shivers, then comes back to the fire.

"Breakfast is served, ladies." Glenda pours coffee that smells as strong as industrial cleaner into four tin cups, squats on a rock, then digs her fork into the pot, pulling out a large chunk of meat and stirring up a hearty scent.

It's not like the rich herby smells I'm used to producing in my kitchen at home, but I'm so starved my stomach growls with eagerness. I snatch a fork and pull out my own chunk of rehydrated jerky.

It goes down well enough.

When Vicky finally joins us, she has a bandana tied over her bleach-blond hair. A few rogue waves stick out, but she's done better than I would have guessed in this environment. I run a hand over my own head and find one side of my hair smashed flat while the other shoots out. I comb it with my fingers then dig an old baseball cap of Calvin's out of my backpack. That's as much primping as I'll be doing. Not much different than most days at home, really.

The air warms quickly as the sun moves higher in the sky. "Time to pack up," Glenda says.

"Where are we going?" Vicky pulls her lipstick from her jacket pocket and does a run around her lips. "What's wrong with where we are?"

"Nothing's wrong with it, it's just not where we're headed. There's a waterfall a few miles from here. It'll be worth the hike."

Ireland nods. This news seems to have brought back her enthusiasm. "A waterfall sounds wonderful. I'm sure that's just what we need."

Vicky wrinkles her nose. "What I need is a good hot shower and coffee you don't have to chew."

My legs begin to shake and my lungs won't draw in a full breath. I can't keep up another day. I really couldn't yesterday, and that was on fresh legs. What if I actually have a heart attack or a stroke out here. Mark was right. I'm in no condition to hike through the mountains.

VICKY

We've been up an hour, and we're only just getting on the trail. There's little organization, order, or rhythm among the four of us. The worst is this woman we call our leader. She's a real piece of work. She refers to us by anything but our actual God-given names. I don't think she has all her eggs in her basket. And someone, I don't remember who, thought it was a good idea to put our lives in this woman's hands.

Well, Daniel will certainly be worried, and for good reason. Or maybe he won't even notice when I don't come home? Will he take the time to find out where I've gone? Or will he settle in with that woman, enjoying a good laugh or whatever while I'm off in the wild, dangerous, and unpredictable mountains?

My stomach burns with fear and acidic coffee.

Though I exercise each day for an hour, my body is still not prepared for this kind of activity. The straps of my backpack dig into my shoulders. The muscles have rebelled and formed tight lumps in order to compensate. *Lord, please heal my aching.*

At the front of the line, Glenda slows, looking up at the sky. She touches her fingers to her lips.

"Vick, you're falling behind," Ireland snaps back at me.

"If you wouldn't rush, I wouldn't be lagging."

Ireland turns, putting both palms together in that infernal way she has like she's about to go all yoga on us. "Even Jenna is managing."

That halts Jenna's feet fast. "What's that supposed to mean?"

"Don't take it like that," Ireland says. "You just don't take very good care of your body. This is bound to challenge you more than others."

"And now I'm supposed to feel better?" Jenna plants her feet and leans forward.

Ireland stands on the incline, making her easily a foot taller. "Relax. Seems like you're more concerned with what I think than with your own health."

Even Glenda's eyes grow wide now.

Jenna takes a step closer.

I can see this going into a middle-aged throwdown any minute. We must manage a way to maintain some dignity, even out here. I come up behind Jenna and start to reach for her shoulder.

She turns like a flash and we collide, her elbow connecting hard with my clavicle.

I reach for the pain as I try to regain my balance, but I can't get my feet to stay under me with the weight of my pack pulling me back. One step. Two. Three, Four. The ground beneath me slopes, and I can't stop the fall. I tumble to the ground, rolling. Thorns, sticks, and rocks cut, scrape, and bruise me, and I only roll faster. I claw for an anchor, my fingernails biting at anything I touch, but I can't get a grip anywhere. Then the thud. I hear it before I feel the pain. My body is stopped by the giant trunk of a Douglas fir.

The world still spins even as my body is finally stilled. This is surely not the kind of death I'd planned. Will they even bother to carry my corpse out of this wooded prison? Or will I be wolf meat?

Crashing sounds make me open eyes I didn't realize I held closed. My vision is blurred with tears, but I see someone coming, sliding down the hill, arms waving. It's a short someone. Jenna.

"Are you okay?" She's still twenty feet up the hill. "Vicky. Please say something."

I manage a moan and wave.

When she reaches me, she touches my cheek first, then runs her hands over my arms, legs, and head. "Where does it hurt?"

"Everywhere." I do a mental inventory of my pains. It's mainly superficial kinds of injuries. I'm sure I'm actually fine, but this really is the last straw. I'm going home. "I'm okay."

I scoot up and rest my back against the tree. My jeans, brand new the day before I left on this crazy trip, are torn down the side of my right leg. The exposed flesh is raw and scraped, but not the kind of thing that won't heal.

Jenna leans in and pulls a twig from my hair.

I run a hand over it and find she's only released one of the larger pieces. My bandana is somewhere between the trail and my resting spot, and I've picked up every loose object between here and there.

Above us, Glenda and Ireland seem to be arguing. Ireland shakes her hands above her head like the homeless man who sits on the street near my gym, ranting and raving to no one in particular. I can't make out their words, but a chill runs over my skin. Can we get back to the pickup tonight?

I try to stand up, but the ground beneath me spins, forcing me back down. A throbbing has begun behind my eyes. It beats a rhythm in my head that matches the thudding of my heart. What did I think I could prove by coming here? Did I think my husband would fall in love with me again if he thought I was an adventurer? Or did I think his protective side would kick in when he figured out I'd disappeared?

There's nothing glamorous here.

Jenna strips off her fleece jacket. "I think you should stay still." She scrunches up the fabric and presses it hard onto the side of my head.

A new shock of pain courses through me, turning my stomach and making lights flash in my vision. "What is it? What's wrong?"

"You cut yourself. I'm sure it's not as bad as it seems."

I'm stunned but somehow more aware than I was a moment ago. Warm and wet, the fleece could be holding my brain in place for all I can see. With that thought the light starts to fade and my vision narrows.

IRELAND

"We're going down there, one way or another."

"So, there's a bit of spunk in you after all, Granola." Glenda looks up at the sky, her features stretched in concentration.

The air chills my skin. It's dropped from balmy to icy in thirty minutes. Dark clouds cover the sun and take away the comfort of light.

Glenda rubs a thumb along her jawline. "They're way down there. A good seventy feet or so. We only have twenty feet of rope."

My heart starts to pound. I look down at Jenna and Vicky. Jenna sits with her back against the tree that stopped Vicky's fall. She's holding Vicky's head in her lap with her jacket pressed to its side. From here, I can't even tell if Vicky is conscious. Or even alive.

"We can drop down to them, then we'll have to hike around to find a better way back out." She bites her bottom lip and looks back to the sky.

The tops of the trees sway like they are dancing to the rhythm of the wind. The tempo picks up.

Glenda ties the end of the rope to a small tree trunk. "Wrap this around your waist and lower yourself down backwards until you run out of rope." She gives me a quick demonstration, then hands me the rough woven cable.

"What happens when I get to the end?"

"You sit down and wait. Do not move until I say. Get going." Her voice is insistent and unusually rushed.

My heart takes another lurch. I swing the rope around me and clasp it together with the other end. Step-by-step, I move down the hill, letting my lifeline slip through my hands enough to allow the descent while keeping me anchored to safety. My feet scuff over tiny seedlings, though I do my best to keep from damaging any of the young plants. Too soon, the rope's end appears. I turn, sitting myself firmly onto the steep slope. The rope slides up the hill, and I hear Glenda behind me.

I turn only my head to watch Glenda, keeping my palms and heels firmly dug into the rocky earth. She makes the descent on her backside, like Jenna, but with a level of control and patience that Jenna lacked. When she reaches me, she hands me one end of the rope again, then shimmies to the side and ties off to another tree, this one barely thicker than the rope but the only one within reach.

I work my way down the hillside again, forcing myself not to watch the tree that holds my safety in its tender hands, but I'm thankful to the Earth for providing it. It's getting steeper here, almost dropping off. Where the rope ends is the worst of the slope.

One of my heels presses through the earth that holds me in place and my leg shoots out straight. My body slips to the side and I slide the rest of the way down the hill, nearly missing Vicky and Jenna with my growing momentum.

Jenna lunges for me, grabbing hold of my jacket.

I bump to a stop, laid flat on the sloped ground, Jenna splayed on her belly behind me.

By the time the four of us are together again, the sky has gone from warning to outright alarm. Dark clouds are nearly black, and there's a rumble rolling over the mountains with the clouds.

Glenda wipes sweat from her forehead. "We'll need to work ourselves down the hill a ways. Can you see where the ground evens out some?"

We all nod. My stomach is sick with the thought of getting us all farther down the mountain and farther from the trail. But looking back up the hill, there's no way we can retrace our steps. The only way out of here now is down.

Chapter 10

JENNA

Every inch of my chubby body burns and aches. I thought that was how I felt this morning when I woke up on the hard ground, but now I know the truth. That pain was nothing. Not even a twinge.

Lucy and Ethel had it easy on their camping episode. I need an Ethel right now. That show was luxury compared to this event. Why didn't I ever watch that survival guy, Bear Grylls, with Calvin? That's the kind of television prep course I could really put to use.

Vicky sits against a massive rock here at the bottom of some kind of canyon. Her shirt is lifted, exposing her skin to the chilly air. I've been dabbing some kind of herbal goo onto her scrapes and bruises for the last twenty minutes. There are tons. She's stick-thin and her skin so white, it's nearly translucent.

I run my finger through Ireland's tin again. The smell is like death. Maybe it's meant to scare away the pain. Or cause the patient to lose consciousness until they're healed.

"That's it." I twist the top back on the stink. This stuff is actually called Big Gun. I almost laugh. Our peace-wielding friend totes her own can of Big Gun.

"Thanks." Vicky pulls her shirt back down and threads her arms into her jacket. "It's freezing."

I turn to Glenda. "Should we get the fire going?"

She's staring up into the eerie sky then shakes her head, but doesn't look at me. "We need to find a spot that's a little higher and flat."

"I can't." Vicky eases herself up. "I can't go another step tonight. Please, can we just stop and hike out in the morning?"

"Not here." Glenda lifts her pack onto her back. She passes us, grabbing Vicky's bag as she goes. "Come on. There isn't a lot of time to chat about this."

Ireland offers Vicky an arm, which she swiftly refuses.

We start walking, my heart already hammering away at my rib cage. I try to play a game with myself to keep my mind distracted from the fear I saw in our leader's eyes. Television theme songs from the eighties. I search for the tune from *Family Ties*, but all I can hear is *Gilligan's Island*. Oh no. That was supposed to be a mere three-hour tour. Look what happened to those people. And it all started with a storm.

The wind is no longer a strong breeze. We walk against gusts that want to use my coat as a sail and knock me over. I duck my head and push on. Fear moves me faster than I managed even our first leg of the journey.

I look back to check on Vicky. Her face is pale and her mouth is wide open. The bump above her right eye has begun to bruise already, but the bleeding has stopped. What if she's hurt worse than she's saying? Maybe this is the time to call in help.

"Glenda, we do have some kind of emergency equipment to contact help, right?"

She pats her vest pocket. "I got a satellite phone right here, but let's not jump the gun."

I expect Vicky to announce her departure, but she doesn't say anything, and that gets me really scared. "Come on. I think we're in trouble. Shouldn't we at least try to let them know where we are? That we're off the path?"

Glenda turns to me, and her eyes are soft. "I can't get a signal out in this canyon. I already tried. But there's nothing to worry about. First thing in the morning, we'll find a way back up, and I'll call out so they can get a location on us. What you need to know about survival is never panic. Panic is your worst enemy."

Great. I feel my enemy knocking at the door.

Vicky's face goes from pale to ashen. Even her lips have lost color. I put my hand around hers and give it a squeeze. She leans into me. Then, as if she's stuck her finger in a light socket, her spine goes straight and she pulls away.

"We'll make a plan, follow the logical course, and be home by tomorrow night." Vicky fishes in her bag and pulls out a notepad and pen. "What do we need to do for tonight?" She taps the end of the pen on her bottom lip. Before we can answer, she goes into super-leader mode. "We'll need a fire. Ireland, collect wood and make a pile. Jenna, you start on the shelter. And Glenda, you keep working on that signal."

This should be good. I look over my shoulder, expecting Glenda's face to flame red at Vicky's demands, not to mentions the notepad and pen, but there's a satisfied smile on her lips. The *Father Knows Best*, I got her just where I want her, kind of smile.

Ireland's another story. "And what will you be doing while we're taking your orders?"

"I've got a plan. How much water do we have left?" Vicky staggers, but regains her balance.

Glenda hands her the jug we refilled with last night. It's barely a quarter full.

Vicky swirls it around. "We'll have to get more water." She looks to Glenda. "How would you suggest we do that?"

"I don't think that's going to be a problem for long." She looks to the sky. Dark clouds seem to be sinking in on us. Holding a palm out flat, she keeps watching.

One drop, then two, then they come down like someone's turned on a shower.

Without another word, we fly into action. I've never set up even a pop-up tent, but I watched Vicky last night, and I had plenty of time during a sleepless night to inspect our structure in the moonlight.

Glenda comes over to give me a hand.

I shiver. That can't be a good sign.

"Pull the ropes tight. We don't want the water puddling on top of us." She starts to dig a trench around the shelter.

Water drips off the hood of my jacket and down my neck. It soaks into the seams around the soles of my boots. My hands slip over the rope as I pull it back with all my weight; then I wrap it three times around the base of a sapling and tie it off. It takes a couple tries with the knot. I can barely feel my fingers.

I motion to Glenda for inspection. She tugs on the rope and nods, then returns to her work. I get the feeling this wasn't in her plans.

IRELAND

Another crack and the sky lights up over us. No fire. No source of light between the flashes. Nothing like I signed up for, but it still may be better than being at home. Maybe I'll die out here. At least I can have the relief of a silent death.

But then what?

We're tucked back into the shelter. No one sleeps.

"What if the lightning hits us?" Jenna's words come out shaky, and I don't think it's because she's cold.

"Unlikely, this far down. What we need to think about is flash flooding." Glenda pulls her knees to her chest and wraps her arms around them. "We came a ways up, but all the water on this hill has to go somewhere, and we're in the path."

"I made a mistake." Jenna is crying now. "I wanted to prove to my husband that I could do this. I thought I could make him proud of me. I thought I could show my kids I'm capable of more than baking. I don't know what I thought anymore. Now I've just proven that I'm a screwup." She sniffs and hiccups for breath.

She's sitting on the end, with only me next to her for comfort. That's an unfortunate placement for her. There's not a maternal bone in me. I've proven that beyond question.

Her shoulders shake.

I pull a sleeping bag over them, then clasp my hands in my lap again.

"I understand," Vicky says. "My motivations weren't all that different."

I grunt. "Come on, Vick. You want us to believe Daniel doesn't know you can do and control anything?"

She's silent for a moment. Another flash and crack. "I think he's having an affair with my assistant."

Now we hit a new level of silent. My mouth is open, but there's nothing to say. Vicky snivels on the other side of me. I'm in an emotional sandwich. And it's making me swirl with unease. The lightning looks like a safer companion.

I reach into my pack and pull out four granola bars. They're from my special stash, my only hope of an animal-product-free week. But I think this trip is about to be cut short, so I'll sacrifice part of my hoard. I give one to each of them then peel back my own wrapper.

Jenna reaches across me and lays her hand on Vicky's knee. "I'm sure that can't be true. No one would cheat on you. You're beautiful and smart. I want to be a fraction of the woman you are."

I notice those words weren't meant for me. No one wants to be like me.

Lightning flashes again, glinting off something where we'd planned the campfire.

"What was that?" Glenda leans toward the place where our fire would be burning if it hadn't turned to a pond.

"I think it's the hatchet," I say.

"Oh for Pete's sake. We can't go leaving important equipment lying around like that. And enough of this 'I'm about to die, so feel sorry for me' talk. The worst thing about tonight is a little discomfort." She throws off the blankets and steps into the rain. Stalking to the hatchet, she makes a show with her flashlight of picking it up, shaking it at us. She hollers over the wind: "See, there's nothing out here any scarier than what you all got going in your heads."

Another crack. Glenda is lit up like a star on a stage. Then another crack, this time as loud as a bomb. *Pop. Pop.* The snaps and cracks climb toward us. I swing my head around but can't find the source until the next flash, and the explosion as a giant tree comes toward us.

"Move," I scream. We're on our feet and clawing away like rabbits from a forest fire.

The earth shakes with the impact, knocking me to my hands and knees.

Then there's just the pounding of rain and the whistle of the air forcing its way through the trees.

I feel around me, locating Vicky and Jenna. "Glenda?"

There's no answer. I yell into the wind. "Glenda? Are you okay?"

Nothing. Standing, I pull the other two to their feet.

"We have to go find her," Jenna says. "She could be hurt."

Water drips down my scalp and across my face. My feet are molded to this spot. The world starts to spin, and I'm grateful for the dark. Sinking back, I sit on the ground, now turned to mud. "I can't."

Vicky squeezes my shoulder. "We need to stay together, and we can't leave her out there alone. Come on." She grabs my hand and pulls me up.

I'm shaking so hard now I can't speak. Can't make the words form. Why can't there be a landslide to wash me away right now. And end this agony.

We feel our way over the ground. We've come farther from the shelter than I thought. Vicky is shining a flashlight into the dark, but the beam is weak and doesn't help much. The wind slows. As fast as the storm came, it's gone. All I can hear is the trickle of water dripping from leaves and flowing by in tiny rivers that run over my feet.

The tree isn't as big as it looked when it crashed toward us. It's maybe twenty inches in diameter at the middle. Surely Glenda is okay. God, if he's there, wouldn't leave Jenna and Vicky in the wilderness without a guide.

Jenna works her way down the trunk with Vicky and me behind, Vicky shining the light at the ground along the tree. Nothing. We keep moving.

Vicky gasps. Glenda's boot sticks out from under the wood. Vicky grabs my hand, then shines the light on the other side.

The image of Glenda's lifeless eyes pulls the last of the warmth from my body.

VICKY

I crawl back into what passes as our shelter and press in close to Jenna's side. My stomach is empty from vomiting caused either by a concussion, fear, or shock. It's accompanied by a pounding migraine. That could also be from the blow to my head, or it could be lack of food and water, or maybe panic.

The Bible says three hundred sixty-five times that we shouldn't fear. I've always taken comfort in the way God lined the commands up for each day of the year. But tonight feels like no other time. It's a day that doesn't fit on any calendar in my life plan. And fear is more real and all-encompassing than I've ever known before. It's like February 30 has set up camp.

Constant shivers pulse my body. My clothes are wet. Our bedding is wet. We are soaked through. If we can't dry out, we'll surely be dead before we can decide what to do about Glenda.

Just thinking about her makes my stomach revolt, but there's nothing left to lose. I'm empty in every way. Heart, soul, and stomach. *Lord, I really tried to do your work. Why have you abandoned me here to die such a horrible death?*

I suppose it's natural to look back on your life when the end is near. My mind passes over pictures of my children when they were young, of times when it was just Daniel and me, together and in love. And even back to Emery House.

Emery was my rebellion. I come from a family of good standing. We're the kind of people who attend Ivy League schools and live in the right sororities. The University of Northwest Oregon served its greatest purpose for me back then. It made my mother crazy. And if my choice of school wasn't bad enough, Emery pushed her right over the cliff.

It was our junior year before she changed tactics and decided to visit me in Oregon. Two years of avoidance had done nothing to get me to give up what she called my juvenile wanderings.

It was spring and the campus lit up with the blooms of blushing rhododendrons. The walk to class was like a stroll through a royal garden. I stopped two or three times as I returned from a psychology lecture just to take in the sweet smells of fresh bark mulch.

But as I entered our block, something changed. It was like the air cooled and a wave of chilled fear ran over my skin. I don't know how I knew, but I did. She was there.

I looked down at the clothes I'd chosen for the day. Sweat pants that had to be rolled at the top so they wouldn't work their way down as I walked and a sweatshirt that belonged to Mark. Oh, Mark. I picked up my speed. I had to save him from the wrath that would cut him into pieces I could never mend.

I rushed up the walkway, then hesitated at the door, adjusting my posture before I entered. I didn't have to go far to find her. There, in the foyer, my mother towered with her back to me. She still wore a designer coat and five-inch heels. And on the other side of her, Jenna stood with eyes wide and mouth gaping. I could only imagine the scene I'd missed, but Jenna never told me.

"Mother?"

Camila Salsubury Stevens turned her entire body toward me. Her face remained expressionless, a sight I was all too familiar with. Tipping her head back, she looked me up and down, her eyebrows pulling together in the slightest way, the evidence of sheer disgust. "Is that the way you present yourself to the world, Victoria?"

I'd worn these same clothes many cool mornings but never felt any shame, until now. My shoulders dropped as the independence I'd gained over the academic year crumbled and fell to a heap at my tennis shoes.

"I'll change."

"I'd say you will. I've made dinner reservations. Go on up now." She patted her hair as if checking to see if my environment had messed with her perfection. "I'd like a little more time to talk with this girl, Jennifer is it?"

Jenna swallowed hard and nodded. But Jenna is not short for Jennifer. I knew that, and I didn't correct her either. More shame.

I rushed up the stairs as fast as I could manage without cracking the brittle thread of decorum that had fallen over our usually comfortable home. At the end of the hall, I burst into our room and threw open my closet, searching for the suit I kept near the back.

"What's gotten into you?" Ireland pulled her headphones to the side. She lounged in the corner beanbag, a physics book on her lap.

"My mother. She's taking me to dinner." That's when the real terror took hold. "Oh no. Mark is supposed to take me out tonight to celebrate our six-month anniversary. I've got to stop him." I sprinted down the hall to the phone booth and dialed the guys' house. But the one who answered told me Mark was already on his way.

I was ready in under five minutes with the help of Hope and Ireland. Sure, the rush job would be the focus of our dinner conversation, but I had to catch Mark before my mother did. Ireland and I ran for the stairs.

After the first curve I could hear her shrill voice. "You say you have an anniversary with my daughter? That's quite interesting information."

My shoulders dropped and my hopes shattered.

"Hey, Mark." Ireland passed me, heading into the foyer. "I really need some help tonight with my physics. It's killing me. And you're the only one I know who understands the stuff. What do you say?" She grabbed him by the elbow and turned him toward the living room.

"Now wait a minute, miss. This young man and I were having a conversation." My mother crossed her arms. "I believe he had plans with my Victoria tonight, and I'd hate to come between two people so clearly committed to each other." Her lips curled up in her signature plastic smile. "Would you please join us? I'm sure I could change our reservation to three, if you don't mind changing yours."

Mark scuffed a shoe on the carpet. "I didn't have any reservations."

"Then you'll join us." Mother eyed his jacket, then blew out a breath. "We do need to be going. I'm sure the maître d' will have something suitable you can borrow."

That was the beginning of the end for us. The night was course after course of humiliation and embarrassment. I've wondered how life worked out for Mark and Jenna. Does she truly make him happy? He deserves to be. My mother thought he wasn't good enough for me. But all the while, I knew it was the opposite. I could never be good enough to deserve Mark.

The sun isn't visible, but a gray light brings morning into focus. I step away from Ireland and Jenna, my side immediately cold where they've been pressed next to me for hours. My feet slosh through puddles as I make my way toward a tree, keeping my gaze away from Glenda.

My boot lands on something hard, I kneel to see and find the one thing that could save us.

Chapter 11

JENNA

I've buried a human being. A real person. With my own hands. It's nothing like *Little House on the Prairie*. There's so much left out in programming. This morning's emotions are deeper and wider than anything I've allowed myself to feel since my own mother died. The grief tied around my heart is tighter than the pain I experienced when notified of my father's death, three months after it happened. My dad had already died to me in so many ways, it was just the loss of hope that he might come to his senses. This is so real. So in my face.

The tree had hit Glenda square across her chest and shoved her into the ground. We could only imagine what broken bones and other internal damage had been done. The tree wasn't budging. Ireland and I clawed through the mud and vines beneath Glenda, but finally gave up on freeing the body. Using the toilet shovel and our hands, we covered her as best we could.

I take the hatchet and chunk out the letters, G. F., the only marker to her resting place.

Ireland leans against a rock, trying to make life return to the satellite phone. But after a good smack by a tree followed by a night swimming in a puddle, I think it's done.

The lighter I found in Glenda's bloody chest pocket is cracked along the top, pieces of the striker had penetrated her skin. It's a total loss, even the lighter fluid has slipped away.

My hands are raw, cut along the knuckles, but at least I'm alive.

I don't even know if Glenda had a family. I don't know if she was married. If she had children. She spoke of God, but I never asked her if she really knew him. I didn't take the time to see her. This trip was all about me. That's what so much of my life has been, all about what I wanted. No waiting on God's timing. Not me.

Since the triplets left, I've been wallowing in self-pity. I've made Mark feel the punishment of that selfishness.

But it started even before the empty nest. It started that day when my father made it clear how little I meant to him. And it continued with me making sure everyone around me needed me, that I was not replaceable. Until I couldn't fool them any longer.

I'm sick with my shame. Sick of being endlessly needy.

Pulling another rock from the ground, I heft it to our shallow gravesite and drop it onto the pile. One of the things I learned while homeschooling, when pioneers died on the trail, the survivors place rocks on top of the graves to prevent animals from disturbing their loved one's remains.

What once was just an interesting fact to learn is now a personal part of my history.

They also drove their wagons over the site to pack down the soil. I guess I could sit my wide-as-an-ox backside on the fresh dirt. It would probably serve the same purpose.

The sun is way past the middle of the sky and burns down on us. Even the ground has stopped steaming and the little streams are gone. The great majority of our clothes lay over limbs, drying in the heat.

Vicky fans through the pages of her survival book, laying it in a new position to dry the soaked pages, another victim of the storm and our half-collapsed shelter.

We were a few feet from needing someone to bury all of us, but there would have been no one. The thought makes my head swim. What was I thinking? This was not fair to Mark and the kids.

Vicky looks up. "We need to get moving if there's any chance of getting out of here tonight." The bruise on her forehead has settled, and now she has a deep black eye.

"There's no way we get out today." Ireland shakes her head. She tests her sweater for dampness, then ties it around her waist. "Not without that phone. We don't even know where out is."

"Just stop it." Vicky stomps a foot into the ground, then grimaces. "Don't even say that. I need out of here. Now. Help!" She screams into the dense forest. "Please, someone, help."

I put my hand on her arm, but she shakes it off.

"I'm getting out of here. Are you with me, or not?"

"Of course we are." I push my feet into boots that haven't dried completely. "But which way?"

Her gaze swings around on me, ready to fight, then she crumbles, tears flowing. "I don't know."

There aren't even our own footprints to retrace. We're alone in a wilderness washed clean of our existence.

"We were headed this way." Ireland points behind me. "I'm sure Glenda had a reason. Pack up. Let's go. We'll look for a way to get back up the hill, then we'll find the path. That should get us right back to the truck. I saw her leave the keys under the seat. Get to the truck, and we're good."

My stomach growls. We haven't eaten anything since Ireland's granola bar. It was disgusting, but I ate every crumb. "How are we for food?"

Vicky rubs her hands together. She seems calmed by the question. I need to remember that. "I've inventoried everything we have." She flips open her notepad, wrinkled along the edges. "There's enough beans and jerky for two or three more meals."

"Jerky. Where?"

Vicky points to Glenda's pack.

The meat is salty and harsh, but I chew until my teeth ache. There's not a lot here, but more than Glenda let on. We repackage every item into our three packs, leaving Glenda's well-worn backpack over the top of her grave, a marker for the authorities. Nothing else gets left—except our leader.

After two hours, my stomach is screaming again. I watch Ireland ahead of me, eating away at another granola bar. She must sense me, because she looks back. "You okay?"

"I'm good." I force a smile to confirm my lie. My feet are on fire. The dampness acts like sandpaper, peeling away any skin I had left. Every step is agony. "If we can't make it to the truck tonight, and we all know we can't, we need to stop soon."

"Stopping is not an option," Vicky says from behind me.

Ireland halts. "Neither is freezing or being eaten by bears."

"What's that supposed to mean?" Vicky's eye has swollen almost closed, making her look like she's winking with an angry face.

Ireland takes one of her calming breaths. "How long do you think it will take us to make a fire?"

I drop my arms limp at my sides. Fire? We'll never be able to do this.

Vicky leans toward a tree, peeling moss from its side. She stuffs it in her pocket. "The book gives a few other methods too. If we each try a technique, certainly one of us will be able to produce a little fire."

I can't help but smile. She's back, and so is that over-the-top determination that comforted me so many times in college. "You're right. We can do this."

Ireland's mouth doesn't move, but there's a hint of a twinkle in her eyes.

The forest seems to close in on us. I let Vicky pass me—favoring her less damaged leg—and set my pack on the carpet of needles. Untying my sweatshirt, I rub it between my hands and pull it on over my head. Before starting again, I fill my own pockets with fir needles. I'm not ready to die. Not like this.

A shadow scoops down from one of the trees. Vicky squats, holding her hands over her head. Right in front of us, an enormous owl glides down and slides effortlessly onto another tree's branch.

"Wow. Did you see that?" I tap Vicky's shoulder.

She brings her arms down and stands. "What was it?"

"A Northern spotted owl." Ireland's gaze remains on the bird. "They're on the list of threatened animals."

"It's so graceful." My mind is swimming. I'm in the worst agony of my life, and I carried triplets for thirty-four weeks. At the same time, my chest is filled with gratitude. Somehow I just can't believe God allowed me to see such an amazing creature so close I could see the individual feathers on its wings.

"Do they attack?" Vicky asks.

Ireland laughs. "No. That owl is not after us."

Seeing Ireland's smile renews me. God won't let us down. Not here. Not now that we're back together again. *Lord, please help us. We're in a big old mess.* It's been too long since I just spoke my heart to God. Too long.

"How about here?" Ireland plants her hands on her hips.

We've been trudging through the dense trees for a couple hours and this is the first place that could be considered a clearing. Small, but there is an area to make a fire. I look up into the trees. No cougar . . . yet.

Vicky flings down her bag and pulls out her tattered survival manual. "Let's get to work on a fire."

IRELAND

The circle of rocks surround our teepee of sticks, waiting on a flame. As the sun edges toward the horizon, the temperature drops, giving our task increased motivation. I should know how to start a fire. I'm the one who actually cares what happens to this planet, the one who's been working her whole adult life to save places like this. But saving nature and surviving in it are two very different things. We are not saviors in this wilderness. We're intruders.

Here, I'm like everyone else. My flesh loves convenience. I miss my ductless unit I may secretly use for the indulgence of air conditioning on extremely hot days. Sometimes I stash my guilt for comfort. Are these compromises the reason the Earth I've tried to save will rise up and murder me?

Vicky has her book out again. She's been throwing orders since before she even took her pack off. It's hard to take her seriously when she has to look sideways at the pages since one eye has disappeared behind a wall of swollen black and blue skin.

I build our shelter while they each try to produce a flame. The tarp has a rip in one side. I can't apply much tension without shredding the material. When I'm done, I pull some brush underneath to form a bed and extra warmth. I don't think it will matter how comfortable we are tonight. After two nights without sleep, my body doesn't care about anything but food and rest.

There are three granola bars left in my pack. Three. That's one for each of us, or three for me. Every ounce of my being wants to gobble all of them while Jenna and Vicky are turned the other way.

"If you're done over there, we could use your help." I think Vicky can hear my evil thoughts. Maybe that's what I get for camping with Little Miss Godly.

"Sure." I tuck the bars deep into my bag, covering them with my extra socks that are already so filthy they'd stand on their own. "What can I do?"

"Jenna's fire teepee is too big. The book says we need a small door. The way she's built that thing we'll never keep the flame going."

I catch Jenna's scowl, but her hands never stop twisting the stick between her palms.

"All right. You're the *boss*." I cringe at how sarcastic my words sound, but I don't look at Vicky to see her put-love-into-the-world response. Rearranging the sticks and needles, I make the should-be fire pit smaller, tighter. But I don't hold out much hope for a flame. What happens if we're here through the night without fire? I'm not so concerned about the cold. It's the animals.

"I've got it." Jenna's voice strikes me with its intensity. "Look."

Smoke curls from her bundle of tinder, rising like prayers to the universe. She lifts the wood block, cups her hand around the needles, like Glenda did, and blows. The smoke fades. She blows lighter and it thickens, then there it is, a tiny flame.

With shaking hands, Jenna slides her treasure into the teepee of sticks.

"Careful." Vick nudges close. "You need to keep blowing." She shoulders Jenna to the side.

"Back off." The words hold more power than Jenna has possessed since our reunion. "If you want to control the fire, you start it."

"Well. I was just trying to help." Vicky stands up, one heel dug into the ground. She folds her arms tight across her chest.

"You know what?" Jenna stretches to her full not-so-tall height. "You're not the only one who can do things. I did that. I made that fire, and I don't want to hear what you think about it."

My gaze shifts to the sticks. There's not much happening.

"That's gratitude." Vicky's one eye blazes.

But the fire isn't catching. "Um."

They both turn on me.

"Never mind." I squat down and blow into the embers, while their terse words fly back and forth over me. A flame jumps to life. It spreads across the needle bed and onto a small stick then climbs the teepee, crackling and snapping. I sit back and warm my hands. I may get none of the credit for this little miracle, but I'm getting all the warmth.

There's silence behind me.

"We did it," Jenna says. Her generosity with the praise is shocking, but I'm not going to argue. "I can't believe we actually did it."

"You did it." I stand. "Good job."

The day is almost over, and we've accomplished fire. Fire, and a burial. Under the circumstances, that's better than I expected.

VICKY

"We have no water left." I lick my lips. They're desert dry and starting to crack. The lipstick slides over them like thick paint on an over-textured wall. The smoke from the fire burns my throat, and I can only see a slit from one eye.

"How much is left?" Ireland asks.

I claw my broken fingernails into my sticky hair. "None."

Tears start to roll down Jenna's face, leaving trails along her dirty cheeks.

"We just need to find that waterfall." Ireland throws another stick on the fire.

"How will we cook the beans?" Jenna rubs her hands up and down her arms. "We can't live very long without water. We need to do something. What does the book say?"

I hold the pages close to the fire for light. A section breaks free and drops into the flames. Without thinking, I reach in and pull them out. Dropping paper onto the dirt, I stomp the fire out of them. But there's not much left. Only corners, ashes, and disappointment.

"Are you okay?" Jenna's jumped back a few paces.

I look at my hand. Realization comes with heat. Two of my fingers are red. One begins to blister. The ground moves underneath me, and I sway with the motion. Jenna and Ireland ease me onto a rock where I give up and crumble into my nagging emotions.

"We can't do this. We're going to die out here. They'll find our picked bones in a year or two. That woman who used to be on television. God didn't protect her. That will be my legacy. The final word from my ministry."

Tears flow, and all I can think is how I can't spare the water. My fingers throb and burn. I run them through my warm tears then hold them over my head. "God, please help us."

I haven't been this desperate for him in so many years. Will he remember me now, or will he give me a dose of my own medicine? My mind won't stop replaying the conversation with the flight attendant. What has become of me? When did I stop caring? Will anyone miss me?

"Whoa." Ireland places a hesitant hand on my shoulder. "Let's not give up before we've done everything we can. Vicky, you go lie down in the shelter. You're exhausted and injured. Jenna and I will work out a plan and we'll go over it in the morning."

"No way. I want in on this."

Jenna cringes. "What about your hand? Don't you think you should elevate it or something?"

"I can do that right here." I hold my hand over my head; the throbbing immediately slows. "We need to find water first thing tomorrow. It's top priority, unless there's a chance of getting out of here within the first few hours of the day."

The sun dips that final bit until we're surrounded by darkness pressing in like the plagues of Egypt. I huddle closer to the fire, but the heat starts my fingers searing again. Somewhere in the distance a woman screams. She calls out in terror over and over again. I jump to my feet. "Someone's out there."

Jenna holds her hands tight to her ears. "That's not a someone. That's a cougar."

"How do you know?" I've practically attacked her with my words, but I don't have any filters left for my mouth.

"Cougars are the mascot of our high school. Mark's been playing the sound of the cougar's cry in pep assemblies for years. It always struck me as weird, both that he'd think this was a motivator, and that the cougar sounds so much like the scream I sometimes hear inside my head."

"What else do you know about cougars?" Ireland asks.

"That's about it." Jenna's eyes are wide, reflecting light from the fire.

I reach down with my good hand and squeeze Jenna's. I need her forgiveness now. Tomorrow may be too late.

Chapter 12

IRELAND

I used to play the sounds of the wilderness as an aid to meditation. The wind through the trees, the call of the wise old owl, they softened the points of my stress and allowed me to do what I considered communing with nature. But those recordings were as fake as one of Jenna's golden oldies television shows.

The last bit of sunlight snaps below the horizon, leaving me to sit alone at the fire and contemplate my life, even if there's a decent chance it will be over in a matter of hours. It's a funny thing, counting our lives in hours rather than years. I'd love the luxury of days even. But the real sounds of the wild mixing with the aggressive roar of my stomach won't let me dream into the future any further than tomorrow morning.

Something rustles in the brush to my back. I take hold of the branch that sits with one end in the fire. As I raise it up over my head, sparks shower down like fireflies, extinguishing before they connect with the ground. I hold the lit end near the place where the noise originated. There's nothing now. But I'm not stupid. We're not alone in our little camp. Eyes are all around, watching our moves, wondering if our food will be left unguarded, if our thighs might be tasty for dinner. I doubt the hidden creature is a vegetarian.

A shiver runs across my skin.

Muffled sobs echo from our half-destroyed shelter. I point my pathetic torch in the direction of Jenna and Vicky, the lucky ones who get the first sleeping shift. The sound is coming from Vicky, but she's not conscious. Her head moves back and forth while she whimpers.

Beside her Jenna lays flat on her back, her mouth hanging open, her breath uneven and punctuated with snores. She's not prepared to survive like this. None of us are.

The fact that the two of them are asleep, even if it is restless, is amazing. Their lives haven't exactly prepared them for the emotional intensity of life or death. Mine has.

I settle onto the smooth rock near the fire. The heat sinks through my pants and I let my skin begin to burn for a moment before I scoot back a couple inches. Sometimes feeling, even if it's unpleasant, is better than the numbness.

I'd forgotten that fact. How much more am I destined to remember now that it's too late to do anything different with my life?

When I came to Emery, I was as lost as I am right now. Maybe more. A foster kid with no one and nowhere to return to on vacations. I turned eighteen two months before high school graduation, and I was one of the lucky ones. My foster family didn't kick me out. They let me stay until September, provided I paid them rent. But what choice did I have? Life on the street? I'd been there before with my mother, and that's one place I would never willingly return.

I came to the University of Northwest Oregon on a bus, all my belongings in the world strapped to my back in a pack not much bigger than the one I have with me now. A grouchy woman behind the counter inside the depot gave me general directions toward campus, and off I went in search of a future. Until that point, my life had consisted of survival.

Funny how my life is coming to an end in much the same way it started.

The walk was only about a half mile, nothing I wasn't used to, and it gave me time to perfect my story. I designed a past with the purpose of giving myself a future. As a lifelong, off-and-on foster kid, I knew well that I wasn't the kind of girl people grew attached to. But in college, hours from the streets of Portland, I could re-create myself. The only thing that remained intact was my name. Ireland Jayne.

I was named by a nurse in a hospital. My mother must not have cared what I was called. The first time she left me was the day after my birth. It wouldn't be the last.

As a child, I thought if I went to Ireland someday, I'd find myself there. I still haven't gone. And now, I probably won't ever step foot on Irish soil.

I've played this made-up role for so long I'm not sure I can fully count on my memory to tell me the truth of where I came from. It's the lie told so many times that it becomes more real than any truth.

In my created life story, I'm the daughter of a long-haul trucker. I don't see him often, but I know he cares. He keeps a picture of me mounted on the dash of his truck. And I'm always on his heart. My mother, a woman who worked hard to give me all the things she didn't have growing up, moved to be near her family in Canada right after my high school graduation. She runs a bakery in a small village. Everyone loves her scones. And she has a cat.

It's been at least fifteen years since I allowed myself to wonder who my parents really are, if they're even still alive. I never met my father. My mother was an addict. She cleaned up every so often. The good times for her seemed to come around the time the state of Oregon was about to terminate her parental rights and place me in an adoptive family. But then there she'd be, professing her love. I was ten the last time I saw her. She left me alone in a bus station downtown. As her bus pulled away, she blew me a kiss. I was there for three days before anyone realized I'd been left. And by the time I was freed for adoption, there wasn't a family who'd take me.

Even with the years of lying my way through the past, I realize I'm still that little girl watching her mother pull away. Rejection leaves a dark aura on a life. And it can't be cleansed.

VICKY

I wake for the tenth time to the deep hoot of an owl. The fire crackles in our makeshift fire pit. It's Jenna's figure silhouetted by the orange flames now. Ireland lays beside me, her back to me.

The night is cool, cold by my usual standards, but nothing like the horrible chill and wet of the night before. The air is still, leaving only the sound of animals and the pounding in my head to keep my mind occupied.

Brushing my hand over my eye, I'm not surprised to feel it's gotten even bigger. I imagine the swelling stretching the skin, creating wrinkles on the canvas I've so carefully protected. None of it matters anymore.

In an effort to go back to sleep, I start my routine of replaying one of my sessions in my mind. The one that comes up first is a segment from last year about managing your family's schedules. I've used this little trick to order my thoughts for many years. It helps me stop the swirling of ideas and plans so I can relax and sleep. It only now occurs to me that I'm actually using my own ministry to bore myself into a place where I can dream.

Recalling each segment of the outline, I recite the lesson in my head. Not letting even the smallest tip be forgotten. I remember feeling that this was one of the most important segments, my words were so vital for my audience to hear. But now, knowing my life is at serious risk, the lecture is revealed for exactly what it was, shallow.

Why didn't I tell them to hug their children close? Why didn't I say that life is fleeting? Why didn't I tell them that sometimes risking your pride in order to humbly apologize is worth the bruise to your ego?

I want another chance.

I need to fix this.

When I open my eyes again, I can see the outlines of our prison coming into focus. Another day is dawning whether I want it to or not. There is so little I can control out here. So much I have to depend on God for—protection and provision. I've been counting on my own strength for most of my adult life. From the outside it seemed to be working.

But my way is a slow driving sickness, and it's invaded the bones of my family. When the news of Daniel leaving me goes public, I'll lose everything else I've collected. Some will blame me, a woman who claimed to know all about how to succeed as a mother and wife. Some will blame

Daniel, a man who looked outside of his marriage for comfort. But no matter what anyone thinks, the result is a solitary me . . . alone in the world.

Jenna stands, stretching. She rubs the heels of her hands into her eyes, then picks up a stick and smacks the brush at the edge of our camp. When she's satisfied that she's scared away any living creature, she steps away with our meager roll of toilet paper. I cringe. What will become of us when we run out? Or won't we survive long enough to finish the roll? It's just one more disaster in the process of our humiliating end.

The same question comes to me again.

Why am I here?

Maybe understanding the answer to this question will be the thing that brings this horrifying lesson to an end. With that, I get to my feet. I have a goal. And I will not die until I'm able to grasp the purpose and the process that brought me to where I am now.

JENNA

I wrap damp soil covered with broad leaves around Vicky's blistered pinky finger, tying it with a strip I've torn from one of Glenda's t-shirts. The dirt may cause infection. I don't know. It seems that being exposed could be worse. We may have to do some climbing today.

"Are you about ready for the great unveiling?" Ireland stands over our black trash bag. We followed the instructions as best we could with half the directions burned away. The plastic is lying over a hole in the ground and secured at the edges. She takes the rock off one corner and starts to pull back the cover.

"I wasn't this nervous my first day of classes." I stand close to Vicky, my arm around her waist. Under that plastic is our only hope. We need water.

Ireland takes the smaller rock off the center where it's designed to form a low point for the dew to run along the black sheet and into our waiting pot.

"Stop." Vicky steps forward. "We need to pray first. This isn't something to leave to chance."

I expect Ireland to protest, a strange change since she was always the one calling us to prayer in college. Instead, she's silent. No agreement. No argument. I miss her. It's a strange time to be hit by that reality. But it's true.

"Lord," Vicky says, "we are in a terrible way. We know you are the provider of all we need."

Ireland clears her throat.

"Lord, we need help." This time Vicky sounds real. Not like television Vicky. Like the Vicky I knew. "Please give us some water and give me another chance. I've really screwed some things up." Her words are choked. "I just want another chance." She doesn't say amen, just stops.

Ireland and I both look at Vicky. I'm waiting for her to explain, knowing she won't.

Vicky kneels down. "Well, let's see our future."

My mouth goes dry.

Ireland peels back the plastic. There in our pot is about an inch of water. It's enough to wet our mouths, but not much more. Fear claws me from the inside. What did I expect, our cup to actually be overflowing?

I go to church every Sunday. Each week I attend Bible study, teaching some of the lessons. My kids were homeschooled until high school. We wanted to send them to a private Christian school, but it just wasn't something we could afford. From the outside, I look like the model Christian wife and mother.

From the inside, there's nothing to see. I'm empty. A vessel. It's not that I don't believe. It's that I don't really care. Not about God. Not about Mark. Not about myself. Maybe it's dehydration. Maybe it's the beginning of my death. My life has never been clearer to me than it is right now. Without my kids, I'm nothing. They're my identity, and my identity has left me behind.

"You okay?" Ireland is staring at me, and I think Vicky is too. It's hard to tell with her eye like it is.

I take a mental inventory. Am I okay? Why are they asking? How could I be okay? I nod. But the phony smile won't come. I've even lost my great fake-it-till-you-make-it skills.

"We're going to be all right." Ireland runs her hand across the plastic guiding every drop into our pot. "You both have family who'll miss you. They'll call in the cavalry. Vicky, your group will certainly have enough power to send helicopters or whatever, right?"

Vicky's mouth drops open. She looks like she's taken a great shock.

"What?" I grab ahold of her sleeve.

"They won't be looking for me. I didn't tell them where I was. I wanted . . ."

"You wanted what?" I'm shaking her arm now. In the back of my mind I've had hope purely based on the public's outcry for their missing Christian home and family leader.

"I thought." She holds her fist to her lips. "I thought that if Daniel didn't know what happened to me, he'd worry. I thought this was the best way to disappear for a week. No one would know where I was."

Ireland takes off her glasses, rubs them on her t-shirt, and shoves them back into place. "Why would you do that? It's crazy."

"No kidding." I start to chew the inside of my mouth. It's already raw from days of worry and nerves.

"I don't expect you to understand." The hot words are thrown my way. "You have the perfect husband, and the perfect family. All we've heard since the reunion is your kids this or that. It's not like that for everyone."

"I've seen your show," Ireland says. It's a bit of a shocker. Ireland Jayne, environmentalist, God-questioner, Christian Home and Family Ministry watcher?

"That show is a bunch of garbage. It's a lie. And it's so well crafted that I didn't even know it until I came back to Emery." Vicky picks up the survival book and starts to thumb through it. "We need to move. The book says to stay in one place, but that doesn't make sense when we're not where we were supposed to be, and no one will be looking for us until one of you doesn't come home."

"No one's looking for me." Ireland's jaw is set. "The only one who'll notice I'm gone is my cat. And I made sure to leave the cat door open so she can go in and out. She'll pick up a meal at the neighbor's. I guess that makes me completely unneeded."

"They'll notice when you don't show up for class," I say.

"What class?" She looks away. "I'm on suspension."

Vicky gasps. "What on earth for?"

"Having an affair with a student, of course. Isn't that the kind of immoral behavior you expect from me?" She picks up the pot and starts to pour its meager contents into our shared water bottle. "Vicky's right. We need to get moving. This is not enough water to sustain us. Maybe if we're quiet, and listen to the wind, we'll hear the water. For there to be a waterfall there must be a river."

Chapter 13

IRELAND

I've become exactly the thing my mother said I was, a burden. At the age of six these were the words she left me to remember her by when she willingly sent me for another tour of the foster care system. But she didn't sign the termination papers. No, she didn't want me, but she wasn't about to give me to someone else. Two years later we were reunited. She said we'd always be together, and she'd missed me so much. *Right*. For forty years I've heard the echo of that one word. Burden.

I went to college on a scholarship for foster children and made up the difference with student loans. There was a time when I believed Emery was my family. Jenna, Hope, and Vicky were the sisters I never had. Then it all tumbled away. I was alone again. Alone, like I'd always been. And a carbon copy of my own mother in more ways than I can bear to look at.

We trudge through the thick trees and cushioned ground. My tongue and throat are desert-dry, making me cough and pant. Water is something we can't live without. That thought keeps my feet moving.

My head pounds like someone beats it with rocks from the inside and my stomach is sour and empty. There's one more granola bar, but without liquid, I would never get it down. The raw skin on my inner thighs has turned to weeping wounds. But we can't spare bandages. Vicky's used most of them already. Conservation is an unknown quality in her wasteful world.

The swelling in her eyes has gone down as we've walked, but that only means she can see me better, and I hate that. Ever since I opened my big mouth about the suspension, Jenna and Vicky have given me pity looks. I know they're praying for me silently in their heads. Don't they get it? This accusation is the least of my losses. It's nothing to me. Nothing like the failures that brought me to my current job in the first place.

My foot falls on hard ground. I look up. A path winds in front of me, starting my heart racing. As I turn back to the others, Vicky collides into my body. "We've found a trail." It's the first sign of a worn path since Vicky rolled down the mountain.

"Is it man-made?" Vicky rubs at her hip.

"Probably an animal path, but I'm sure there must be water somewhere along the way. We're not the only creatures dependent on it to sustain life."

Jenna shakes her head. "Cougars and bear." She plops down onto the ground. "I don't know if I can go much farther. I'm starved, and I hurt so bad, I can't take it." She crosses her arms on top of her knees and drops her head onto them. The next thing she says is a muffle of grunts. Great, we've lost the perky one. We're doomed.

"Maybe we should take a break." I drop my pack. Without the weight, I feel like I could almost float.

Vicky leans against a tree. She pulls the bottle from her bag. "Here's to hope." She takes a swig and hands it to Jenna.

Lifting her head, Jenna studies the jug. "This is it until tomorrow or a miracle. Are we sure?"

I nod. "There may not be a tomorrow if we don't find more."

She takes her drink then hands it to me. I pour the last bit into my mouth and hold it there as long as I can. My tongue swims in this luxury. But my stomach won't be held out on. Without my consent, I swallow, the pleasure is over, leaving me with a mouth as dry as it was before.

Part of me wants to give up. I wasn't meant for life. No one planned me, counting each day until I arrived. I've been an inconvenience since my very birth. If I lie down here on the cool earth, I could fade away and no one would be hurt. Not one life would change.

Except Vicky's and Jenna's. They need me, if only for this little part of history. I can't give up on them. "Come on. We need to keep moving. We can make it two or three more hours today. Surely there's water within that distance. The path heads down."

"The truck is up," Vicky says. "Isn't the truck the goal?"

"I'd love to agree, but I've been doing some thinking. We don't know for sure how to find it. If we go down, we're likely to come across a stream or something. With water, we can survive longer. Either way's a risk."

Vicky cocks her chin higher. "We have to stick with the plan. I say we keep looking for a way up the mountain."

"This isn't a dictatorship," I say.

Jenna flops back, her arms splayed over her head, her body flat on the ground. "I vote for down."

"Up," Vicky says.

I evaluate them both, giving every perspective a fair thought.

But Vicky crosses her arms in a stance that looks like an issued challenge.

"Down." I'm not about to let the last moments of my life be defined by a bully.

VICKY

I will not die in the pits of filth because these two have a different plan. I said we go up, that means we go up.

"Come on." Ireland keeps moving along her path. "You can fight us on this when we come to a place where climbing the mountain is even possible."

We've emerged from the trees with the mountain now a sheer rock at our right side. Heat radiates off the stone, cooking my dehydrated body. I'll look like a piece of jerky by the time we get out of this nightmare. If we ever get out. I rub my hand over my face. Once smooth, now it's rough and pitted with scrapes. My hair feels like I'm aiming to join the hippie crowd. I hope there isn't press when they find us. I hope they find us.

The ground at the left side of the trail plunges down. If we miss a step, it'll be another roll down the side of the mountain. This fall will be deadly. We've gone at least half an hour. Ireland drags her hand along the rock. I practically claw at it.

We come to a corner where the cliff juts out, forcing us to duck under the jagged stone or take the tumble.

Jenna hollers behind me.

I turn. She's holding her palm to her scalp. Blood oozes through her fingers.

My stomach churns. Breathing in through my nose, I try to keep from losing the only fluid in my body.

"Jenna, is it bad?" Ireland edges back to us.

"I don't know. It sure hurts." She pulls her hand away. There's a pool of blood in her palm.

I squat, putting my head between my knees. The ground rises and falls beneath me.

"Vicky, I need to get around you." Ireland warms my already hot shoulder with her hand.

I start to stand, but my body sways. Grabbing my arm, Ireland thrusts my side into the stone. It scrapes, but the pain feels safe. She squeezes past me, pressing me hard against the jagged surface.

Rolling back, I keep my spine tight along the wall of stone.

"It doesn't look as bad as I thought, but there's plenty of blood." Ireland puts the hem of her t-shirt into her mouth then rips, taking the bottom inches off in one piece. Tying this around Jenna's head, she holds her hand over the wound for a moment longer. "Can you go on?"

Jenna nods. "I'm a little dizzy, but I felt like that before I hit my head."

Ireland leans back next to me. "It's kind of funny, you know?"

I roll my head to look at her. "I can't believe you could find anything funny out here."

"The shortest one of us cut her head on overhanging rocks. Come on. That's a little funny." She presses her glasses higher onto her nose.

Jenna's laugh is like a child's giggle. I can't help but join in. Though dying like this isn't really humorous at all. It must be delirium.

We start out again. Soon the trail becomes steep downhill. My argument is pointless now. We somehow lost our way from the direction we came in with Glenda. We're in completely new territory.

Loose rock rolls out under my feet, and I slam down on my backside. Pain shoots up my spine and burns at scraped flesh. That may have been the only place I didn't already hurt. I'm completely battered now.

Without a word, Ireland reaches out for me and yanks me back to standing as she continues past. I don't think we miss a single step.

At the bottom of the hill Jenna startles us to a stop. "Listen. Do you hear that?"

I hear nothing over the scratching of my tongue against the roof of my mouth.

Ireland shakes her head. "What?"

"Water. I think I hear water."

I shake my head. "Sounds like you're having visions of a mirage except with your ears. There's no water." I start to walk again, passing Ireland. The crunch of their feet on the path behind moves us into a steady rhythm. I can't stop. If we take a break, I'm done.

The trail evens out and the soil becomes softer under my feet. There's a smell in the air I can't place. It's fresh, not that there's been a bad smell, but this is clean, new, almost rejuvenating.

"I hear it." Ireland grabs my arm. "Listen."

"Maybe." I'm not sure if I just want to so bad I think I hear the distant gurgle, or if it's real.

Jenna pushes around us. Her short legs speed forward. "I told you. I said I heard water. You should listen to me once in a while."

We take off after her, my throat burning with dehydration and anticipation.

I'm sure of it now. There's water somewhere out there. It's all I can do not to rip through the brush and go straight toward the sound. Maybe we'll make it.

JENNA

They never listen to me. They never did. No one does.

I hear these words over and over in my head, and I know I should fight them, but my brain is throbbing, and my mouth feels like it's been open to a hot wind all day. There's actual pain in the back of my throat, and I wonder if it's cracking like my lips.

I start to jog, puffing for air. I need this water more than I need to breathe. Or as much.

The sound is so loud now. I crave it like I crave my past. Crave the babies that are grown and gone. Crave the feeling of being needed by someone. By anyone.

The trail takes a gentle turn, and now I smell the water. Actually smell water in the air. It crashes, roars. I pick up speed until it's there. Right in front of me, more water than my body will ever need in this lifetime tumbles over a cliff and pours into a pond then rushes away in a gurgling stream.

I push myself forward, feeling the mist as it sprays my skin. At the edge, I drop to my knees, plunging my face into the cold, almost icy waters. I suck it in, pulling it through my mouth and down my throat, gulping like an animal until my lungs scream for air.

Coming up, my eyes are blurred by drops on my lashes. I swipe them away just in time to see something, someone disappear through the brush. Standing, I blink, my heart in a race for life. A person, I know it was a person. If there's someone here, they can help us. They can save us.

I stumble forward, my legs not moving as fast as the thoughts in my desperate brain. "Wait." I try to yell after him, but the sound is rough, raspy. "Please. Wait." I don't evaluate my next move, only fly forward on pure instinct, crashing through the bushes in the direction I saw the figure.

Branches and berry vines grab for me, but I shove through, whipping my head from side to side. Where has he gone? Why won't he stop? I'm lost now, no idea which direction he's taken. No idea how to find our only hope somewhere in this endless wilderness.

There's a rustle off to the side. It's breathing, panting. He's watching me. My gut goes sour, but I need this man to help us. "I hear you in there. Listen, my friends and I are lost. We don't want anything from you, just help getting out of here." I'm reminded of Grizzly Adams. He lived in the wilderness with a bear for a companion because he'd been wrongly accused of a crime. Maybe this guy is in a similar situation. Maybe he has a bear.

"Please. We won't tell anyone about you, if you like." Grizzly Adams always helped out, even at his own risk. I step closer to where I hear him. Maybe if he gets a good look at me. I'm harmless. All of five foot four.

I pull back branches and there are eyes meeting mine. Low eyes. Cat eyes.

My heart slams against my chest as I take three strides back. Adrenaline buzzes down my arms. I can't pull oxygen through my clamped throat. This isn't the way I want to go.

The eyes follow me. Edging forward, he comes into the light. Soft, sleek fur shines against taut muscles. He crouches, his gaze intense on mine, his tail twitching with anticipation. The anticipation of the attack. The attack on me.

I can't run, can't even move. I'm paralyzed with the fear of the thing I can't stop.

He pumps his back legs, his ears standing up straight. I watch every tiny action, knowing it will be my last observation.

With movements ever so slight, his weight shifts, and it's time, he's preparing to lunge. I cover my face with my arms, watching through the crack between them.

He pulls back, tightening his springs.

The air echoes and cracks. My ears ring. There's another shot. This time I turn and see Vicky, her eyes closed, her hands wrapped around a gun.

My chest pounds. I look back to the cougar, expecting him to lie dead in the dirt, but he's not. His eyes blaze as if the bullets only made him rage. There's a jagged roar, and I fumble back as he bounds, claws forward, down on me.

VICKY

My arms buzz like my veins are filled with bees. I've missed. Twice. The gun is heavy in my hand. I can't lift it to try again. My legs collapse and I'm in the dirt.

Ireland grabs my elbow, ripping the gun from my grip.

I wrap my arms over my head, squeezing my eyes tight.

Two more shots ring out, but I can't look. I can't face what's happening. I wish the bullet would have pierced my heart. My screams block out all other sounds. Over and over I hear my own desperate voice crying out, and I can't rein it back. My body tumbles onto the ground. I'm done.

"Why am I not dead?" Jenna yells.

It's the last voice I expected to hear. In my mind, she's already gone.

I lift myself up on an elbow and pull my hands from my eyes. They're covered in muddy tears. The trembling is too much. I can barely sit, forget ever standing again.

Jenna is on her back, the cougar sprawled across her lap, one claw clinging to her sweater. He twitches, then he's still.

Jenna's gaze swings from the dead animal to Ireland and back to the beast on top of her. She wriggles her legs free and scoots on her bottom until she's put ten feet between the animal and herself. There are four blood-streaked lines trailing down her neck.

"Where'd you get that?" Jenna points at the gun in Ireland's hand.

Ireland's narrowed eyes are drilling into me. She doesn't have to ask.

"It was Glenda's. I thought it might come in handy." I bite my lower lip, hard.

"You were carrying a weapon, and you didn't think you should tell us?" Ireland holds the gun out in front of her, flicks open the cylinder and spins it, then clicks it back into place. "Looks like there's one bullet left." She shoves the pistol into the back of her pants.

Jenna climbs to her feet. "Good shot. Thanks."

Ireland doesn't respond. She doesn't even take her gaze away from me. I'm sitting squarely in her judgment seat.

My face goes numb, and my stomach pitches. On my hands and knees I lunge for the brush where I heave the nothing from my stomach.

There's a hand on my back, rubbing gentle circles. "It's going to be okay," Ireland says. "No one died. But the way you shoot, it's amazing Jenna's still here. You're more of a hazard than that mountain lion ever thought to be."

I push up onto my knees. "I'm sorry."

"Why didn't you tell us you had it?" Ireland grabs my hand and pulls me to standing.

She's talking to me like a child. I wipe my palm across my mouth. "I was afraid you'd take it away, just like you did. I don't want to die out here, and I don't care what you think about gun control."

Ireland crosses her arms. "A lot you know. I have a revolver like this at home, but mine's a twenty-two. This is a thirty-eight. Don't make judgments based on societal stereotypes. You don't have to be an every-Sunday churchgoing Republican to appreciate the right to bear arms. You could have killed Jenna."

"She would have been killed if I hadn't shot." The fire is returning to my gut, and I relish the empowerment of its flame.

"Hello there." Jenna waves her hands over her head. "I just faced death, and the two of you are fighting over your stupid pride. Get over yourselves. Ireland carries the gun from here out. If I'm going to die on this trip, I don't want it to be because I was shot by the people who are supposed to be my friends."

She stomps away, grumbling something I can't quite make out.

Chapter 14

IRELAND

Twenty years of moving in the crowd that strives to protect animal rights, gone. Living on the brink of my own ruin has my mind spinning with confusion. This beautiful animal, who simply wanted to feed herself in the only way she knew, is dead at my feet. And I took her life.

I run my hand over her silky fur. So beautiful. She's a majestic queen even in death. I'm sick we've come into her territory and taken her very breath. We have no business being here. No business hiding from our problems in the wilderness. No business bringing our issues into a place that's still clean of human contamination.

But here we are, and there doesn't seem to be any way out.

The gun is cool against my skin. I hate how it makes me feel empowered to have the metal snuggled against me. Never in my life have I considered using a gun on an animal. A human, yes. But never an animal. They don't come after people with the intention of causing pain. That cougar, she just wanted dinner. Not really much different from what I'm feeling now.

"We need the meat." Jenna's face doesn't reflect relief or disgust, only fact.

I shake my head. "I can't do that."

"What choice do we have?" Vicky says. "I'm so weak, I can't make it much farther without some protein."

I reach down and pull Vicky to standing. The three of us loom over our catch. A beautiful cat. No, this is not the way I turn my back on my morals. No way. "I can't do it."

"Then he dies for nothing." Jenna's words sting.

I kneel down, running my palm from the crown of her head along her back. She's massive, so much like the nature I claim to worship. Her tail lays thick and long, still in the dust. *Your life needs to mean something. Thank you for sharing it with us.* My eyes water, but I blink hard and pull back my focus. "I can't be here. You'll have to do this on your own."

"I've cut up Mark's deer. It can't be that different. We'll need a section of the rope and a knife."

Vicky's eyes round. "Do one of you have Glenda's knife?"

Jenna and I shake our heads.

"Then it's . . ."

I finish the sentence for her. "Buried with Glenda."

❖ ❖ ❖

There's blood on Jenna when they return to the pond. Blood on her clothes, on her skin, and covering our only cutting device, the hatchet.

Vicky carries the metal canister that used to contain our beans and jerky. She holds it away from her body, like a bomb ready to explode. There's not a drop of blood on Vicky.

No words are spoken about what just happened. I heard the sound of the blows over the rush of water cascading down the cliff. That's enough for me forever. Vicky tucks the canister into the shade and joins us at the water.

We sit at the edge of the pond, Jenna facing away from the water, her eyes intent on the brush. Our stomachs are filled with the sweet liquid, and the throbbing in my head has lessened. I strip off my layers, placing the gun on the dirt, and dunk the clothes into the water, swirling them around. The days of sweat and dirt fade away. I wring out my t-shirt and lay it on the rock next to me.

The sun is high overhead, but it isn't as hot as yesterday. Maybe it's the icy water cooling the air here. Maybe it's the new fears that have settled into our veins.

I plunge my pants in and out of the pond, then stretch them flat on another rock.

The water cuts into me as I step in. It steals my breath and stills my movement. Prickles of pain give way to hardening numbness. I cup water in my hands and run it over the raw flesh on my inner thigh.

"What happened?" Jenna kneels at the water's edge.

"Just some rubbing from my pants. It's fine." I draw in air, then dip under the water. It rushes over me, freezing, refreshing. Lifting my head into the open, it's warmer now. I feel . . . alive. And I smile. The sun shines down on my face, blessing me with the kiss of her warmth. With both hands, I push water around my body. "You should come in. It's an amazing feeling to be weightless and clean."

Jenna takes another hard look at the brush.

"Don't worry. We've made so much noise, there's probably not an animal for miles."

Jenna steps in without taking off her clothes. She holds tight to a tree limb like she's afraid she'll wash away in the four feet of water. Blood clears from her skin, mixing with the crystal clear liquid.

I step farther away.

Vicky hasn't said anything in twenty minutes. She stares down at her feet, gone away from where we are.

"Isn't that better?" I ask.

Jenna shivers. Her teeth chatter. "Yes. So. Much. Better."

I laugh as she rubs her arms vigorously and her shirt floats around her chest. It's enough to crack a smile on her face.

Cold water sprays me. She's actually splashed me. I jump back, flatten my palm, and smack the surface, sending droplets all over Jenna's head.

She squeals and sounds like the girl I knew again. Her mouth tightens. Her eyes dart from me to Vicky, nodding with a smile barely contained.

I get the message and we both sneak up behind.

"Vicky?" Jenna says.

Vicky turns, confusion evident on her face.

Then Jenna covers her with water.

Vicky screams, jumping to her feet. "What did you do that for?"

"You seemed like you needed cooling off, and I owe you one." She splashes again.

Vicky's eyes soften. She glances around as if she doesn't want to embarrass herself, then runs full force into the water, dipping under the surface. When she breaks free and stands, even scratched and bruised, she's like a mermaid, water dripping from her blond hair and lashes. This is why so many women worship her and seek her wisdom. Vicky is stunning. She's the kind of woman we all want to look like. She's the one every guy stares at, and who is never without a date. Even at our age, I'm sure she gets plenty of attention.

I don't think a man has considered me that way, with no strings attached, maybe ever. That's not true. Skye looked at me like that. I lift myself onto the hot rock and watch the water roll off my body, turning the stone's light gray to dark.

"Did I scare you out?" Vicky investigates me with her one good eye.

"No. Just needed some warm air. You're beautiful, you know." I have no idea why I'm telling her this, there's just this nagging feeling that she needs to hear it.

Her smile flattens. "Not so much anymore. Not without all the help I can get from cosmetics and lotions." She brings her hand down her face. "I've been thinking about surgery."

"Why?" Jenna asks.

"It's not so easy getting older when you have a camera in your face all the time. Everyone is waiting to see me fall. There's no shortage of women ready to take my place."

"But you work in a Christian ministry." Jenna sits on the bank, dangling her feet in the water. "It's not about how you look."

Vicky's smile is sarcastic. "You'd be surprised."

"You've got Daniel, and I'm sure he loves you even with a wrinkle or two," I say. "Really, Vick, you're gorgeous. But that's not all that matters."

"Daniel doesn't find me attractive anymore. Apparently, my thirty-year-old assistant is more to his liking." She dips her head back into the water, emerges, and wipes the drips away with her hands. I wonder how much of the liquid is from tears.

Jenna slips back into the water and wades toward Vicky. "That can't be true. I've seen your family on television. You look genuinely happy, and you must be the perfect wife."

Vicky shakes her head, but doesn't add anything.

Vicky

I'm exposed. Raw. My failures open for Jenna and Ireland to see. And it feels more like I'm home than I've felt in Texas for at least ten years. Even if this is the end, and I could go to my grave without anyone knowing I screwed up my marriage and my husband no longer loves me, I'm glad Jenna and Ireland know. It's not everything, but there's a weight lifted.

We're filling our jug and canteens with water, then we'll leave the waterfall and pool behind for the night. Ireland pointed out tracks from various kinds of animals. We don't want to be camped where they all converge.

I have three sets of clothes, and I've worn all of them. Two sets I washed in the pond and laid out to dry. The cleanest, I'm wearing. Tomorrow we'll come back and I'll wash the other set.

Pulling my t-shirt from the branch it's been hanging on, I notice little hand prints in the moist soil. It looks like a baby was here, pressing her fingers in and leaving a stamp. My gaze follows them to the rocks beside the water. It's there. "No." It's meant to be a scream, but my voice only manages a whisper.

Jenna and Ireland look up.

I point to the creature on the rocks, his eyes behind a dark mask.

His paws are in my pack.

"It's a raccoon," Ireland says.

I want to thump her for stating the obvious. "Yes, but what do we do? Should we shoot it?"

"Are you crazy?" Ireland turns to me.

Jenna steps closer to him. "We're not going to kill you, little guy. We just want you to leave Vicky's stuff alone, okay?"

The raccoon tilts his head and runs a hand over his mouth, then reaches in my pack again. He pulls out the survival book, tipping it one way then the other.

"No." I hold my palm out like a stop sign. "That's not for you."

With both paws, he grips the book and pulls it tight to his chest, then sniffs the binding.

I step back. "He's going to take the book."

"Just stay calm." Ireland crouches down. She pulls a bag with a half handful of seed out of her pack. Where did she get that? I thought we were sharing our food.

The raccoon sets the book down, half on the rock and the other half hanging over the water. My stomach tightens into a stone.

He eyes Ireland and the seeds.

She tosses one near him.

Easing to the edge of the rock, he looks down at the food, sits on his back legs, and stretches his body tall.

Ireland tosses a few more. One lands beside him.

The raccoon picks it up and presses it into his mouth. Then rubs his hands together. All at once, he jumps down, knocking my pack and the book into the water.

We all lunge forward. Jenna yanks my bag out, but the book hits the current and tumbles away from us down the creek. I splash into the water, staggering after it. Pages separate and sail away. I grab for every paper my hand can snag, but more escape than are saved.

Rocks roll under my feet. I trudge through. I can't see where they've gone. My foot lands in a hole, sending me toppling under the surface. I gasp before my face comes back out. Water burns my airway. I choke and cough, sputtering for breath until my breathing becomes hard sobs.

That book was the only thing that gave me hope. I need to have answers. What will we do now? My thoughts flash to my cell phone inside my pack. No. Not that too.

I push up against a rock that slides under my weight, dropping me down hard on my elbow. Pain shoots needles up my arm and nausea engulfs my middle. A hand grasps my other arm, pulling me upright. It's Ireland. I fall into her embrace and cry. "I can't do this anymore."

"You don't have a choice. Just like you don't have a choice about your marriage. When you get home, and you will, you're going to fight with every ounce of your tiny body to keep your family together. Don't give up on surviving, and do not give up on Daniel."

I pull back and look up at her. "Why are you saying this?

"Because I know what it's like on the other side. It's a very lonely existence. You have to fight. I ran away." She tugs me toward the dry ground. "How many pages did you get?"

I open my fist. A clump of unreadable paper. They're useless. There's no point finding the rest. This is the second time the book has been waterlogged. Maybe God is trying to tell me something. I never listen the first time.

JENNA

My culinary skills have arrived at a new level. Whether that's a compliment or an insult is still to be decided, but I'm actually here in the middle of nowhere, cooking cat meat on an open fire.

I boil one piece with some water in the pot, and another I hold over the flame using two green branches I cut from a baby tree. The smell is amazing, even without spices or seasoning. It's been two days since we ran out of jerky. Opossum might be tasty before this journey ends.

"When Carrie was little, the only thing we could get her to eat was beans." I stir the coffee pot of boiling water with our last handful of beans mixing with the meat. "I could cook them any old way, and she'd scarf them down. She didn't eat meat until her sixth birthday. Mark came home the week before with an elk he'd downed. Carrie wanted to try it, just to please her father. There was no going back after the first bite."

Ireland nods, but she's silent. I can't read her anymore. It seems like everything I say offends her. Was it the mention of eating meat? Or because I go on about my family relentlessly? I know I do it. I can hear myself, but I can't stop the flow of memories that cross my tongue. It's like I need to relive every moment of their lives before I'm gone. Like I'm committing them to eternity. I just wish I could get her to eat the cougar.

"Mark turned out to be a pretty good husband." Vicky combs her fingers through her hair. There's no expression on her face as it glows in the light of the fire. "You were a good choice for him."

My jaw tightens. There it is. It's been stewing for years and it's finally out of the pan.

"I was the only and best choice for him." I regret the words as soon as they leave my mouth. This is not the place to destroy each other. Not when we need to stick together now more than any other time. "I'm sorry. I think I've been consumed with jealousy for so many years, my tongue gets away from me." I stand up and pace around. "I literally hate that he loved you first."

My hands shake in front of me. I squeeze my fists and turn back to the fire, rotating the meat on the sticks. It's shrinking like it's drying out.

Vicky shrugs. "He never loved me. He never even knew me."

"Two years is a long time to be with a man and say he never knew you." I keep my gaze on the hardening rock that will be dinner. "I don't think that's true. Do you know how many times I've watched you on television and thought how happy Mark would have been with you?"

My face is growing hot, and I don't think it's because of the fire. It's all bubbling up. More than I knew was down there.

"You have no idea what you're talking about." Without even looking her way, I can see the glib expression.

"Why? Because I'm just a mom? Is that it? I couldn't possibly have anything of value in my brain, because I haven't used it for all these years, right?"

"Whoa." Ireland steps back. "Let's not have a battle of who has it worse or who should have been with whom. None of us is perfect, but the two of you have it pretty darn good. That's enough negative energy. Oh my goodness, Jenna. You have a husband and three children. Yeah, they left for college. Did you really expect them to sit around the house for you to serve forever? If they had, it would only prove that you hadn't done your job."

She turns to Vicky. "And you. If your husband really doesn't find you attractive anymore, he's nuts. That isn't on you. But my guess is the guy probably wants you as you, not as some television evangelist. You can't manipulate every situation. Be real."

"What would you know about being real?" Vicky's voice throws flames with her words. "You have no idea who I am. And you certainly don't have a clue about who you are. This act"—she throws her arms in the air—"I'm not buying it. I know exactly who I am."

"Do you?" Ireland's question is meant for Vicky, but it hits me hard and dead center.

"I don't," I say, almost in a whisper.

They both stop, staring at me. At least I could deflect the argument for a moment.

"I don't have a single clue who I am." I squat back down, sliding the meat onto a rock and stirring the beans again. "All I wanted was to be a wife and mother. I gave everything to have those babies. We used all our savings, put another mortgage on the house." I shake my head. "I don't regret it, any of it. But, sometimes, it's like I sold my soul for the chance to have children. Now they're gone, and there's nothing left of me. They were me."

"Do you love Mark?" Vicky asks.

It seems like a horrid question coming from the woman who gave him up because her mother didn't approve. She left a scar on my husband that's made me furious more than once. But the question remains.

"Of course I love him. He's my husband. It's not about loving, it's about living. It's about caring for someone else so deeply you're willing to put them first."

"When do you come first?" Ireland stares into the fire. "When do you just be you?"

"I don't know who *I* am, so how can I ever just be me? Something happened this year. I woke up from a dream. It was a very beautiful dream, but when I went to sleep, I was someone else. And now, I have no idea who I am. I'm not her anymore, and I'm not the woman in the dream. I'm lost. I'm just wandering around in the world, one of the lost people who don't know why they're even here."

"I get that." Ireland touches my arm. "We come from very different lives, but that thing you said about not knowing who you are, about being lost in the world, needing to know your purpose here. That's me. I'm one of them too."

I squeeze her hand, and she grips my fingers.

Vicky's shuddered breath draws my attention. I walk around the fire and pull her down into my arms. "I'm sorry. I wasn't kind. It's hard to remember you're a real woman when you look so put together on television."

"That's not me." She sniffs. "That's a made-up character that gives the audience what they tune in to get. It's not me on the show. It's not me when I do speaking engagements. And it's not even me when I go home. I don't know how to turn it off. I'm so afraid that if I don't do it well enough, I'll lose my family." She shakes her head against my shoulder. "Who am I kidding? I'm out in the middle of nowhere, and I still put a spin on things."

She stands straight. "I've lost my family. My daughter can't stand me. She spends all day and late into the night with a boy who looks like a wannabe gang member. My son was picked up with marijuana last year. We did a lot of legwork to keep that one under wraps. We're a mess. Daniel's interest in my assistant is merely a tiny symptom of our family's cancer."

Chapter 15

VICKY

I hate it here. I hate it, but part of me doesn't ever want to be found. The more truth, reality, and sadness that spills from me, the more I know I can't bear to go home. I will never fit into that life again. The denial has passed. With it went the fit. I can't manage my family, my life, and my marriage like I do my calendar for even one more day.

Jenna lies next to me under the shelter, while Ireland takes a turn manning the fire and watching for danger. I know Jenna is as awake as I am. The conflict between us is heavy. It's like another person under the tarp, taking up space and air and comfort. It's more than Mark. But it is Mark.

I walked away from him to protect him. My mother would have made his life miserable, but he may have made my life wonderful. Daniel was a law student when Mother introduced us. He had this amazing future before him. There were political aspirations, following in his family's footsteps.

It wasn't until years after our wedding that I discovered the man I married had no interest in the law or holding office. He'd come home exhausted and bury himself away in the garage with his tools.

That was when I started to push forward on my own power. Maybe it was a way to deflect my family's attention from Daniel. Or maybe I want to remember it that way because it makes me look better when I deny my frustration with our unwritten contract. I married a man who was supposed to make me into the woman I'd always failed to be. In the end, I had to create the image on my own.

Without thinking, I let a long sigh escape.

"You want to talk about it?" Jenna's voice is groggy.

"It's nothing."

"We both know that's not true."

I readjust the sweatshirt under my head. "Why didn't you tell me when you started to date Mark?"

She's silent so long, I wonder if she's gone to sleep. Then she shifts her weight so she's facing me. I can't actually see her, but I hear the direction of her breathing. "I was scared. I didn't want you to come and take him back. Mark took it so hard when you ended it at graduation. I meant to console him. Honestly, there was never any intent for it to go further."

"You were right to keep it from me."

"No. I should have been honest."

"I would have come between you. I was right to end the relationship. My family would have destroyed Mark. But, you know who I am. I would never have let you have him."

"Mark wanted to call you and explain it. He always felt bad about how it worked out. He feels like I lost my best friend because of him."

"That's not the story I told myself. When I got your letter, the one saying you were engaged and all, I decided you'd been planning it all along. I told myself you loved Mark when we were dating, and you were just waiting for a chance to get your claws in him." Saying the words brings the anger back, even if I know it's not true. I turn my head away from her, hoping she can't sense the fury I still hold inside.

"I promise you, I didn't. I didn't really even know him when you were together. And I never, not even once, looked at him that way. We started talking one night. You were already gone, and I was still in town working at the restaurant until I could start my teaching job. We were the only people left from our graduating class. And he needed someone to talk to."

"So, you heard everything? I bet he had a lot of horrible things to say about me."

"No. And in the end, we both realized how God was in it from the beginning. I love my husband. I'm not going to apologize for that. In fact, that's the reason I'm going to do everything I can to get home. I've taken him for granted. When I figure out who I am and what God has me here for, I'm going to spend the rest of my life striving to do my best at that and at my marriage."

"I hope you have that opportunity."

"I hope we all do. Everyone deserves a second chance. You, me, and Ireland. And we deserve each other. I don't want us to drift apart ever again."

"You don't know what you're saying. When we get back, I'll be a joke in the Christian community. You won't want to be associated with me in any way."

A sound escapes her mouth. It's something between a giggle and a sigh. I can't read her intent. "Don't fool yourself. I don't love you for the image of you. I love *you*, Vicky. And I love Ireland. You're the sisters I never asked for." I can hear the laughter in her words now. When was the last time someone had the courage to tease me?

I reach out and touch her arm. "Thank you."

"It's nothing."

"No. It's really something. I can't believe I gave this up."

"Yep. You wasted over twenty years not being stuck in the wilderness fighting for your survival. What a pity."

The dam is broken. Laughter bursts from my chest. There's no holding back. No reason to be proper. No one to impress. And it feels like a fresh spring afternoon. Like life.

The covers move beside me and I feel Ireland squeeze into the shelter. "No need to fend off the wild tonight. I'm sure you've scared away anything looking for a meal."

I nudge her with my shoulder.

There's the tiniest giggle, then a snort.

"You love us," I say.

"Oh gag."

And Jenna rolls over the top of me, tackling Ireland in a full-on hug.

IRELAND

My head snaps up and my foot kicks forward, knocking into a stick from the fire. Embers sparkle and rise toward the sky. I stretch my hand in front of me, tip my neck to one side then the other, and try to breathe oxygen into the deepest parts of my lungs.

Just about to step onto the stage, the sun glows at the edge of the sky. I've slept little, mainly due to the growling pain in my stomach. Maybe I should give in and eat the cougar. But then who am I?

There's a natural draw toward survival. It's a physical instinct that screams from the core of our humanness. But for me, there's another desire in my soul. Maybe deeper than anywhere else. I long to be done. To say, I'm finished. To close my eyes and let whatever power holds eternity punish me however I deserve. I want to face the end, and find the nothingness of it.

I stand, ensuring I won't doze off again, and look up into the sky. It's a whole different world here. The stars shine like they've been turned up and millions more joined them. They're only dimming now with the sun. If God is out there, he doesn't care about me. For twenty years I've tried to walk away from him. I've tried to have the same attitude. If he can leave me, abandon me like any parent on Earth, why can't I walk away and forget him?

The sky is too big above me. I'm supposed to be comfortable in nature. I've dedicated my career to saving this planet, this view, this fresh air. But I want to curl up on my mattress at home and watch a senseless television show. I want to drive to the movie theater with friends. Yes, with friends. And I want popcorn no matter what kind of chemicals they use to produce it. And I want butter. Lots of slimy, gooey, slippery butter. So much butter the salt has no choice but to stick.

The brush behind the shelter shifts. The sound is slight, but in this still morning, I can't miss it. I run my hands over the cool metal of the revolver, keeping my finger off the trigger, but ready to move in an instant.

From the fire, I pick up a burning stick. Its flames soften as I bring it away from the rest, but there's a bit of light, and I need it. If I have to, I'll use the fire to protect us first, saving the one remaining bullet. If we survive, there will be other predators.

Two steps closer, and I hear it touching the tarp. Jenna and Vicky are sound asleep. Soft snores come from Jenna's side.

My heart races. If it's something big, and I scare him, he'll certainly kill both of them before I can do anything. I'll be in the wilderness. And I'll be alone again.

I don't want to be alone. Not in this decision and not in my life. I'm tired of that lifestyle. I'm tired of protecting myself.

Stepping around the side of the shelter, I lift the flame high, the gun pointed in the direction of the last sound.

I suck in breath and jump back.

My motion wakes Vicky. She sits up, rubbing her eyes. "What is it?" Then she registers my alarm and starts to kick away the blankets.

It's too late. The torn flap of the tarp moves and she's face-to-face with a skunk.

"What is that stink?" Jenna rolls over and answers her own question.

I still can't speak. There's nothing I can say or do. I can't shoot the thing. He's too close. And if I did, he'd probably spray.

Vicky scoots away in a crab-walk kind of motion.

In a second, Jenna is up. She stumbles toward me, alarming our visitor and screaming at the top of her lungs.

He twists, raises his tail, and lets a stream of nasty shower everything in his reach, with a direct hit to Vicky.

Her screams join Jenna's.

The smell could make a landfill seem like the place to build a home. My eyes water, and I'm choking on the stink that's so thick it has a flavor. It's ridiculously horrible. I keep backing away, but the stench follows me.

The skunk, without even an ounce of remorse, saunters off into the brush. He's left us like the aftermath of an atomic bomb. Jenna gags, losing what's left of the water and cougar she had for last night's dinner.

My eyes water so fiercely I can't get them clear enough to see the mess we're in. Some sentry I am.

JENNA

It burns. My eyes. My lungs. Everything is on fire. I'm too freaked out to cry, but my eyes run like I've lost my entire family in a tragic accident. My throat feels like it's swelling shut, probably the body's way of stopping this putrid odor from making it farther inside.

I swat my hand around looking for the jug of water. When I find it, I unscrew the cap and gulp, then pour the rest over my face. It helps for a moment, then the burn strikes back.

Somewhere behind me, Vicky is screaming. I think she's been doing that since before the skunk sprayed, but I'm not really sure. There's a hand on my cheek. I hope it belongs to Ireland, because I know it's not Vicky and I'm suddenly reminded of the man I thought I saw by the waterfall.

"Did you get the spray in your eyes?" Ireland asks.

"I don't think so. It's just the smell. It's like acid in the air."

"I know. I'm so sorry." She sets me down on a rock, and I feel the warmth of the fire on my legs.

I blink rapidly until the world comes into a bit of focus. The sun is rising and pink clouds color the sky, casting blue shadows across the ground.

Ireland grabs Vicky by the shoulders and gives her a hard shake. "Stop screaming," she shouts.

Vicky collapses into Ireland's arms, sobbing like a little child.

"It's going to be okay. This isn't forever, and we're all fine, all right?"

A snotty yes is muffled in Ireland's shoulder.

"The sun is coming up." Ireland guides Vicky to my rock. "We can go to the waterhole and clean up."

My stomach shrinks. I'm sure our dinner was not the only mountain lion on the block.

"No." Vicky stands upright. "The book said to avoid places like that at dawn and dusk. This is bad enough without trying to play hide-and-seek with bear and cougar we can't even see." She wipes the back of her hand across her swollen eyes. "Can someone hand me the water jug?"

Now I'm really sick. "I'm sorry. I panicked."

She stomps her foot, presses her hands into her sides and whips her head around to face me. She's off by about three feet, but I'm not going to mention that right now either. "How could you? That was so selfish."

"I wasn't thinking."

"I'll say you weren't. If I'm blinded from this, well . . . You'll hear from my attorney."

"Ha." I jump up. "Good luck finding a lawyer or a court for that matter out here in Skunkville. And for your information, you can have everything I've got. That consists of two t-shirts, a sweatshirt, and a pair of pants at least three inches too short and five inches too big around the waist for you."

"Fine," Vicky says. "I'll take them, and the clothes you're wearing. I can make a tent from my winnings. My own tent. Where I don't have to share space with takers."

"You're calling me a taker?" I push way into her personal space. "Is this about Mark again? You have a lot of nerve. No wonder your husband doesn't want you."

Ireland steps closer to us. "Are you two serious? Did the skunk spray make you nuts? Just knock it off."

My emotions are a jumble. One minute I want to hug Ireland and Vicky, the next, I'm spitting insults at her face.

Vicky uncrosses her arms. "I'm sorry. I lost it. But you didn't need to yell at me."

"Yes, I did. But I'm over it now. How are your eyes?"

"Terrible, but I can see."

Ireland clicks the safety on the gun and returns it to her waistband. "We need to do better if we're going to get the two of you home to your families."

My family. I imagine Mark seeing me verbally attack Vicky and flush with shame. Ireland is proving to be more levelheaded than we are. Who does Ireland have missing her at home? I'm sick with what I've neglected. And I'm sick with what I've taken for granted. I have everything.

Chapter 16

VICKY

It's still cold when we get to the waterhole, but I jump in without taking time to adapt. The icy chilled water soothes my burning eyes. I gulp, drinking until my stomach is so bloated I can't stand the tension.

The smell seems better, but my olfactory senses may have surrendered in the Skunk Wars. It's possible that I'll never enjoy the scents of Thanksgiving dinner, fresh picked roses, or baby shampoo ever again. Permanent damage.

My body shivers.

Ireland and Jenna sit next to me. I imagine we look like three women soaking away our troubles in the warm springs at a resort, but we're not warm, and this isn't relaxing.

"What are we going to do?" My voice is soft. The tissue in my throat so raw and angry, it's like I've been screaming at a football game for days.

Neither of them answer. Hope is running out of us, and God hasn't shown up with a miracle yet. Matters continue to get worse each hour. My stomach growls. I'd love another piece of cougar meat. And I hope no one ever finds out that I ate a cat, and I liked it. That's one of the many secrets we'll share if we ever get out.

I watch Ireland drip water off her fingertips onto her arm. She stuck to her guns last night and only ate beans. It must be killing her. A tear prickles behind my eye. Have I ever felt so passionately about something that didn't benefit me in some way? Even my service to the Lord serves me. So is it really service?

There's a shadow at the edge of my vision. I turn my head and my

147

breathing stops. A man, dressed head to toe in fur, scratches the top of his matted head with a stick. Around his waist a vine ties his clothing tight. It must be years since his last shave, maybe tens of years.

I tap Jenna with my finger and point in his direction. He hasn't seen us, but by the way he's wrinkling his nose, I can tell he's picked up our odor.

Jenna's expression goes wild. She nudges Ireland, points to her eyes and then to the place where we killed the cougar. "I saw him yesterday," she whispers in my ear.

His head extends higher, and he looks around. Then he spots us.

"Wait," I say as he backs toward the trees. "We need your help. We're lost." I stand and step from the water. Cold rushes my body, and I convulse with a violent shiver.

He won't make eye contact with me, only continues backward, some kind of grunting coming from his throat.

"Please." Jenna is beside me. "Show us how to get out of here. We won't hurt you. We just want to get home to our families."

He leans forward, squinting at us, taking us in one at a time.

I reach for my pack and pull out the cell phone that doesn't start up anymore and the flashlight, another casualty of the raccoon. "Here. You help us find our way out, and we'll give you these." I hold them out for him to see.

He backs away, cringing as if he's Superman and I'm offering him kryptonite. Then he bursts through the brush and down the hill, sticks cracking and crunching with each leap. I run after, but he moves like he's part of the wild and I'm . . . not. Giving up, I turn back.

"What was that?" Ireland stares, unblinking.

"I knew it." Jenna pushes past me. She cups her hands around her mouth. "Wait. We're not going to hurt you."

"Really?" I shake my head. "You're worried the crazy guy who lives in the woods, probably with the skulls of all the lost people before us, is scared of three half-starved, bruised, cut up, and stinking-like-a-skunk women?"

She turns back. "I saw him yesterday. That's why I went ahead without you both. That's why I ran into the cougar."

"So, he's a real gentleman, huh?" I'm less than impressed by this guy. He probably couldn't help us if he wanted to.

"Why didn't you tell us about him?" Ireland asks.

Jenna's mouth cocks up in a half smile. "I thought he was just in my imagination. I was so hungry and thirsty. I assumed I made him up, and I was embarrassed. I didn't want you both thinking I couldn't hack it."

"We know you can't." Ireland nudges Jenna with her elbow. "None of us can. But we will anyway."

"With the help of God." Jenna runs a finger over her cracked lips.

"Then I'm in good company. God wouldn't let you and Vicky die out here." Ireland smiles, but her eyes are deep with sadness.

What happened to the girl who taught me who God is?

IRELAND

Today is like giving in to the reality of our deaths. We don't hike. We don't break down our camp. We're utterly lost, waiting for someone to save us. And it's like waiting for a miracle. They never actually arrive.

This morning my stomach was growling like a hungry bear, but now even my digestive system has given up. There hasn't been a rumble from my belly in hours. And it's not because I've eaten. In a panic yesterday, while Jenna and Vicky were hacking up that mountain lion, I ate my last granola bar. And then we finished the beans.

"I wish we had some cards." Jenna sits on the edge of a log, looking into the fire pit. She hasn't moved in at least an hour.

The scent of skunk has softened. When I walk near the shelter, I'm hit by the lingering burnt rubber smell that still hangs on. It doesn't sting my eyes, so I think we'll make it through that little disaster with no more than another bad memory.

Vicky returns from a billionth march around the campsite. "If Glenda said we were coming to the waterfall, then there must be a path out of here. Why haven't we found it? The only place that looks like it's been walked on is the trail we came in on."

I scratch at my scalp, bumpy with dirt and forest fragments. "Could be that somewhere along the line, the path to the truck tied in to the path we were on. Or maybe it's farther past the waterfall and the original plan was to come at it from the other side." It's so hard to pull my thoughts together to form sentences. My mind swirls and jumps from one idea to the next. Do we wait on the old guy to return? Do we keep moving? Do we start to dig our graves? "Or we could be at a different waterfall altogether."

A cold wind whips up the side of the hill and across my bones. I'm too tired to shiver, too weak to pull my sweater over my head. There won't be many more choices for me. I think this is day five, or maybe it's day six. Either way, we're close to the time when we should be home. And I'm counting on a search party for Vicky and Jenna to save my life because I don't have the strength or the desire to save it myself.

JENNA

I am the master at fire starting. It's a superpower given to the one least likely. It's something I can do that no one else here has managed. In a weird way, it makes me feel more alive than I have in months. Isn't that funny? I feel more alive when I'm facing my death. Irony, I suppose.

We kept the cooked cougar meat in the bean can under the surface of the creek today so it remains cold, but I'm still leery about eating it again. Of course, we have little choice. We could go without a meal or three, but tomorrow the meat may be bad. And we don't have much to waste. Butchering a cougar with a hatchet isn't efficient.

I stick the rest of the meat in the pot and pour some water in. Ireland has found a few mushrooms. Some of those go in the pot too. I'm tempted to throw them all in, forcing her to have some meat. She looks depleted. Her skin is pale all the time, and when she stands, she has to steady herself. I'm scared.

She sits on the edge of our campfire, peeling a mushroom and eating the thin pieces. The sun is starting to fade, but we still have good light.

We decided to stay here for another night. Where else could we go? We've lost ourselves in this canyon. We vaguely know which way is east and west, but none of us can commit to the direction of the truck.

"Ireland, please have some meat. It's so much better than you think." I pierce a hunk and hold it out toward her.

"It's not that. I'm sure it tastes fine. It's just what I do. If I eat the meat, then what's left of me if we make it out of here?"

"I won't pretend to understand." I keep stirring. "But I'll beg if it will do any good."

Vicky drops a pile of wood at my side. "I'm lying down for just a moment. It's my turn first for watch tonight."

I nod, but don't say anything. I'd much rather stay awake on watch than be woken by another skunk.

With Vicky in the shelter, now's as good a time as any I'll ever have. I sit on the ground, poking the fire with a stick. "Ireland, what happened to you? Why don't you believe in God anymore? Why didn't you ever have a family?" I'm way out of line, but who knows what adventure awaits us next. There may not be a tomorrow for Ireland, or me, or Vicky.

"What makes you think I wanted a family? That's your dream. Maybe it's not for everyone." She's chosen not to respond to the first question and her answer to the second seems convenient. Even after twenty-five years, I know the core of Ireland, and I know she's not being honest with herself or with me.

"Sure. Not everyone wants a family. But you wanted one more than any of us. And you deserved one."

She blinks fast. "No. I didn't. It's so much more complicated than you think."

"Try me. I'm a good listener, I've been told. In fact, I've been told that by you." I offer her a smile, and it strengthens me that she returns it.

"It might be better to go to the grave with my secrets."

I'm sure we all have those things we don't want anyone to know, but for me, they seem less relevant when tomorrow is actually in question.

"Do they hurt you? Keeping them bottled inside. Is it the way you're choosing to punish yourself, like walking away from God?"

She tilts her head. "I'm not walking away from God. He didn't want anything to do with me. It's always been that way. When we were all together, it was easy to believe that I was loved, and then easy to believe God was looking out for me, for all of us. But the real world is different. When you get out there, you become the person you're born to be. You're your parents' child, all the way through."

"No." I rub her arm. "That can't be true."

Her eyes go cold. "I have a son. He lives with his father, and I haven't seen him since he was a baby. Now, what kind of mother do you think I am?"

My stomach turns. She's hit me where I'm soft. How can a mother walk away from her child? I remember the pain of my father leaving. It's still so real, I could reach out and physically hold on to it. That's been well over twenty years. And I was a grown woman. Those are the wounds that never seem to heal.

"What would make you do that?"

"I'm my mother's child, Jenna."

"Your mother works at a bakery in Canada. What does she have to do with this?" My voice is rising out of my control.

Ireland tips her head, looking at me from an angle. "That mother never existed. My mother is a drug addict. The last time I saw her, I was ten. We'd been *reunited* by children's services four times by then. Four times I was taken out of safe homes to live with my mother until she chose heroin over me again."

I'm shaking from the inside, shocked at the story that's unfolding. Ireland's past never made sense. The pieces didn't fit together the way she told them. But deep in the corners of my crazy imagination I couldn't have thought up this truth.

"I didn't know my dad. I'm just a statistic. A foster child who aged out of the system." She stands, looking away from me, and walks away from the clearing.

I should follow, tell her that I love her, that God loves her, but I can't move. I'm a coward who stays by the safety of the fire. My fire.

❖　❖　❖

The glow of the sun behind the filter of clouds sinks below the horizon. I add more wood and continue watching the crackle of the flames. The meat has boiled until I'm sure not even one microscopic bacteria could survive. I wonder if any of the vitamins or protein will still be in there.

The coffee pot sits near my feet, the meat cooling in the air which has turned icy. I scoot closer to the heat.

"Where's Ireland?" Vicky settles next to me. The crease along the side of her cheek tells me she was able to sleep for a while. Unfortunately, that means she probably didn't overhear my conversation with Ireland. Do I have to tell her what I know or is that gossip?

I shrug. "She walked that way." I motion with my head to the part in the trees where I last saw our friend. A woman I really have never known.

"How long ago?" Vicky reaches into the pot and takes a misshaped chunk of cougar then tries to tear the end off with her teeth.

"Not long after you laid down."

Vicky drops her cougar-holding hand to her lap. "That's been a couple hours, I'd guess, by the sky. Didn't you ask where she was going?"

I shake my head.

"Was she upset? Was she sick?" Vicky gets to her feet. "We need to find her. That's too long to be gone. It's dark."

"Duh." It's about as mature as any third-grade response, but it's the best I can do.

"Are you kidding me? That's what you have to say?" She shrugs her shoulders then stomps away from the fire. "Ireland?"

The only answer is the hollow hoot of an owl.

"Are you coming?" Vicky's question is a command. I don't have a choice. I get up, grab a piece of meat and follow her. With the cougar in my mouth

I won't have to answer any more questions. No amount of chewing will break up this culinary disaster.

"We can't go far because we could get lost and freeze to death, but we can't leave Ireland out here alone. I don't know what to do." She looks at me as if she cares about my opinion. When I don't answer she shakes her head and takes another set of careful steps into the darkness. "Ireland. You need to answer us."

"I'm here." The voice is flat, uncaring. Like a mother who would leave her child behind. I hate that my mind went there so easily. "Sorry. I'm going to bed." She bumps past us and soon we're back within the glow of the campfire. Ireland doesn't say another word before climbing into the shelter.

"What was that about?" Vicky brushes off the surface of a rock before sitting on it.

She thinks she has the right to know everything.

Chapter 17

JENNA

After completing my morning ritual, a trip to the trees to relieve myself, I come back into camp and stand near Ireland and Vicky. Enough of this waiting to die. I have a home to return to and a life to salvage. I cock my hip and extend my head as high as I can stretch. "We need a plan, and we need it now. We can't stay here waiting for winter. What happens next time a storm hits?"

"A plan for what, though?" Vicky seems wired, probably by the mention of planning. "That guy, Grizzly Bob or whatever you want to call him, he must know the way out. I can't believe he lives out here like an animal year-round."

Ireland digs a hole in the dirt with her boot. "I don't know. He didn't look like the kind of man who works in a bank during the off-season."

"Maybe not, but he has to get supplies, doesn't he?" Vicky lifts her eyebrows. "It's not like he's making his own soap and whatever."

"How do you think the pioneers got their soap?" Ireland asks.

"They bought it before they left."

Ireland adjusts her glasses. She's lost one of the lenses somewhere. "I make my own soap. And I live in the middle of town. It's better for you, no sulfates. And it's better for the planet."

"Does it stink?" Vicky wants to know.

"Do I?" Ireland waves her hand in the air. "I mean, did I before this trip?"

Vicky shrugs her shoulders. "No. You smelled like lavender. I remember that because I wanted to ask what kind of perfume you were wearing, but I didn't think you'd like me noticing."

"It's the lavender I put in the soap. And I don't mind. I just come off as a grump sometimes. It's not because I'm mad at anyone except maybe myself."

I've lost them completely. The subject is supposed to be how to get out of here, and they're discussing the finer points of homemade soap. I'm beginning to think I'm the only one who wants to go home. "Okay, back on task here. How do we get this guy?"

"We're not kidnapping him." The way Ireland says this makes it sound like that should be obvious.

I don't say anything right away. The truth is, I've thought a lot about it. "What if we can't track him? What if he refuses to help us?" I tuck a chunk of hair behind my ear. Kidnapping may be the only way. "There are three of us and only one of him. And . . . we have a gun."

Now I have their full attention. Lunatics get that much anyway.

"I'm not a murderer," Vicky says. "I just want food. Real food from a grocery store or a restaurant. But even so, I think I'd prefer to live my whole life, what little there may be left of it, in the wilderness rather than in a jail cell."

"Real food doesn't come from the store or a restaurant." Ireland stares into the fire. "It comes from the earth."

Vicky stands and throws another stick into the fire. "Blah. Blah. Blah. I don't care where it comes from as long as it's not wild before I eat it."

I wave my hands to get them back on track. "We could take the bullets out of the gun before we threaten him with it."

"You've lost your mind, you know." Ireland stands and starts to pace. "It's never a good idea to threaten with a gun that's not loaded. What if he's packing? He'll just pull out his pistol and boom, boom, boom, we're dead." She wraps both hands around her throat, making a gagging sound. "And we don't have *bullets*. We have one bullet, singular."

"So, we track him," I say. "He's come to the falls two mornings in a row. Surely he'll be there again today. We scared him off before he could get any water."

"What's to stop him from taking his water farther down the river?" Vicky asks.

"Giardia." Ireland says. "Seems like the chances of it being contaminated would be higher in the creek than from the water flowing off the mountainside. I wish we still had that book."

Vicky's mouth curves in a satisfied smile.

"I have a plan." I pick up a stick and draw a diagram of the waterfall and surrounding area. It's more like stick figure drawing, but they get the point, I'm sure. "Vicky, you tuck yourself over here to the left of the falls. There's that high brush. You'll be completely covered." I mark the spot with a V. "And Ireland, you can be here, just past where the cougar came out." I mark an I on the drawing.

"Can I be anywhere else?" Ireland covers the eye with the missing lens and evaluates my map. "And I'm not saying I think this is a good idea."

"Okay, I'll be there. And Ireland." I rub out the I and put it on the other side of the falls. "You go here."

"This is crazy." Ireland runs fingers through her hair. "What if we catch him? What do you really think we're going to do with him? We can't feed ourselves."

"We only grab him if we can't get him to listen to reason."

"I like the tracking idea." Vicky jumps to her feet. "I can't believe I didn't think of this. If his house is so close to here, there must be a road. We only need to find the house."

"There wasn't a road on *Grizzly Adams*." They both look at me like I've said something crazy. "Okay, there was a road to the Ingalls's place. Better?"

❖ ❖ ❖

Before the sun is overhead, we're putting out the fire and preparing to pull off the greatest plan in all of Emery House history. Those college day pranks have nothing on three middle-aged women fighting for their one chance at survival.

Ireland hugs the trunk of a tree. I know she's dizzy, but I won't say anything. She doesn't take questioning well. My initial shock at Ireland's coming clean about her family is softening. With so little known time on our hands, I don't want to hold on to anger. That's not how I want to die. It's not even how I want to live anymore. I take a couple steps toward her, not enough to make her uncomfortable, but so she knows I'm there.

"Once, I saw an episode of some show where the character actually ate the bark from a tree. It's vegan, you know."

Her mouth squishes up.

"It might be worth a try." I want to beg her to eat, but I turn my back to give her the opportunity to do it on her own.

A moment later, I hear the hatchet, and the guzzling of water. I'm sure wood doesn't go down easy.

She steps to the place where the fire was and dips her fingers in the ash. Swiping them across her face, she begins to disappear in the darkness.

"Vicky, look." I point to Ireland. "We need to do that too. Great idea, Ireland." I scoop a handful of soot and rub it into my skin. The particles burn my throat and make me choke, but I keep rubbing, making sure every inch of white skin is covered.

Vicky takes a step back.

"What are you going to do about the stink?" Ireland flares her nostrils.

"I don't stink." Vicky lifts her chin.

Ireland's eyebrows rise. "You smell like a skunk with BO."

I giggle. For some reason I see Vicky standing on a stage, giving one of her inspiring messages with green squiggly lines rising up around her.

Vicky isn't amused. She crosses her arms tight across her chest. "He'll just think there's a skunk at the waterhole. So?"

"So? Would you go to the waterhole if there was a skunk there?" Ireland asks.

Vicky's shoulders droop. "Not after the last run-in. I'd rather face a bear."

"Hush." I hold my finger to my lips. "We don't need to put any ideas out there."

"Into the universe?" Vicky says with a mocking voice.

Ireland either doesn't notice, or doesn't care. She walks to the path and yanks at a broad leafed plant. "This one has quite a smell. Rub it all over. Maybe it will disguise the skunk stink."

I crush the stems and leaves in my hand. The scent is bitter and strong, but nothing I'd worry about if I were heading for a drink first thing in the morning. I smear the juice across my clothes and through my hair. Then I turn to Vicky.

"No. Please. I can't do this." She backs away toward where our shelter was. We've packed everything up so we're ready to travel. "Can you imagine if we're found like that?" She points at me.

Ireland gives me an up and down look then grins. Her teeth shine next to the darkness of her face. "I think your family will be proud that you did what you had to do to get back to them." She's still looking at me.

"Your son will be proud too," I say.

Her smile fades and a tear draws a line through the soot on her cheek. "Maybe."

"You'll just have to find out. There's nothing to lose."

She swipes at the tear. "Let's do this."

We both take a step toward Vicky.

She raises both hands. "No. This isn't a tubbing. Stop."

I cross my arms and tilt my head. The memories that word brings back. Tubbing. It was an initiation, being dumped completely clothed into a full bathtub. We were carefree and overflowing with humor, not bent on finding fault with others, like the world is now.

"Okay," she says. "But I do it myself." Vicky kneels by a tree and snaps off a handful of leaves, then rubs them up and down and over her face.

"You're still white as snow." Ireland cocks an eyebrow. "You'll need to do the hair too."

Vicky's eyes are plate-size. "I'll never get it out."

"They'll fix it at the salon." Ireland doesn't even laugh at this.

Huffing as she walks, Vicky goes to the fire pit. She dips one finger into the ash and paints a thin trail across her forehead.

"That's not going to do, and we have to get moving. Either slap that on, or we're going to do it for you."

Vicky fills her hands, a sob being held back by teeth tight on her bottom lip, and rubs the soot into her skin and hair.

"I wish I had a way to take a selfie of the three of us right now, only teeth and eyes."

"Not a chance." Vicky yanks her pack onto her back and we're off to our designated waiting spots.

"Let's go catch us a man," I say.

They don't laugh.

Vicky

Running through the plan helps me pass the time. I've never felt so useless and pathetic. We hide in the brush, listening for Grizzly Guy to show up. If he actually does, we'll watch until he decides to leave again and follow him to his house, which we hope has running water, electricity, and a telephone.

Of course, there's the chance, which seems rather high to me, that a bear, cougar, or another skunk will attack us before we are able to become the predators instead of the prey.

I scratch at the back of my neck. It feels like there are bugs crawling over my skin. The thought sends shivers across my body. In the dim light, I inspect my arms for any manner of insect, bug, or other critter. There's nothing moving, but bumps are starting to form under the soot.

Something shifts on the far side of the falls. Every muscle tenses as I wait to see if this is salvation or condemnation. I'm betting on the latter, but, Lord, please let it be the former. The itch on the bridge of my nose is worse than any other torture I can imagine. I crinkle it, but it's no good. The twinge is so overwhelming, I can't focus on our plan.

Moving as slowly as I can, I reach one finger to my nose and press what's left of my ragged fingernail into the offending spot. The sensation is better than warm chocolate drizzled in caramel floating over my tongue.

Why do I always have to think about food?

My heart catches. He's here. I see him lean down to the water. He can't be more than five feet from where Ireland is hiding. My heart thumps so hard, I'm afraid he'll hear it over the rush of falling water. What if he spots her? Will he hurt Ireland before we can stop him? Could we stop him?

My breath comes in puffs. We're out of our comfort zone here. Three women who just wanted to get away from the world, turned renegades, probably soon to be kidnappers. The media is going to love taking me down.

Grizzly Guy opens some kind of sack. It looks like it's made of an animal hide, the fur still intact. From the bag he pulls a gourd. He fills it with water, drinks it down, then fills it again. While this is not evidence that he lives in a state-of-the-art abode, I'm unwilling to give up hope. No one lives like an animal all the time.

A thought strikes me. I'm sick. What if his morning routine involves bathing? Lord, please, no. I've had about all the stretching and growing I can take for a lifetime. He pulls a hunk of jerky out and lets it hang from the side of his mouth while he runs water through his thick, curly brown and gray beard.

Jesus loves him too. God loves everyone. We're all his children. My mind is chanting, surely an early sign of insanity.

My stomach wants to revolt, but I keep telling myself that he's one of God's precious creations. That's so much easier to do when I'm holding a newborn baby and cooing to his mother about the blessing he is than when I try to have compassion on a man who lives like an animal and has refused to help three lost women in the woods.

The sun rises over the trees, and I feel completely exposed. A deer ready for the hunter to take down. Finally, he tosses his bag over a shoulder, wrings his beard out, and picks up his water-filled gourd.

At the beginning of the trail he came in on, the man stalls. His back straightens, and he slowly turns, looking over the area where we're hiding. Can he hear my heart? Can he sense the craziness that's crawling over my skin? I'm two seconds away from diving into the water and freezing the itch from my flesh. I need these ashes off.

Just in time, he turns back to the path and heads away from us. I start to count. We've agreed that twenty seconds is the best amount of time. One Mississippi. Two Mississippi. I scratch my neck so hard I expect to bleed. Eight Mississippi. Nine Mississippi. Stepping forward, I hold one arm out into the light. The skin is raised and so red I can see the irritation under the soot. Forget the Mississippis. I'm out.

IRELAND

Vicky emerges too early. I wave my hands in the air trying to get her attention, but she's hopping around like one of the Riverdancers. Like she's gone and lost her last marble. I glance toward the path, the one that goes right by Jenna's hiding spot. It's clear. As quickly as I can, I get to Vicky.

"What are you doing?" I ask in a kind of whisper-yell.

"I can't take it. I itch everywhere. I'm going nuts." She holds out her arms. They're pimpled with a rash that oozes under the ashes.

"Did you look closely at the leaves you rubbed on your skin?"

"No. I did what you and Jenna did."

"I think not." I shake my head. "That's a poison oak rash."

Her eyes start to water and a whimper escapes her mouth.

I touch one finger to her lips. "No. You've got to hold it together. I promise you, when we get to civilization, the first thing we'll do is get you cleaned up and treated. You have to do this. I can't leave you behind."

She shakes her head. "No. I need to soak in the water. Just come back for me later."

"What if we can't find you?" The reality is, we'll probably never make it back here again. "We have to leave now or we'll miss this chance."

Her head nods yes, but her eyes are pleading with me to do anything else. It breaks my heart to say we can't, the greater good and all.

I take her hand and we head toward the way he left. At the corner I look around before going farther. Jenna is about twenty feet ahead, ducking behind a rock. We come close and she motions us to tuck our bodies close to the barrier. After a moment, Jenna gives us the "let's move" motion and we start our descent farther into a canyon and, I hope, in the right direction.

We keep him in our sight, but just barely, which is our only salvation because Vicky is scratching so loudly it's like sneaking around with someone who has sandpaper taped to their inner thighs. "Quit."

"You could have an ounce of compassion." Vicky scowls.

Her arms are raised with bumps, but it's her face that's really taken the worst of it. One look in a mirror, and this adventure would be over. She'd scream and sob for hours, but we don't have a mirror, and I'm grateful, not for the first time, about that fact.

The farther we go down, the denser the trees become and the closer we need to follow our prey.

"Let's spread out a bit," Jenna says. "If we keep the person in front of us in view, we won't get lost, but we won't be making as much noise."

"Sounds reasonable." I scratch my head. Vicky is making me itch vicariously.

"You go first." She points to me, then the direction the guy went.

This would be a very bad time to laugh, but she looks like an older version of one of Charlie's Angels the way she motions like a cop on a stakeout. I bite my bottom lip.

With careful steps, I head out, watching for his movement ahead of me. One minute he's there, then I can't make him out anymore. I whip my head back and see Jenna behind me. Raising my hands, I shake my head.

Jenna freezes, one foot ahead of the other. She turns her ear, like she's listening to the trees. In a moment, she's caught up with me. We both scour the horizon, but he's gone.

I drop to the ground, my head spinning for need of protein, fat, anything to add fuel to my body. The muscles in my legs scream. And the headache is back, pounding the left side of my forehead.

Vicky catches up. "Why are we stopped?"

"We've lost him," Jenna answers.

I'm so grateful that she says we.

Chapter 18

JENNA

We've got to find something for Ireland to eat. She's wilting in front of us, lying in the grass like she's given up. Vicky isn't any help. For twenty minutes she's whined and begged to go back to the water. I'm not sure Ireland can make the climb, and she may need to get it out of here more than any of us.

I nudge Vicky. "Did the survival book say anything about what foods we could eat?" I've asked this before, but it seems important to ask again.

"All I remember is not to eat red berries. I don't get that. Strawberries, raspberries, cherries, they're all red, and we eat them all the time. So, why not red?" Vicky buries her face in her hands.

"I hear you back there." Ireland doesn't open her eyes, but her head tips toward us. "Stop talking about me."

"What makes you think we're talking about you?" Vicky tilts her chin up. "We could be talking about anyone or anything."

"Sure," says Ireland. "And you have to whisper so the bear doesn't get offended, right? That's so very kind of you both."

I step closer to her. "Ireland, we're just worried about you. You need to eat something. The vegan thing is all well and good." Honestly, I don't get it. I think she's gone plumb crazy to give up even eggs. "But this is another kind of circumstance. Your life is actually on the line. Don't you think God gave us meat for a reason?"

"Who says God gave us meat?" Ireland opens her eyes. "He gave us the animals to watch over, but where does it say that he thought we should slaughter them and eat their flesh?"

"But, you agree they were created by God." Vicky eases herself down next to Ireland on the grassy hillside. "I knew you still believed."

"You make God sound like unicorns." Ireland spits the words. "I don't know if God exists. Really, I just don't know. But I think he probably does."

Vicky claps her hands twice.

"The thing is, it doesn't matter if he exists. He hasn't chosen me. I'm not part of the plan." She raises herself up on her elbows. "He doesn't want me." There's a tear in her eye, a drop of humanity.

I sit next to her and do the only thing I know to do. I pull her to my chest and hold her tight. She doesn't fight it, and as I rock side to side, her body relaxes into mine. I stroke her hair and feel her tears soak my t-shirt. "You've spent so long feeling unwanted. I don't know if you can recognize how precious you really are."

Vicky fidgets with blades of grass. Worry lines her forehead, and I realize how uncomfortable she is with this level of emotion.

My mind shifts to my own children. I see the results of how each of us were raised right here in every single move we make. My father walked out of my life and my mother died. I grasp on to my family, holding them so tight they try to squeeze from my grip.

Vicky's mother held her at a distance, pronouncing emotion as a weakness. She was never satisfied, never pleased, so Vicky is stuck in an endless circuit of trying to be perfect. To be set above. And she'll always fail. It's a lifetime prison sentence.

And Ireland, she may have had it the worst. No one took the time to love her in any way. She was thrown out like the trash, a burden to the people who should have treasured her very breath. Now she can't even feel the love of God. I hold her tighter. How could I have let us slip apart? I'm one in the long line of people who've let her down.

"Ireland." I relax my hold on her.

She sits back and wipes tears from her bloodshot eyes.

"I need to apologize to you."

Her eyebrows tighten. "Why?"

"After college, I got so wrapped up in my life. I didn't take the time to stay in touch with you. I should have been the one to make the effort, because I know you. I knew you wouldn't do it. And I was so mixed up about Mark and how Vicky would feel, I walked away. It was my way of hiding."

"Ugh." Vicky shakes her head. "I didn't love Mark. Never did. Do you really think I would have let him go just for my mother?"

"Yes. I do." I nod with the words.

Vicky smiles. "Okay, I would have. But here's a secret you don't know. I love Daniel. I fell in love with him on the first date my mother arranged. His eyes, oh my, they were green, not hazel." She looks up. "I was overcome. We talked about things that had nothing to do with all the political hopes my mother had been assured of. He was so real. So passionate about life. I felt like I was getting away with something."

"I wish you had told me," I say. "It would have really made a difference." There's a wave of heat pushing into my face, but I remind myself we're not here all these years later, with a canyon of time between us, because of just Vicky. I'm the most guilty. I'm the one who wanted to hide. "But maybe it wouldn't have. If I hadn't walked away then, I would surely have walked away later. When I couldn't get pregnant, I was so sure that everyone else on the planet could. I isolated myself from friendships, especially with women."

"But we could have been there for you," Ireland said. "We could have loved you through the hard times."

"And I could have loved you when you were making hard choices. I could have been the person who reminded you how important you are and how much your son needs you. He still does. Ireland, when we get out of here, I want to help you any way I can to get your relationship with him back."

"Me too," Vicky says. "I don't know what happened, but I want to be there for you, no matter what. You're that important." A tear slips down

Vicky's smudged face, clearing a trail across her skin raised with a red rash and decorated with bruises and scrapes. She looks nothing like the woman on television, and I think this is the best thing that could have happened to her.

Vicky kneels beside me, and I slip my arm around her tiny waist.

My sisters.

VICKY

Our wannabe stealthy moves to catch the mountain man have left us on a hillside overlooking another valley. A beautiful piece of God's creation lies before me, but it's like a copy of a portrait I've already seen. Just when I think we've traveled as deep as the land can go, we find a place to weave farther into this endless expanse. The wilderness stretches on for eternity. Instead of farther up and farther in, we're farther down and losing hope.

I lace my fingers together, using every droplet of my remaining strength to keep my hands still, away from the luscious indulgence of scratching. Which will lead to open sores. Which will end with scars. Which will be a forever reminder of this trial. If we survive, I will not need a reminder. This nightmare will live in my mind like a movie repeating over and over until my death. Will I still see it playing when I'm in heaven?

We didn't follow the exact path that man did, but it only makes sense that somewhere around here there must be a sign of his passing.

We know he goes to the waterfall daily. That's all we need for a solid plan. The three of us march out in different directions searching for a sign, while staying close enough not to get separated. It would be bad enough to die out here, but at least we have each other. I'm not willing to lay my friends out as a sacrifice.

After days with so little food that I'm already feeling my hip bones protruding, my mind seems clearer than it has in years. I can see all the blunders, all the faulty thinking, every place I took the wrong turn. Maybe that's how it is when you near the end. Maybe it's only when your life is fading away that you see the path you've traveled and the mistaken ways you've turned.

I left home with a plan to manipulate my husband into wanting me. My biggest focus was on the public humiliation I would face if he left me for my own assistant. I don't know when I became so detached, so much like my mother, but the time out here fighting for life and survival, it's cleared up my priorities. My husband isn't perfect. He holds fault in this too, a lot of fault, but I love him. I want us to work, not only for show, but because I want to grow old with the man I married. And I want to be the woman who walked down the aisle to him.

My foot catches on a rock, and I look down. It's faint, but the dirt is exposed here. It's the path we've been searching for. I look over my shoulders to tell the others, but they're too far to risk calling.

I snag the purple shirt from my pack and tie it onto a baby tree, then wander down the hill after them. My foot lands on a stick and it snaps, loud in the quiet around us. Ireland turns her head, and I wave for her to come my way.

She gets Jenna's attention as she plods up the hill to me.

"Did you find something?" Jenna asks.

"I think so. It doesn't look much different than a deer trail, but I'm sure it's his."

The three of us stand in a small circle inspecting the dirt beneath our feet. "What do we do now?" Ireland wipes a hand across her forehead. "We can't knock on his door and invite ourselves in for dinner. For all we know, he's a serial killer in hiding."

The sky darkens with a curtain of clouds, and the temperature is dropping. I untie my sweatshirt and pull the once vibrant material over my head. "We could sneak up on him while he sleeps."

"And what?" Ireland swats at a bug. "Hit him over the head with a rock?"

"No." I shrug. "I don't know." My shoulders fall. At home, problems come across my desk all the time. There's always an answer, sometimes two or three, and I need to decide which is the best. The thing is, there is always something I can do. Here, I know less than nothing. All my training and knowledge is useless. "Do you have a better idea?"

"No. But I'm thinking."

I look at the fading light. "We don't have long to make a decision. It's getting cold. If we're not going, we need to make camp."

"I . . ." Jenna's forehead is tight. She fiddles with some strands of hair at her ear.

Ireland and I stare at her, waiting for her to give her opinion, but Jenna seems stalled. "We're listening," I say. "What do you think?"

She rubs her hands together. "If he goes to the waterfall each morning, isn't he going to go again tomorrow?"

"That's a fair assumption." Ireland pulls her hood over her ears. "So?"

"What if we wait for him to go to the water, then follow the path to wherever he lives?"

"You're a genius." Ireland looks up at the darkening sky. "He must have a radio or some way to contact others."

"I don't know about that. We're not talking about Mr. Congeniality here." I look at Jenna. "But I think you're right." I jog in place, trying to keep the cold away. "We need to set up camp and make a fire."

"We can't do it on the path. He'll see that we've been here and it could scare him off." Jenna points up the hill. "The smoke won't be as obvious up there."

The rest of our light fades away as we use the dregs of our energy to climb straight up the incline. Pine needles slip from underneath my feet, and I fall to my knees more than once. I grope the ground in front of me like a blind woman. Moisture soaks through my jeans, chilling me. I shiver. How will we know when we've gone far enough?

In the not-as-far-as-I'd-like distance, coyotes howl. As much as I understand the reasoning for not going to the mountain man's house tonight, I have to ponder if a bad plan is better than another night in the woods that could easily be the end of us.

JENNA

I've found a bit of myself out here in nowhere. For an hour or so, I didn't even think about the kids. I didn't wonder if Mark would run off with the first twenty-five-year-old who crosses his path. I was doing what I needed to do to save my life, and as crazy as it sounds, there was a touch of power in it.

Our only remaining but very dim flashlight is all we have to illuminate the land. Clouds have drifted in and covered the moon and the stars. Thin trees form a maze that we've wandered into, but we'll be concealed from Grizzly Adams. In front of me lay the supplies I need to start our fire. Me. I'm the person who takes charge of one of our most important tasks. Every night since we lost Glenda, it's been me. Being the only one who can manage this feat is a secret pride.

A couple of times Ireland and Vicky have tried, but they've never gotten past the first smoking stage. This makes me important and needed. It makes me a valuable member of our threesome, not a chubby tagalong.

I press the moss into the hole in my board and begin the twirling of my stick. My palms warm with the friction and the muscles in my arms start to burn. I release my right hand and shake it out, then the other. Starting again, I lean close to see if there's anything happening, then adjust the flashlight as if that's the problem. After adding more fuel, I begin again.

I know my muscles are begging for nourishment even if I have enough chub to live off for a month or two, but that's no excuse for the fire not starting and my arms beginning to feel like heated rubber.

Behind me Ireland and Vicky struggle to put up our damaged shelter in the dark. It sounds rough, but better than I'm making out.

"Jenna?" Vicky comes up behind me. "How's the fire going? We can't see a thing back here."

"Maybe if one of you held the flashlight. I can't see. I'm sure that's the problem."

A hand picks up the light and holds it above my work. "Better?" It's Ireland.

"Yes. I'm sure it won't take but another minute." But I'm not sure at all. My head is starting to spin, and I'm about to topple over. I don't know how long I've been at this task. Maybe half an hour. Maybe an hour. It hasn't taken this long since my first night.

"Do you have enough moss in there?" Ireland squats next to me.

"Yes. I have the same as every other time. Would you like to try?" I hold out my stick.

She sits back. "You keep at it."

"I'm sorry. I'm tired, and this isn't working. Maybe one of you should do it."

Vicky huddles at my other side. "What if we can't get it started?"

"Don't say that." Ireland rubs her hands together like she would over a fire. "Jenna will get it. She has every night. Why should tonight be any different?"

"Because there will eventually come the night we don't get by, just barely." I hear the scratching of Vicky's fingernails on her rashy skin. "Tonight could be the last night."

Ireland gasps. "Wow, Vicky. Throw a little more negativity into the universe, why don't you."

"I'm saying it straight. If we don't make a fire, how will we keep the wild animals from making us into a midnight snack?"

A cold tingle washes over me, runs down my arms. What if she's right? We could all die because I can't do my job.

Chapter 19

IRELAND

It's cold. So very cold. We're dressed in every bit of clothing we have with us, and huddled tight together, but the breeze cuts through with iced air that burns my nose and fingers. I tuck my face into my shirts and huff moist warm breath into the space. I used to stand in a field near my home and embrace the power of the wind. I'd let it blow away the negative energy and fill me with renewed power. How foolish I was. How very unenlightened.

After probably two hours of trying to start the fire, Jenna collapsed into a sobbing heap. We tried to console her, but only after we each gave the task an hour of effort. She feels heavy against my side now, hopefully because she's sleeping, not—I can't face what will surely come next. In the brush somewhere behind us, I hear movement. Sticks crack under the feet of something larger than a bunny.

Twenty years of worshipping nature, I never considered it could be that very thing to take my life. And the lives of my two closest friends. The best parts of my experience in the universe were the years the four of us spent together. Hope, Jenna, and Vicky were my sisters. Our connection will be forever now. No chance to walk away again, because there's very little hope we'll have a future to walk away into.

"This isn't working." My teeth chatter any time I try to speak. "The shelter doesn't keep the chill or the moisture out. I think we need to take it down and wrap it around ourselves."

"Are you sure?" says Vicky. "This is how Glenda had us set it up. She must have had it this way for a reason."

173

"That was a lifetime ago." Jenna's voice is a whisper barely above the sounds of the trees. "I'm willing to try anything."

I start to rise, but Vicky's hand grabs me and pulls me down. "Did you hear that? The noise?"

My body freezes as I strain to hear what I'm afraid she's talking about. Another snap. This one much closer than the one I heard minutes ago. I'm shaking with cold and adrenaline. This could be the end. I run my hand over the handle of the gun tucked into my waistband. It's pitch dark, and I don't know which way I should shoot.

Standing up straight, I grab hold of the tarp and rip it free of the ropes, waving it madly in the air. "You will not eat us tonight. Go away." I scream into the night. "No. Not tonight. I won't let you." The tarp snaps and whips in the air, crashing away the peace and the fear.

My chest burns with the intensity of my emotion. Forget peace. Forget calm. I'm ready to fight anything that has the nerve to take us on. I'll throw that creature down with my bare hands if I have to. I'll rip him up and stomp on his head. I will not die tonight. And I won't sit still while my friends' lives are whittled down to food for some wild beast.

Vicky and Jenna stood up sometime during my rant. I feel their grips on the sides of my sweater, their bodies tucked into mine. Suddenly, my arms are too heavy to hold up. I let the tarp fall to my feet, my body going limp. I sway, but the girls hold me upright.

"I think it's gone." Jenna rubs a hand over my cheek. "Yeah. Take that, whatever you are. You don't mess with Emery sisters and come out happy. Got it?"

Something bounds through the woods, the sound getting softer as it moves farther away.

"I think we just threatened the life of a deer." I cover my mouth with one hand.

We laugh until the warmth from the anger and fear cools, then we crouch on the ground, pulling the tarp over us and tucking it under our legs. I squeeze my eyes shut and ask God to keep watch over us through the night. It's my first request since I gave up on being a mother and wife.

Inside our little house is warm, but damp, our breath clinging to the sides. There's a sense of safety even if the walls protecting us are only a thin sheet of plastic.

JENNA

We're not going to make it out of here. If only I had a piece of paper and a pencil. I want to leave something for my family. A note to tell them what a privilege it was to be a mom to Calvin, Carrie, and Caroline, and a wife to Mark. I want them to know how sorry I am for holding them too tight and for leaving too soon.

But I can't do that any better than I could light the fire.

"What would you do differently, if you could go back?" My question is for both of them, but mainly for myself.

There's silence aside from the rustle of the tarp for so many minutes that I assume my question is offensive.

"I would never have started my ministry." Vicky's voice is dull like the life has begun to leave her already. I'm not the only one who's facing the end tonight.

Ireland shivers at my left side. "Seriously, Vick? Why?"

"I gave it everything and in the meantime lost the people who were important. I lost you all and my family. The first people I should have been speaking God's love to, are the people I didn't take the time to remember."

"It's not the ministry that took those things." I pull the sleeves of Mark's sweater over my hands. "You've been a great mentor to many women. It's just the balance was off. You can't throw it all away."

"No kidding." Ireland sniffs. "Really think about that. If you'd have put all your crazy-making energy into your family, they would have been out here hiding years ago."

I brace myself for Vicky's anger, but instead she starts to laugh.

"You still know me very well." Vicky reaches across me to Ireland. "I guess I don't know what I would do differently, I just know it would be different. Maybe I'd make my family my first ministry. And I know I'd stay in touch with all of you. I would have been there for Hope. I would have stood by you, Jenna, when you were trying to conceive. And Ireland, I wish I could have been there to hug you."

Ireland tips her head onto my shoulder. "I wish I'd stuck it out, but then again, I left my family for their own good. I just can't remember exactly what that meant."

"If you could have seen yourself the way we saw you, none of that would have happened." I run my fingers through Ireland's hair. Instead of stiffening at my touch, she relaxes into me. "We were all selfish. I hope you'll forgive me for leaving you behind. In a way, I did the same thing your mother did." My voice catches with the guilt of my actions, or inactions. "We've hurt each other, and we've hurt others. This isn't the way it was supposed to work out."

Ireland squeezes my hand. "No worries. The three of you gave me the best years of my life. While I was at Emery, I had a family. It's better than I thought I'd ever have."

"I know what you mean," Vicky answers. "Emery gave me a glimpse into a warm world. I can't believe they've closed the house. How many other girls will miss out on the opportunities that kind of home has to offer?"

"If I had the money, I'd buy it." But I'll never have that kind of cash. If we ever do make it back, we'll jump into the world where money matters and it separates people into categories. Vicky and even Ireland are not in my group.

Vicky straightens, sending a puff of ice-cold air into our warm, damp, body-odor filled bubble. "Why don't we do that? We could buy Emery House. Well, not we, but Cambridge Ministries could."

"It's not a Christian house. And if it had been, I never would have come to Emery," Ireland says.

"One of the great things about Emery is the different kinds of people that end up there. There's an opportunity to meet God in a natural way. I'm not sure that's how to say what I mean. It's just that Emery didn't make me love God. It didn't make me love all of you. Emery gave me the chance to love it all."

"And that's the way it should remain." Vicky is sitting tall now. Her head pushes the tarp up and allows a whiff of chilled air to creep in near my leg. "We won't make being Christian a requirement to live there, but we'll keep the rent low and we'll give the students the opportunity, like Jenna said."

The smile pulling across my face feels unfamiliar, like purpose is growing up through the cold ground and blooming in my chest. It feels like something else to live for. Like that moment when you say something and the people you love nod in complete agreement.

"I want a piece of that action." Ireland reaches across the space to Vicky and clutches my hand with her other. "There's a purpose here I really want to be a part of."

It may be a fantasy that we'll come together and make this crazy plan work, but it's a dream I'm willing to throw myself into if only to give my legs the added encouragement it will take to get out of here.

At our backs, somewhere in the dense woods, a stick breaks.

❖　❖　❖

I peer from a gap I've made in the tarp. The first glow of sun rolls over the mountain. We made it through the night. I really didn't believe we would. There wasn't a minute of sleep, but I don't even care. We're alive and not injured any worse than before.

A week and a half ago I could barely make it out of bed in the morning because of the self-pity consuming me. Now, I'm charged because a bear didn't slice me up and make kibble of my flesh. It's a new perspective, to be sure.

I nudge the girls. "We should get ready to move."

With little noise, we pack up the few things that aren't already on our bodies and move to the edge of the trees. From here we should be able to see Grizzly Adams make his way to the waterfall. Then off we go. By tonight, we could all be home.

I look over Vicky. She should probably spend a day in the hospital getting that poison oak under control. There's a crusty ooze caking her ash-smudged face and arms and her eye is still quite swollen from the fall. I hope there isn't a mirror at Grizzly's cabin.

Ireland leans forward. I follow her gaze. Way off in the distance, barely visible in the dim dawning sunlight, our mountain man makes his way along the path. There's so much hair on his head and face, the features are hidden. He could easily be mistaken as an animal. Maybe we've found the real Bigfoot, but his feet aren't especially large.

A chill shakes my body. Vicky lays a calming hand on my leg.

The next step is ours, and I can only pray we find what's needed when we follow his path back to wherever this man comes from.

Once he passes over the ridge, and we can't see him anymore, we rise together and start down the hill. Our pace is fast, quicker than I thought we'd be able to move. There's a mix of excitement and nerves fueling my body where protein is absent.

It doesn't take long and we're somewhere we've never been before. The path becomes more beaten down here and runs back and forth along a hillside. "We don't have time for this. Let's go straight down."

"The switchbacks are here for a reason." Ireland looks back at me. "But I think you're right. No tumbling, though." She looks at Vicky with that statement.

"Got it." Vicky sits down on her rear end and starts to slide down the hill.

I set my pack on my lap running my arms through the straps backward and start down. The ground bumps beneath me. It doesn't take much to keep the momentum going. My palms burn with the friction of the grass and dirt. Every twenty or so feet, we find the path, scoot over and slide the next section. I can't believe Grizzly Adams makes this climb every morning. He must start the second the sun begins to rise.

When we come to the end of the steep decline, we follow the path. We're all looking hard to spot evidence of anything that points to human life, but I see nothing yet. Finally, around a large rock, we come to a cave opening where the path gets wide before going off the other way.

"I think this is it." My heart plunges with the realization that this guy doesn't have a cabin like the real Grizzly Adams. I guess I should be thankful that he doesn't seem to keep a bear as a pet either.

"No way." Vicky shakes her head. "That's a cave. I'm not going in there. With my luck on this little adventure, there'll be bats or hyenas in there. There isn't a spot on my body that hasn't been mangled. I have nothing left to give."

I step closer to the entrance. It's wide. Tall enough for me to stand as I go in, but Vicky and Ireland would have to duck. "It smells like food." I stick my head into the opening. "Yes. There is definitely food in there." My mouth waters at the thought of a real meal.

Vicky comes two steps closer. "What kind of food?" I knew that would get their attention.

I sniff deep. "I think it's some kind of smoked meat. Maybe fish."

Vicky turns to Ireland. "You eat fish don't you?"

"Vegan, Vick. It means no animal and no animal products. Fish are animals, aren't they?"

"Technically, they're fish. I think that would be an okay exception this time." Vicky nods like she's the new vegan authority.

Ireland chews her bottom lip as if she's running through her options. The mother in me really needs her to eat something, but another part of me, the part that loves her just as she is, roots for the vegan to win.

Ireland rubs her dust-covered cheek. "I don't know. I've been hungry so long that my stomach doesn't even bother to growl anymore. I feel like I'm floating away, and I can't get back." She shakes her head. "Maybe I could have a small serving of fish. Halibut smothered in buttery citrus sauce, with scallops and shrimp. And garlic cheese rolls." She slurps and swallows.

I think we're losing her.

Chapter 20

JENNA

This cave thing. I have to be the one to do this.

I failed them last night. The fire is my thing, and I couldn't do it. I downright failed. The taste of it is bitter in my mouth. I haven't been able to swallow it away. It's the only meal I've had since the cougar meat. There were so many cold sleepless hours to toss the letdown around in my head, to feel the guilt as Ireland and Vicky shivered next to me. Even as we made our pretend plans for a future, I could feel their ends coming and my part in bringing it.

I need to make it up to them. I need to do it for myself.

I try to step forward, to enter Grizzly Adams's home of sorts, but my feet will not make the move. *Please, just go forward.*

A tear swells on my lower eyelid, blurring my vision. *I give up, Lord. I'm worthless. I can't do anything.*

My body fills with warm strength. That's it, isn't it? The truth. It's not all about what I *can* provide. It's not even about making it out of here alive, though I certainly hope we do. It's about not giving up, but giving my problems over to God.

"I'm going in." I feel something tap my arm. It's the flashlight, a precious tool because we have no idea how long the battery will last. Vicky holds it out to me, but she doesn't come any closer than she has to.

"Please, be very careful." Vicky looks at me like I'm leaving for the war. Maybe this is something like that, I don't know.

"I'm going with you." Ireland grips the top of the entrance. "Vicky, you stand guard out here and watch the path very carefully." She squats and picks up a stone. "If you see or hear anything, hit this rock on the edge of the cave three times then hide over there." She points to the brush edging the cave's opening.

Vicky nods. She seems too terrified to speak, but she takes the rock and holds it to her chest. Her head dips, and I assume she's praying—an act I really appreciate right now.

At the mouth of the cave, rocks form a fire pit with smoke still rising from the ashes. Along the wall, wood is piled. The pieces are ragged and rough, not like the firewood most people stack in neat rows. This stuff looks like it's been cut without benefit of saw or hatchet. There's a stack of moss and pine needles farther in.

The ground rises then begins to dip slightly. We walk deeper in, but I have to duck now. My heart is beating so loudly I wonder if he'll hear me from wherever he is and come back to get us. That frightens me, but the reality that I'm wandering into a cave filled with spiders, that is terror. I imagine them crawling all around me. They're watching me, ready to drop down into my hair. I start to fidget. Without Ireland I would have run screaming out of this horrible place already.

I shine the dim flashlight around. It's what I *don't* see that is the big disappointment. There is not one sign of technology here. Nothing man-made. A pile of furs, lots of them, in one corner. This must serve as his bed. And a stack of rocks, that's about it.

Ireland crawls around, rubbing her hands across the dirt floor.

"What are you doing?"

"There must something there. Maybe he has a trap door or a hidden compartment."

I lift one of the stinky furs. "I don't think this guy has seen *Scooby Doo*. And I doubt he feels the need to have great hiding places. This may be it."

"It can't be. I know a woman who sold her home and moved into a tiny house. It's only eighty-four square feet. She owns only what she needs to get by, and it's a whole lot more than this guy has. He'd consider her a hoarder."

My light picks up something deeper in. "Look." I edge closer. My arms go numb. There's a stack of bones. Long ones and short ones and a few that are wide and flat. "Why do you suppose he keeps these?"

"I don't know. But I'm starting to feel very uncomfortable. The aura in here is dark."

Tingles run over my skin. "We haven't found anything though. This looks like we're out of luck. If Grizzly isn't the way"—I shake my head—"we're never getting out of the wilderness."

Ireland rubs my arm. "Don't talk like that. There's got to be an answer here. This is a temporary setback. Don't let it get you down. We're not at the end of the cave. Maybe we've missed something."

I turn back, but I can't see the entrance from where we are. The cave curves to the left, and it keeps going. We go deeper and the air starts to feel like someone left the refrigerator door open. Wouldn't it be great to find a fully functional fridge stocked with food? I'd really love a cup of coffee with half the cup being caramel creamer.

It doesn't take much for me to start picturing a complete kitchen back here in the nowhere. An oven, table, chairs, even a microwave. This is my oasis in a tunnel. Deserts have nothing on the wilderness.

Along a wall, a hide is stretched. It's attached to a frame with what I think must be sinew. If I hadn't homeschooled, I'd have no idea about this, but now I have the honor of being a touch more grossed out than before. My imagination remembers the girl in *Island of the Blue Dolphins*. She was lost, but in a different way than us. And she was alone. At least the three of us have each other.

We're still going deeper, when my ear picks up a faint noise. "Did you hear that?"

"There was something." Ireland leans toward the way we've come.

The sound echoes again, and the reality of what the noise is hits me like a truck. "Vicky. She's giving the warning." I shine the light toward Ireland in time to see the fear in her eyes.

Crouching, we make our way back. The pounding becomes panicked then stops. We wait, listening before we go any farther. There is movement, rough movement, not Vicky's kind of sounds. Ireland pushes me against the wall. She puts her finger across my lips and takes the flashlight from my hand, switching it off and leaving us trapped in the dark.

She doesn't have to tell me. My voice is paralyzed along with the rest of my body. All except my heart that's raging so hard, I feel it in my throat. I can't even swallow.

In the darkness, our breathing sounds like a speeding train.

He's at the entrance. I can hear his grumble, low and wild.

Ireland pushes me deeper into the cave. We're trapped. I need a moment to sit and cry, but there isn't that kind of opportunity here. I'll die without the chance to throw a final tantrum.

VICKY

I always run the scenarios when faced with a new situation. In the mental list of all the possible outcomes, this one did not exist. It didn't exist because I couldn't allow my mind to go to a place this awful, this bleak. It's the worst of all possible results from our ill-planned strategy.

Okay, maybe not the worst, but it's bad. Very bad.

I pull my knees tight against my chest as the cold of the rock behind me seeps through my clothes and into my bones. Brush grabs and snags my sleeves and pant legs. Even my breath is sharp and sudden, my lungs convulsing in the wake of my fears.

And he's there, maybe ten feet away. The smell of him, stale body odor and dead animal skins, permeates the air. It curls around my stomach. Clasping my hands together, I mimic the slow purposeful breathing I've seen Ireland do every time I start to ride her nerves a little too hard. Any gagging, and I'm done for. And if he spots me, Ireland and Jenna won't stand even the slightest chance of survival.

He grumbles like an animal warning off a rival. Thuds accompany his steps as he makes his way into his home, and toward the only two people I have left on this earth. My face tingles with tears. Jenna and Ireland are trapped. At this point, the idea of being alive without them is far worse than a reality of death. My mind grabs for any plan that can bring them back to me.

But being a savior is a skill I do not possess.

I could run now while I have the chance. Maybe I could find help before it's too late. No. If that were possible we'd be out of the endless wilderness and home sharing stories of our adventures over cups of hot tea. I can't leave my post if there's any chance I can save them.

Beside me all three packs are tucked in a hiding place alongside the cave. I have the extra clothes, the tarp, and even our water. They've left me with what I need to have a chance, but how can I ever go on without them? This moment, even if I survive, will haunt me for the rest of my life, and I wonder if the memory will even follow me into eternity.

I hear him come back out, but there hasn't been a struggle, at least not that I could pick up. Jenna would surely scream if he'd found them. The thought gives me the only hope I have right now.

There's a solid whack of something hard coming down on something soft. The scent of blood fills the air. I peek around, unable to let my mind wonder what he's mutilated. A rabbit's body lays lifeless on a stone. Mountain man's back is toward me. I watch him peel the skin from the pink muscle. Tears sting my eyes, but I don't cry. If I've learned anything out here, it's that sometimes animals must be food. It doesn't seem real when your plate arrives at a restaurant or it's packaged at the store.

He takes a flat, white object and scrapes it over the inside of the skin, pulling off the fat that clings and dumping the slime into a hollowed-out gourd. I can't help it. My stomach growls. I really want some of that rabbit. I think I'd be willing to try it raw if that's the only choice I had. He ducks back into the cave with the hide. The meat lays out on a rock. I could grab it. He'd assume it was an animal.

I'm on my knees, ready to make my move when he comes out again. This time he takes the rabbit with him.

The loss of the raw, probably parasite-ridden meat, makes me shiver with mourning. Beside me, a tall sprig of sage grows. I pull off a branch, inhale its sweet herby scent, and start to chew on the leaves. I salivate with the pleasure of the flavor on my tongue.

After an hour or more, my legs are cramped and my mind is screaming to move them, but he's still there, so close he could hear any move I make. So close, I can't run away. I can't get to my friends, and I can't even take the chance of opening the canteen for a drink of water.

IRELAND

The stink on this guy reminds me of the week I spent protesting a particular logging site. We started out as a group of over a hundred, blocking the road to save the precious spotted owl from losing her habitat. But by day three our numbers were cut in half. And by the time the police came in with the order to evacuate or be arrested, there were five of us.

Skye and me, plus three other graduate students willing to put their spring break to good use for the cause of preserving nature. Not one of us bathed that week. But we didn't mention the smell, only encouraged each other to stick to the plan.

Skye was the one with such force of conviction. His leadership was strong and noble. I fell for him in an instant, and I was ready to follow him anywhere for any cause. But there was something we didn't share. He had so many reasons why God didn't exist. I think convincing me to join him as an atheist was his most passionate cause.

At night, he'd read to me from writers who'd spent their lives searching out ways to prove the nonexistence of God. During the day, he'd give me his explanations for the things I considered miracles. He always had an argument for self over a greater power.

After a while, all I wanted was him. I let God slip away like a fairy tale from my childhood—if my childhood had included stories and books. We shared a cottage, protested, and worked for a better world for those who would come after us.

We'd been together for years when I found out I was pregnant. Skye wasn't happy. He'd always told me this planet was not equipped to handle more people, and we should do our part by not procreating. This hadn't been a big deal to me, a girl who feared the idea of becoming her mother far more than tear gas and billy clubs. We wouldn't be part of the problem, but part of the solution. He suggested I terminate, for the good of the child, but I couldn't take that step.

For months, he looked at me as if I'd broken a promise. Then the day came, and I delivered our son in the bedroom we shared. Skye fell to his knees, his arms wrapped tight around the one thing I'd done right in my life, and he wept.

I thought his tears were for our son's hopeless future on a dying planet until he lifted his chin and I saw the first real smile I'd ever seen light his face. He was crying with the depth of his love for our son. My heart was so full I could feel the strain, the stretching of the muscle, the places where it weakened, ready to split.

Jenna's hand silently wraps around mine as if the grief in my heart could be felt in hers. She is my sister. Jenna, Vicky, and Hope were the only family I've ever known aside from my time as a partner and mother.

We're far enough back into the cave we may be safe until he goes out again, I just hope he makes one of his journeys soon. This is no place to spend the night, especially with our water all carefully hidden outside with Vicky.

We've pushed our way deeper in. There doesn't seem to be an end, but we can't turn on the flashlight to see what surrounds us.

I run my tongue over my lips, hoping to sooth a bit of the dryness, but it's hopeless. Water has been what's sustained me for days, and now even that is inaccessible.

Vicky must be scared to death. I pray that she's okay out there on her own. As scared as I feel in here, at least I have Jenna beside me. After all the years I've spent isolating myself from everyone, there's a deep hunger that's fed by having her alongside.

Chapter 21

Jenna

I wonder if our Grizzly Adams started out like us, lost in the woods until he adapted so much to his surroundings that he lost his mind. All day, every day without a single modern convenience. No television or laptop. No Netflix or Hulu. I wonder if he has a mother somewhere who still holds out hope that he's alive, that he's safe, that someday she'll see him again.

Tears don't come with the emotion. I don't get to wallow in my self-pity, or even cry for a stranger. The only action I can continue is the one of breathing in and out, over and over again, with the hope that this is not the day I will die. That I don't leave this life without a body to bury or solid closure for my family.

Hours crawl by, and he seems to do almost nothing. He moves in and out of the cave grumbling and growling as if he's communicating with a bear. As if he *is* a bear. I shiver.

His fire crackles, and I wonder if the day is fading. For all I know it could be noon. I've grown used to my stomach aching for food, so it no longer is an indicator of time. It's like when you go to the movies in the middle of the day, then walk out into the sun, somehow expecting that it should be nighttime. My perspective is off.

The scent of meat cooking over an open fire floats through the cave and to my nose. I grab Ireland's hand to keep from lunging forward and snagging a bite of whatever he's cooking. I'd eat snake about now, or a dog, or really anything. I believe I've developed a deeper sense of compassion for the Donner Party.

He comes in closer to our hiding place now and must be on his pile of furs. I can hear the crunch of burned skin and meat as it's ground up by his teeth. My mouth waters and my nose stings with the smoky smells. Couldn't he toss a bit this way? I lean forward. Wouldn't even this wild man have a touch of mercy if we stepped out and begged for a little nourishment?

Ireland must sense my thoughts. Her hand tightens around my arm. With her other hand, she turns my head toward hers. I sense more than see her shake her head. Then she pulls me closer, and I rest my cheek on her shoulder.

It brings me back to the long-packed memories of my mother. Once, I was a loved daughter. Before I became an abandoned adult. I've avoided this area of my life for so many years, the good times only making the ending somehow sharper.

My parents always wanted more children, but after me, no more came. Maybe that's part of what made me go a bit nuts when I wasn't able to conceive. I spent my childhood longing for a sibling, thinking all would be perfect if I could just have brothers and sisters. Then, as an adult, I faced the real possibility of not having children at all. It was like the same grief visiting twice.

When I was in the crazy middle school years, my mother was in the even more crazy world of chemo and radiation. My dad never gave up. He prayed over her night and day until the treatment was complete and the doctors gave a happy prognosis.

My senior year of high school, the time that should have been filled with dreams and excitement, was lost in the shadow of cancer coming for another call. This time it swooped in fast and dark. My mom was gone before spring break. Before she could see me off to college. She left me alone before I had the chance to leave her.

What was I thinking, coming out here like this?

I wonder what will happen with Mark after I'm gone. Will he lose his faith like my father? A smile creeps onto my face. No. Even though my dad was a pastor, and Mark is a public school teacher, their faiths are even more different. In some way, my dad's belief required the Lord giving him what he thought he was owed.

God is not on a leash that we hold. He is the creator of everything. We can't even begin to understand his timing or is ways.

If this is how God sees fit to end my life, then I have to trust he knows what's best.

I close my eyes and offer the only worship I can, giving my family, my kids, and my future over to the only one who cares more than I do.

VICKY

I shiver in the icy air that whips around the cave. If that man would stay inside for more than a few minutes, I could at least retrieve more clothing from the packs. But he insists on constant movement, in and out of the entrance. With the increase of the wind, it's hard to tell when he's coming until he's there again.

Smoke drifts my way with the scent of cooked meat dancing in smoldering flames. He's made a fire at the mouth of his home, I assume this is his way of keeping animals from joining him in his living room, uninvited. When I haven't seen or heard him for at least thirty minutes, I sneak around the corner and huddle as close to the fire as I can without being spotted from inside.

A bone flies past me as he uses his entrance as a trash receptacle. In the glow of the fire, I can see the remains of flesh still clinging to its white surface. With a quick motion, I grab for the treasure then sit back against the rock, listening for his footsteps.

Nothing.

I shove that bone into my mouth and suck every scrumptious morsel from the smooth surface. Then, I can't even help myself, I crunch through the bone and suck the tender marrow. Lobster and steak have nothing on this meager meal. Because this is real. It's here, and I actually taste its goodness. My life, however short, will never be the same.

I run my tongue over the bone. It wasn't enough to satisfy, but it's more than I assume my friends have inside what must be a horrible prison. Maybe I should start to scream. I could run into the woods. He'd surely come after me, and Jenna and Ireland could escape.

But then what?

This new life with no answers weakens me. I'm as broken as the bone I chewed to the core.

This is me, Lord, nothing but me. Am I worth anything to you this way?

I actually don't expect an answer. I'm exactly how I always feared I'd end up. I'm useless. I have nothing to give. I am only the shell of the woman the world thinks it knows.

Maybe it's the beginning of my end, but I hear a voice that speaks directly to my heart. A voice that carries my soul on its words. *I love you where you are.*

There isn't a fire in this world that could bring the warming comfort that heats me to the depth like those words. All my works have meant nothing. God loves me here, in the middle of nowhere, with nothing but my dying body and mind to offer. To the world, I'm as valuable as that tossed-aside bone, but to my Maker, I am a treasure.

Daniel may not see me that way anymore. But his opinion doesn't matter out here. Just as it doesn't matter if my fans turn their backs on me. I wasn't put on this planet to fear the disapproval of my mother, my husband, my children, or strangers. The beginning of understanding swells in my chest. I believe I was created to love without reservation. And all I've had my entire life is control and formality. Now that I'm dying, I want to truly live.

My eyes are heavy. And my soul has found peace.

We didn't sleep at all last night, and though I know drifting off could mean the end for me, there's a big part that doesn't care. I can't stop my eyes from closing, my body from dropping out of this misery into a dream world. I let go.

❖ ❖ ❖

A loud noise startles me awake. I whip my head to one side then the next, taking in the scene and trying to make sense of where I am. The night has passed and the morning is greeting me with fresh terror. I swing my gaze around in the early light. Then I hear the scream I've been dreading, but I think it's Ireland who made the sound. He's got them. This is it.

I lunge back into my hiding place, the rock I used as the warning sign tight in my hands, ready to be my weapon.

JENNA

We must have been sleeping. In fact, I think that's the deepest I've drifted since I left my own bed to head out on what was supposed to be a vacation. It was Ireland's scream that woke me. My heart still races from the shock.

Above us, Grizzly Adams's silhouette towers. He doesn't say a single human word, and I wonder if he's been out here so long that he's lost his ability to speak.

He grunts then lifts one arm, smacking his wrist with his other hand then pointing to us.

I hold out an arm. Maybe I should fight, but my muscles don't have the strength left for the struggle. Even this exertion is exhausting. He ties my wrists together then binds Ireland's. The sinew is tight. It cuts into my flesh, burning the skin. With some kind of rope that appears to be made from vines, he ties leashes onto our bound hands and tugs.

Pressing my palms into the ground, I get myself upright. My face heats with the effort, and I'm dizzy from thirst.

Ireland's expression hangs, her eyes dull. Her glasses with the one remaining lens crunch under my foot. She doesn't seem to notice, only holds her gaze on our captor.

Another grunt and he tugs us forward.

The dawn light is blinding after a night in a cave. I blink, but my eyes still buzz with the adjustment. "What are you going to do with us?"

He looks back, narrows his eyes, as if evaluating me, then yanks on the rope causing my feet to trip forward.

Ireland trudges on without protest. It's not that we have a choice to move, he's stronger than the two of us put together, even before a week of very little food. But there's a sense that Ireland's given up in a way. I need her to be with me. I need her strength.

"You can't do this," I say. "There will be people looking for us. Lots of people."

His footsteps don't even hesitate at my words. Our week's adventure has passed. They must be searching by now.

"If you harm us, you'll end up spending the rest of your life in a jail. They'll make you live in a crowded prison with lots of . . ." I search my mind for what this guy would hate most. "With lots of metal."

His face turns toward me for a moment, but he keeps moving.

"Yep. That's right. You're looking at years of metal all around you. Metal bars. A metal bed. They'll even make you eat your meals off a metal tray. And there won't be any of this wild food you're accustomed to. No. In prison you'll eat processed chemical food. The kind of stuff that kills you from the inside, rotting your guts."

I look to Ireland. Her mouth hangs open, and I don't know if she's mortified by me or impressed. But I see a flicker of life and that's enough to keep me fighting.

"Can you just imagine what it will be like locked away? No freedom. No mountains. No fresh air. Oh, the air in prison must be very stale. You're breathing the same air the guy next to you just had in his lungs. Come on. Let us go. I've got your best interests in mind."

"We won't tell anyone about you," Ireland says.

The sound of her voice brings a smile to my face. I'm no longer isolated in my quest to rattle this guy.

But even together, with Ireland and I both pulling hard on the ropes, yelling horrible consequences, Grizzly Adams marches on, and we're pulled with him. When he slows to climb over a rock, Ireland twists her back to me, and I see the handle of the gun poking out of her waistband.

At the first chance, I'll get my hands on it. Then we'll see who's in charge.

"I take it you don't much care for company. Well, in prison, you'll be surrounded by other people, and you won't be able to tie them up. And there will be television. They'll turn the volume up and the laugh track will echo off all that metal."

I think there's the slightest cringe. Maybe he understands what I'm saying. Maybe he's already been to prison. Maybe this won't be his first murder.

Chapter 22

VICKY

By the time I am able to move without the tree blurring into swirls of green and brown, the man has dragged my friends from the cave toward who knows where. I had jumped to my feet at the shock of Ireland's scream. Too many days with insufficient nutrients and sleep left me weak. I think I passed out for a couple minutes.

Ireland and Jenna's fading pleas refocus me. Jenna keeps talking, her voice strained, but I can't comprehend her meaning.

I rush to catch up while staying unseen, a real feat in my bright pink coat.

A sob catches in my throat. I'll kill him if he hurts them. The fire in my gut consumes me and takes away my hunger and my pain. Jenna is making so much noise I don't have to worry about being heard behind them, and I'm sure any wild animal has been scared miles into the mountains. When they get far enough down the trail, I strip off anything of unnatural color and tuck everything into the packs. Then I slip out of my hiding place and begin my trek as close as I can manage without being seen.

After an hour, my back aches and my legs burn. I'm carrying my trusty rock and the weight of all our supplies formerly distributed among the three of us.

I can't go any farther this way. I step into a clump of trees and drop the bags, dumping everything into a pile. Then, with quick decisions I choose what we must have and tuck it back into Ireland's muted pack. The rest I shove into the other bags and stash behind a rock. Hopefully we'll be able to find this location again after I free them.

Throwing the backpack on, I head out again. Somewhere ahead, I can't see where, Jenna bellows about the food they force you to eat in prison. I chuckle. Our timid little friend has fire in her veins now. Mountain guy doesn't stand a chance.

Even with the lighter pack my shoulders ache and my legs wobble. It must be mid-morning, but the overcast sky is dark, ominous. An angry cold wind whips up the mountain, cutting through my clothes and burning my skin. My nose has gone numb with the chill, but my back is damp with perspiration.

I scratch my cheek and feel blood drip down my jawline. Wiping it away with the back of my hand, I lean down and grab a leaf, careful not to pick poison oak again, and press it into the cut like a man does with toilet paper after a shaving nick.

If my fans could see me now. Would they abandon me because I'm a mess or applaud my willingness to fight on? It doesn't matter. This isn't about how strangers perceive my worth. God didn't put me on this earth to show others all the things I can do better than they can.

After my epiphany, maybe this is my first test. What could possibly be more important than saving my friends? Eventually this beast of a man will wear down. He has to go to sleep, and I will be ready. My grip tightens on my rock. The one I will use to exert my power. One hard smack to the head, and even a guy his size will be off to dreamland.

IRELAND

Blood flows from my wrists where he's bound me and taken away my independence. I'm nothing more than a dog on a leash. Nothing more than helpless. I hate that word, helpless.

I can't catch my breath, can't take a minute to center my spirit. All I've built my life on was stolen in a moment. I screamed. Like a child at the mercy of a kidnapper. Where is my empowered life now? There's only prayer remaining. I've been stripped down to only me and God. Even the gun in my waistband is out of my reach.

One of my boots flops more with each step through the sloppy earth. The lace is undone, making it an unrestrained weight on the end of my leg. My toe catches a rock and I'm down. The ground slams my body, my arms are yanked above my head by a tug on the rope, and the air bursts from my lungs.

I struggle to pull my knees up, but with each inch I gain, our captor drags me another two and lays me out again. My loose boot slips off my foot, leaving my wet sock-covered foot exposed to the cold.

"Stop." Jenna's plea is shrill, like the cry of a wounded animal. In the second that he hesitates, Jenna yanks me up. I stumble, but I'm on my feet.

Every bit of me is soaked through. The core of my body aches with the chill. We can't be long in this life. Not now, with the air frigid to the point that ice is forming on ground.

A creek gurgles in front of us so loud even Jenna's constant flow of consequences is drowned out by the power of the water. Surely we can rest now, get a drink, dip our cuts in the stream even if we're already freezing.

But he barely even slows down. His uncovered feet splash into the water, and he pulls us along with him. The cold cuts through to my bones, making them feel as brittle as kindling. The pain is too deep to stomach. I cry out, but our forward motion continues.

As we scale the bank on the other side, Jenna slips, her feet dragging back into the current.

The guy tugs, but Jenna can't get her feet under her body again. He looks at me and grunts. I'm tempted to lie down next to her. What can he do with both of us flat on the muddy ground? But I see the angry blistered skin on Jenna's wrists and how the rope tears into her flesh.

I squat down in front of Jenna, like I'm taking a moment to catch my breath. Her intensified grunting tells me she's gotten the hint. A moment later, Jenna stumbles up the bank and collapses on top of me. I feel the gun slip from my pants.

When he tugs hard, Jenna gasps and I hear the splash of something heavy hitting the water.

"No." Jenna's cry is so loud he startles. "No. This can't happen." She screaming like she's finally lost her mind. "No. No. No." Collapsing onto the ground, she kicks and wails, her face a fiery shade of red. "This is not going to happen."

He turns, his eyes flaming. Behind him dark clouds roll over the sky as if God himself feels the same rage toward us.

"Jenna." I plead with my eyes. "You need to get up."

"No. I will not. I'm not moving any farther. If he wants to kill me, let him do it right here. This is as good a place as any."

The man steps close. He ties the rope around his waist and glares down at us.

I can hardly take a breath. I'm paralyzed. With his hands free, he's ready to break our necks in half, and I don't have much strength left to fight. Jenna still screams and cries next to me. She hasn't even looked up. She won't see him coming. I envy her.

In one quick motion, he leans down and grabs Jenna. I hold onto her, begging him not to, but he rips her away from me. Throwing her over his shoulder, she hangs like a newly slaughtered animal, but her screams have stopped. Her eyes are wide, and her mouth is open but quiet for the first time since we left the cave.

He moves forward. I stumble to my feet, a rock cutting through my sock and piercing the arch of my foot. My jeans, soggy with creek water, pull down a bit with each step. The wind picks up power; cold, icy strength. My lungs fight for oxygen but cry out with each freezing breath. *Please, Lord, if we have to die out here, make it quick.*

VICKY

I saw the gun slip from Jenna's grip and hit the water, but I'm forced to wait until they've moved farther away before I can begin to search. The screaming has stopped. It's abrupt. With Jenna and Ireland out of my view, my stomach clenches so tight I can't stand straight. Are they alive? Is this the end?

The way the freezing wind howls through the trees cuts off the sound of any footsteps ahead of me, if there are any. Supposing they are still moving, I only have moments to find the gun before I'm too far behind to locate their trail again.

At the creek, I barrel into the frigid water, pressing my palms over the rocks at the edge. The gun is heavy and couldn't have floated downstream, but the water rushes over me, taking away my bearings. My fingers go numb, like I'm searching the creek bed with a hammer rather than my hands. One after another, I yank up rocks thinking I've found the weapon, but each time I'm disappointed.

Flopping onto the bank, exhaustion claims me. Every day out here I learn how much further my body can dip without actually dying. My eyes start to close, my mind begs to drift off into sleep even if I never wake up on Earth again. At least I know there's heaven waiting. Will my mother be there? Did she really know God, or just religion?

I think about the memorial they'll hold in my honor. The crowds that will attend, and how many of those people really don't know me. I hope I've given my children a glimpse of the person inside of me, but I have very little confidence that I have.

Tears wash over my face, hot on my cold skin.

How can I die without ever being known?

When Brooklyn and Cameron were little, I was the mom I wanted to have, but then I lost my balance. It seemed like a good thing, dedicating my time to minister to other mothers and wives, to show them how they could make their homes a special place where their children and husbands could be surrounded by good food and a beautiful atmosphere.

I put the pretty in and took the love out. Wouldn't it be better to live in a shack and eat mac and cheese for dinner every night but have love? Jenna's children will know what life is truly about. She goes on about them all the time, and it annoys me, but that's because I'm jealous. She's given them the one thing I was afraid to give. The thing that I couldn't spare. She gave her children her heart.

Will Daniel even look for me? Will part of him rejoice when he realizes I'll never be back? He can go on with his life, form a new family with

Cori. Maybe she can do a better job with the kids than I've done. Maybe it's for the best.

Get up.

My eyes snap open, and I whip my head around. There's no one here. I rub my palms over my face and blink my eyes until I see clearly. Light from somewhere in the cloud-darkened sky hits on something in the water.

I dip my hand in and my fingers wrap around the gun's handle. Pulling it from the water, I let it drip as I stare in amazement.

How long have I been here? I shove the gun into my pants. The icy metal shocks me and I gasp, but I scurry to my feet and jog in the direction I saw them go. Rain starts to fall and the wind pushes hard against me. The spray hits like needles piercing my skin.

Each step is like climbing a mountain, but I have to catch them. I have to keep going now that I have the gun. It's the only chance any of us have for survival. It can't be night yet, but there's not a bit of sunlight left in the sky. Thunder rolls over the mountains and I brace myself for the lightning but it doesn't come until I've relaxed, then the sky lightens, giving me a brief glimpse of their silhouettes ahead in the flash.

We have one bullet. I raise the gun over my head, pulling back the hammer like every western movie hero. He won't know if I'm out of ammunition. But it's gone dark again, and I've lost my opportunity. I keep moving in that direction, the gun in front of me, cocked, held tight with both hands.

"Stop," I yell into the wind. My legs carry me farther, until my foot hits something and I fly forward. On impact, my finger hits the trigger and our last bullet flies unaimed into the storm.

My grip loosens, and the gun slides from my hand. I scurry around on all fours, rubbing my palms through the mud. Useless as it will be now, it still seems important to have that gun. Huge raindrops plop onto the ground and my back, water dripping through my hair and down my scalp. Sobs wracks my body, and I smack my fist down, splashing my face with filthy water.

Chapter 23

JENNA

A crack breaks through the air. And I don't think it was the thunder. The sound seemed to come from the ground. Even with the wind whizzing past my ears, I heard it. A gunshot. I lay loose on Grizzly's shoulder, not fighting, but listening with all my strength.

Ireland keeps moving forward, her head ducked as if she heard nothing. But I know I'm right. I know it all the way through me. Vicky is back there. And she has the gun. It's so similar to the sound of a tree splitting or lightning hitting, but yet I'm sure it was a shot.

The man halts and turns back toward where we've come from.

Ireland runs smack into the side of Grizzly Adams. She looks up, and I see the shock in her expression. Where has she been?

There's absolutely no doubt now. He's waiting for our pursuer to catch up. He must know it's Vicky. Or maybe he knows she only had one bullet left and she couldn't hit him even if she could see in the dark. More likely, Ireland or I would die by the weapon that was supposed to save us. It could be a blessing that the last bullet is gone.

He drops me onto the muddy ground.

Without warning, Grizzly Adams yanks us forward and we're off on his path again. My ribs ache from being bumped along on his shoulder, but I'm grateful to at least move on my own feet.

Beneath my feet the dirt has turned to slop, my boots get heavier with each step as more mud clings. I tip my head back and stick my tongue out to collect rain. It feels better than champagne in my parched mouth. Drops run across my arms and soak around the ropes, cooling my raging wrists.

Lightning strikes again, and I get a glimpse of something in the distance.

He pushes us down into a puddle, my back hitting against something rough, then he pulls a sharpened bone from his pouch and saws the sinew until it pops free.

I rub my wrist and stretch my arms. Knots scream in my shoulders.

Next to me, he frees Ireland. This could be my chance to attack, but I don't. My back stays tight against the wood, and I wait for his next move. When he finishes, he pulls the ropes together and tucks them into his pack.

I brace myself, but I don't look away. Keeping my gaze glued to his shadowed eyes, I dare him to take my life while I watch.

He scowls, scratches his head, and then turns, running away into the darkness.

Ireland grasps my hand. "What's he doing?"

"I think he's leaving us here. Maybe he thinks it funny to let us die in the storm. Or maybe this is his way of protecting his secret. We'd never be able to retrace our steps back to the cave and out him to the authorities."

Ireland climbs onto her hands and knees.

"There's more to it." I know I'm right, but I can't figure out what's happening. "We have to find Vicky." I reach back to pull myself up, my hand gripping the tree behind me, but it's not a tree. The shape is wrong, rough and angled. Standing, I run my palms over the surface and my finger catches on a plank coming out horizontally.

"Ireland," I yell into the wind. "It's a fence." Tears run down my cold and already wet cheeks. "It has to lead to somewhere." I turn my face toward the way we came.

"Vicky," Ireland yells before I get the chance. "Vicky, are you out there?"

There's no answer.

"We have to go back for her."

Lightning strikes, illuminating a figure in the distance for a split second.

"She's out there." I strain my eyes into the dim light. "Vicky. We're here." I pull my soaked sweatshirt off and then my long-sleeved t-shirt and tie them together. "Take off your sweater."

"Why?"

"We need a rope."

Ireland takes off three layers and I tie those arms together with mine. We don't have a lot of length, but it gets us out into the open. I hook one end to the fence then hand the other end to Ireland. "Hold my hand and we'll go as far out as we can."

We start screaming into the storm, my hair slapping me in the face. Her voice comes to us and we yell more. I catch a glimpse of her shadow, then we're close enough.

Vicky runs through the slop and falls into our arms, the gun dangling from one hand. "Where is he?"

I hold her tight. "He's gone. It's okay. We're safe."

She steps back, waving the gun in the air. "This is not what I call safe."

Ireland grabs the gun. We'll all freeze. We're out of bullets. If we run into trouble now, we're on our own. *Lord, we need you.* Well, that's been the truth the whole time. We've needed God to guide us through, and he's done just that. We're alive, and we have the fence.

"The temperature is dropping. Let's move."

We pull ourselves back to the fence. The rain pelts us and turns to hail. Of course it turns to hail. Why wouldn't it? It stings and burns my skin, but it's too much of a struggle to get back into my wet sweatshirt. Hand over hand, we work our way along the fence posts. Ice collects on the ground. Talking is useless.

The wood railing is the only thing keeping me from falling on my face. But there's no sign of it ending, the storm or the fence line.

IRELAND

I have proof of civilization in my hand, but I can feel the end is coming near, and I have nothing to say for my time on this beautiful, dangerous, cruel planet. I have nothing but a stack of articles with my name as the byline as evidence I was here. Even my son won't know the difference. To him, I've already been dead for years.

Sharp pain rips through the skin on my palm. I yank back, instinctively cradling my hand at my chest.

Vicky bumps into my back, then staggers, slipping on the mud.

"Wait," I yell to Jenna.

She turns. "We can't stop. No breaks."

"Vicky fell, and I have a chunk of wood in my hand."

She slides by me, literally, and takes Vicky's hand, pulling her up. Without hesitating, she starts again. One hand on the fence, the other on Vicky. "We can't stop," she yells over her shoulder. "I'm really sorry about your hand, but it will have to wait. I'm getting home to my family, and no ice or sleet or wind or even a splinter is going to stop me. Come on."

I start to argue. This isn't a splinter. But given the choice of death by freezing or a pillar through the palm, I think I take the pillar. Sliding my injured hand into my shirt, I use the other to grip the belt loop of Vicky's pants. We're a sorry train heading for somewhere. I hope it's the station.

"Hey, there's something on the fence here." There's joy lacing Jenna's words. A bit of that cheerleader is back, but we're not going to be saved by a sign. "Can you read it?"

I squint, my face close to the metal sheet. The letters are hard to decipher in the near dark of this storm, and I don't have my glasses.

Vicky leans into my shoulder, murmuring a prayer for help.

"It's . . . No trespass . . ." I rub the ice layer off the sign.

Vicky grabs the placard with both hands. "Enter without permission, and you will be shot."

My stomach drops. I'd almost claimed a bit of Jenna's optimism. "What do we do now?"

"We keep going." Jenna tugs Vicky, and they start moving along the fence again.

"Are you crazy? I don't think that's the kind of thing you post just for the fun of it."

"We're not robbers. Anyone can see that." Jenna's feet trudge forward, one step after another.

I've lost all feeling in my shoeless foot. The one that still has a shoe feels plenty—the pain of open blisters and wet skin rubbing against hard seams. When do we resign ourselves to the inevitable? When do we just lie down and die?

"Here's another one. That must mean we're close." Jenna picks up speed.

"Since when is it a good thing to get closer to a gun-toting maniac?"

"You have no way of knowing that," Jenna says. "Maybe they're just a nice family who's cautious about strangers."

Vicky knocks the ice off the new sign. "Think again." She points to the words. "Trespassers will be shot without question."

A shiver runs down my nearly numb spine. We're in a lot of trouble here. Jenna presses on.

Ice pelts my face like pebbles hitting stone. The Earth is claiming her prize. Maybe I'm growing delirious, but the picture my mind forms is of our three heads, mounted in a giant showroom. I'm slipping into the fantasy. I see the room all around me now. There are other heads, other prizes. I see what remains of corporate CEOs who leveled natural habitats for the sake of profits. I see those who lived plush lives on the backs of the oil industry. They're all sneering at me. Laughing at what's become of me.

"Look!" Jenna shakes me back to our current torture. "There's a light up there."

It's dim, but I see it too. Maybe a hundred yards away, but it might as well be ten miles. I can't keep moving. Vicky is practically being dragged by Jenna. How does she keep going?

My bare foot slips out from under me and I topple to the ground, pulling Vicky down by the belt loop. It's too late for me. My cheek sinks into the slush, and I close my eyes.

Before I can fully give in to sleep, I'm tugged up, Vicky under one arm and Jenna under my other. "Leave me here. I'm done with life anyway."

"Good try," Vicky mumbles. "It's not up to you. There will be no giving up."

VICKY

When we reach the building, it becomes clear that this is not a house, at least not for people. I think it's the stench that brings it home to me first. Sickly sweet and pungent, even from outside I expect the smell to have a color—green. Not just regular green, split-pea soup green.

Jenna listens at the door then squeezes a spring and flips up the hook-and-eye latch and cracks it open. We slip inside as if we're about to pull off a major bank heist. A guttural moo stops my heart and breath.

"Milk cows. Thank God!" Jenna pushes us in, and closes the door behind us. "This is just the break we need."

No. She's gone off the steep side of the mental cliff. Steam is literally rising off piles of cow . . . leavings. The huge eyes of about a dozen mammoth creatures stare us down with nothing to keep them from trampling us. What little flesh I have left is going to be eaten by bovines. On the other hand, being able to see by virtue of electricity-powered lightbulbs makes me almost giddy.

Ireland slides down the wall. For the first time I notice her missing boot. How long has she been like that? "Jenna."

She turns and takes in Ireland's state. "I thought *you* were in rough shape."

The comment stings. I run my hand over my bumpy skin. There are more hills and valleys on my face than the most acne-affected teenager.

Jenna kneels near Ireland. "We're safe now. You're going to be okay."

Ireland's eye blink, then go wide.

I follow her gaze. Posted on the side wall are three posters of former presidents. They're all decorated with bullet holes.

"Okay, maybe this isn't the friendliest farm." Jenna tosses our one bag at her feet. "But it's tons better than where we were living in Nowhere, Wilderness."

I shake my head. "I don't think we can trust them without further information."

"Agreed." Jenna's shoulders slump. "We may not be exactly saved yet, but we're getting closer."

"Closer to one end or another." The wet nose of a cow nuzzles my neck, sending me into a hard battle with paralysis. "Help."

Jenna shakes her head. "Get back now, Bessy. We're not here with treats." She pushes on the animal's shoulder and it takes a couple steps back. Jenna helps Ireland up and moves her to the side of the barn where hay is stacked. "First things first. We need to have a safe place if they come back. I'm not saying these are horrible people, but a few minutes to observe them would be good." She walks up to the backside of a cow. "Hey there, old girl." Running her hand down the leg she continues on to the bulging sack that hangs below.

My stomach wavers, and I hold my hand in front of my mouth.

"Looks like they haven't been milked yet. That's good for us." She cups her hand and sprays milk into her palm then tips it into her mouth. "That's the best thing I've had in maybe forever."

"Clearly that's the starvation talking." I don't usually drink milk, but when I do, it's organic and it's skim, and it definitely has gone through serious pasteurization. But my stomach is hollow and desperate. "Can you get me some?"

A smile lights Jenna's eyes. She pulls a bucket from a nail on the wall and places it under the cow. "There's something strange going on here. This is a hay barn, not equipped for cows to live in." Milk echoes off the metal. After about ten streams she moves to the next one. "I don't want it to be obvious that we've been here."

When the bucket is half full, Jenna hands it to me and motions for me to drink. I've come a long way from crystal goblets and imported water.

The milky scent fills my nose and mouth before the warm liquid pours over my tongue. It's thick and smooth like satin. The taste is more of a feel than a flavor, a sensation. It's heaven to the starving. The heat rinses down my throat, and I gulp, taking in more and more. Just as I'm sure my feet will lift off the ground in ecstasy, Jenna pulls the metal rim away from my lips.

"I think that's enough. You're going to get yourself sick swigging it like a drunk sailor."

I wipe the back of my hand across my mouth, removing a layer of cream. "Nice image."

She grins.

We return to Ireland. She's so still, I shiver with the fear that she's already left us.

Jenna shakes her shoulder. "Ireland, I need you to wake up."

She stirs but her eyes stay closed. How could I take the time to feed myself when Ireland lays helpless on the edge of a mountain of hay bales?

Chapter 24

JENNA

I have to stay positive, but I want to crumble onto the floor and cry. Ireland doesn't look good. I search through all of our decisions since entering the cave. Was there something we should have done differently?

I've filled the pail again. Steam rises off the surface of the milk. I try to take the sock off Ireland's bootless foot. The wool seems stuck to the skin. Is it better to leave it or take it off? My instinct tells me the sock has to be removed. It's wet and the skin can't warm this way. She whimpers as I do this horrible job. It gives me that same sick feeling I had while changing Calvin's bandages after he fell in the campfire the summer the triplets were nine. I'm shocked by the swelling and redness. This isn't something she'll be able to push past. Ireland needs a doctor. Then I see her hand.

There's a stick, this is not in the splinter category, woven into the tender tissue of her palm. It's terrifying, but we've landed in a reality where that will have to wait.

I want to go home.

Digging a hole in the straw, I settle the bucket on the floor and position her foot so the sole lies against the warm metal. I wonder if dipping it into the milk would be better.

Ireland cringes, pulling her foot away. "Hot."

"No. It's only warm. It won't burn you." I place her foot back on the pail.

Vicky comes to us with a ladle. "Look what I found." She dips it into the milk bucket and squats next to Ireland. "Take a drink. The fat does wonders."

I grab the ladle. "You can't do that."

"Why on earth not?"

"She's vegan. Don't you remember?"

Vicky drops her chin to her chest. "You're kidding me, right? I'm sure with the choice of starvation and death over an animal product, anyone would choose life. It's not even meat, for crying out loud."

"Convictions mean something." I'm overwhelmed with a wave of protectiveness for everything that makes up Ireland. "It's commitment. If we don't stick with our commitments, what are we?"

"Alive. We're alive." She settles her fists into her sides.

I can't answer. And I can't make Ireland break. And I can't watch her die. It's a world of can'ts.

"Fine." Vicky tosses the ladle into the bucket. "Feed her hay. But we have to give her something."

I hold up a hand, my mind spinning with sudden realization. "Grain. There has to be grain in here. It will be packed with nutrition and it's not an animal product."

"No. Just a product *for* animals."

"Desperate times, Vicky."

She doesn't respond, only takes to scratching the rash on her arm. If those guys walked in right now, they'd probably run away. Vicky looks like a carrier of leprosy.

I scan the crowded room for anything that would indicate feed. Along the stacks of hay is a metal garbage can with a bail placed on top of the lid. "Vicky, help me move this." I push a cow out of my way.

Vicky edges toward me, her back away from the animals, but she does come.

"We need to lift this bale off the top. Can you take one end?"

She nods, but her gaze doesn't even come close to the task.

I take hold of her hands and press them into the twine bindings. "Lift." In a moment, I'm opening the top. My heart races at the treasure inside. I unfold the top of a feed bag and fill my pockets with rolled oats, corn, and barley, all covered in molasses.

When we've put the container back like we found it, and I've given Ireland some grain to suck on, it's time to move on to shelter. Is this really how pioneers lived, one life-saving task to the next? Vicky and I try to move some bales from the middle of the tall mountain of hay. We've been weakened by our Fantasy Island vacation, and this just about takes my body to the breaking point.

"There's too much lying on top." Vicky plops down on a bale. She holds her head in her hands. "I can't do this. I can't do any more."

"What are you talking about? We just have to use our brains instead of our muscles." I hold back my thoughts on the fuzziness of my thinking lately.

"What's the point? We die here, or I go home and wish I had. You have no idea what it's like to know your husband doesn't love you anymore. You can't understand what I'm facing."

"No." I put my hand on her shoulder. It shakes with sobs. "I can't. Mark has loved me through the worst of me. And I've never even appreciated that. But you're stronger than you're acting right now and, Vicky, this isn't all about you. Now get your backside off that bale and help me." I stand, my arms crossed and my face forced into a serious stare, but in my heart I want to hold her, stroke her hair, and let her cry until she's better.

To my shock, Vicky stands and brushes hay from her wet jeans. "What do you want me to do?" Her voice is still weak, but I can sense the tiger inside of her.

"Grab that pitchfork. Wedge it under the bale on top and pry it up. I'll pull."

She sticks the tines in and lays her body across the handle. The hay rises and I pull.

There's a slight movement, but it's like trying to pull a Jenga piece out of the tower and realizing that it's been glued in.

"You're going to need me." Ireland's voice is soft, scratchy, and determined.

Tears catch in my throat. "Yes, we will."

IRELAND

For the first time in what feels like months, I'm in a warm place. Jenna is the genius behind our quarters, the superstar in this play. By rearranging a few bales of hay, we're tucked into a tiny house of sorts, insulated on all sides.

And now that there's heat, it actually brings with it pain.

My foot aches and burns, the skin taut with the throbbing flesh.

With my good hand, I take more grain from our pile and lay it on my tongue. It's sweet and sticky with molasses. My mouth waters with the sensation. It's almost more than I can bear. I take a drink from the canteen newly filled from the cow's makeshift water trough. My stomach pinches with the deep, primal desire for milk, but there's something that tells me this commitment of mine is no longer about me. It's about Jenna. If I give it up, even though I have no true memory or understanding of why I ever made vegan my lifestyle, I'm afraid Jenna will see that as the time to give up hope. She holds on to my needs like I'm a child giving her life purpose. And she's so strong right now, I can't stand to be the fault that brings her down.

"Are you doing okay?" Jenna rubs my leg. "Do you need anything?"

I start to speak but choke on a piece of rolled corn. "I'm good," I lie. The truth is, I'm pretty sure I'll be the first one of us to experience the sweet relief of death, and I feel guilty about this. Really, after everything Vicky's been though, dying first is a feat. Maybe I should be proud as my body gives up the fight. In an odd way, this is a win.

A tear burns as it slides across my cheek. Jenna and Vicky will walk into heaven together. I don't know where I'll be sent, but it surely will not be through the pearly gates of eternity.

I figure my sadness is well masked by the dark of our hay bale home, with only two slivers of light slicing through, but I'm wrong. Jenna pulls my head over to her chest, and I snuggle into her, breathing to the beat of her heart.

"We're going to be okay," she says.

I can't answer. I can't tell them what I'm really thinking. It's not about the now. It's about the forever.

"She's right." Vicky's at the other end, her boots at my hip. "I don't believe God would bring us out here without a reason. It's a trial. That's all. And trials help us to grow. And growth is meant to be shared, so others can learn from our struggles."

"Wow. You're going to turn this into a sermon." I sound angry, but really, I'm impressed.

"That's not what I mean. I just think the three of us have a message. I've learned more about myself through this than I did in the forty years before. I'm praying that God will give me a chance to change. And, don't be offended, I'm praying that for both of you too."

I'm too overcome with emotion to answer her, so I squeeze her leg then pat it, nodding my head. I want that chance too. But I'm not as convinced God will give me a second, who am I kidding, a billionth do-over. And I know Skye won't. And, River, my baby boy. I've abandoned him in my desire to protect him from my rejection. The idea is so ridiculous. But I've become my mother in a way I didn't see coming. A part of me always longed to hear her say that she loved me and was sorry. I can give that to my child, if I live long enough to deliver the message. If not, I know two women who can do it better than me.

JENNA

There's a crash as the barn door hits the siding. I've woken from the best sleep I've enjoyed in weeks, maybe years, and I've done it instantly. My heart pounds against my ribcage. They're here. What if my hideout isn't as hidden as I think?

Ireland moans in her sleep.

I shake her shoulder then lay my finger over her lips as she awakens.

At the other end of our little house, Vicky curls into a ball, her knees tucked to her chest, her face close to one of the open slits.

"Which one of you idiots left the door unlatched?"

I can't help but look. My face is jabbed with hay as I press close to the view hole.

"Do you realize what could have happened here?" A man with a belly as round as my ready-to-pop-with-triplets one had been sets a shotgun against the bottom of the hay bales. It looks like the one my husband uses for goose hunting. He scratches rough fingernails through thinning hair. In his other hand he holds a wool-lined hat.

If only we had half of the warm clothes he's wearing right now.

"I'm sure I locked the door, Pa." I can't see the owner of this voice, but he sounds at least as old as my son, maybe older.

Our vision from here is extremely limited. And so far, this doesn't look like a friendly situation. If they realize we're here, we'll be helpless targets.

"Well, that doesn't explain the open door, now does it?" The older man looks all around him. "Seems like all's in order." He shakes his head. "We'd have an awful time coming up with how Johansen's cows got all the way over to our field if they got out. I'm already feeling perty itchy about them being in the barn."

"Kyle said he'd be able to bring in the trailer tonight if it cleared up. He doesn't want to chance sliding off the road and having to explain the herd to a state trooper."

"The boy's a coward. We should have done this ourselves. The sooner these cows are in Wyoming, the better for all of us. Well, maybe not Johansen." He lifts his chin and bellows with laughter, spittle dripping from the corner of his mouth.

The boy walks into view, a stack of metal pails held in his mitten-covered hands. "Pa, are you really sure this is the right thing to do?" Metal screeches as he pulls apart the buckets.

"You're not turning coward on me too, are you, son? Johansen has this coming. Those prize animals of his and the money we're getting for them won't begin to make up for my trouble last summer. The old man thinks he owns all the water in this valley. Well, he'll think twice about cutting off our stream next year."

The sound of milk hitting the bucket's bottom makes my stomach growl and my bladder spasm. I bite my bottom lip. Vicky was right to question the character of the barn owners. I'm so grateful I didn't drag Vicky and Ireland up to the farmhouse's front door. Right now we'd probably be buried at the bottom of a well instead of cozy in our hay bale castle.

Vicky flinches then draws in a deep breath. My gaze snaps toward her. She's pinching her nose, trying to stop a sneeze. I look back at the man who will surely kill us if that noise gets out.

Lord, please. All I can do is beg God from my heart to save us.

Another flinch from Vicky then she lowers her hand, breathing deeply.

I tap my palm against my chest indicating my relief.

"Milk's less on this one," the boy says. "Suppose we should be feeding them more?"

"That's no concern of ours. I'm not fattening up these cows, just keeping them going until they're out of my hair." He smacks his hand on the backside of Bessy, the first cow we milked when we got here. The one that gave me some hope to work with.

My skin crawls. I'd like to punch this scum.

"Move your boney hind end over." He slaps Bessy's caramel-toned skin again.

Crossing his arms, he leans back, evaluating the boy's work. "You're not giving that bovine what she needs. Grab hold and pull harder. We've got our own chores to get to. When you finish this one, throw a bit of feed at them. Forget the others. One bucket's enough for us."

I bite my bottom lip. I imagine all the chores around this place go much the same way as the milking. He bellows orders, and the boy does the work.

Chapter 25

VICKY

Jenna doesn't wait five minutes after the truck rumbles away before she kicks aside the door bale to our cubby. Her face glows so red I think at first she was having some kind of allergic reaction to the hay.

"I can't believe the nerve of that man." Jenna paces back and forth in front of our hay home. "Leaving these animals half-fed and most of them not even milked. We had a cow when I was a child—"

She must notice the she's-lost-her-mind-again look on my face.

"What? We did. That's not weird. My mother milked her faithfully in the morning and again at night. Every morning and every night. She said that Mavis took care of us, and it was our duty to take care of her." Jenna walks right up to the head of a huge bovine and hugs it around the neck. When she looks back at me, her eyes are filled with tears. "We have to get these cows back to their owner before something awful happens to them."

We've left Ireland in the hay, and I'm glad of that right now. The last thing I need is her bleeding-heart environmental argument to join with Jenna's off-the-wall thinking. "Listen, I know you're a mom, and you just want to love on every creature in the world. Trust me, I think that's very commendable. I'd like to learn how you give your heart so easily, but this isn't our battle. We have a friend who's in serious need of a doctor."

A tear drips over her cheek. "I know. You're both a mess."

I raise my eyebrows, giving her a mock-offended glare.

Jenna's mouth turns up in a smile. "You're right, but we can't just leave them here like this." She runs her hand down the cow's boney back. "Help me milk them."

"If we do that, they'll know we were here."

"Not if we're gone before they return."

My pulse beats loud in my ears. It's not like we could stay here forever, but I thought we'd have more time to get healthy. "Ireland isn't ready to move. Her foot is a mess."

Jenna nods. "But that foot isn't going to get better without a doctor's help." She opens one of the feed bags. "You know I'm right."

I draw my fingers over my skin. Most of the itching has faded, but what was once soft and supple, is now bumpy and hard. "Daniel will never be able to find me attractive again, you know. When I left, I didn't expect to come home without my looks. I thought he'd be worried. He'd remember he loved me. And then there I'd be, and his heart would come back to me."

"Sounds like the Disney version of life." Jenna pats the hollow along the side of a cow, then she sets a bucket under it. "It's not your face Daniel loved. It was your heart. He just needs to see that the same heart is still in there." Milk sprays into the pail. "It is going to take time, but I have never known you to be the kind of woman to give up easily, or at all."

I pull my shoulders back, straightening my spine, but the confidence that should come with the posture fails to appear. "I'm scared."

"I know you are." She stands, bringing me the bucket. "Here, take a good long drink, then help me finish the milking. We need a plan."

Dipping my fingers into the milk, I slide a layer of cream off the top then rub it into my face.

Jenna wrinkles her nose.

"Skin cream." I hold back a laugh. "A girl's got to do what a girl's got to do, right?"

"Always the princess." She nudges me with her elbow and sets another bucket at my feet.

After drinking down all my stomach will handle, I take the remaining milk to Ireland while Jenna is busy. "Here. Do you want this?"

Ireland takes it without hesitation and drinks until it's almost gone. "Don't tell Jenna." She winks.

And I understand. I wipe my fingers across my lips.

Ireland gets my hint and cleans the foam from her face. She's still beautiful even with chapped lips and wind-burned cheeks.

"What's taking you so long?" Jenna calls.

"Just checking on Ireland." I approach the cow. Behind her is a large pile of steaming excrement. The scent curdles the fresh milk in my stomach.

"Just reach down and gently grip the bottom of the udder." She holds a hand out, squeezing her fingers one by one into her palm.

The action looks simple enough, but the actual touching of the cow in a place like that, ugh. This is not the kind of homemaking I would have taught on my show. The cow's skin is warm to the touch. To my surprise, she doesn't kill me for being down there. My first few attempts bring nothing, but then I remember how Ireland marched through the cold without one of her boots and how Jenna hollered at that crazy man. And how we buried a woman on the mountain, and kept going without a guide. I will not be undone by a milk cow.

Taking a firm hold, I squeeze just how Jenna showed me. The milk sprays out. I've done it. I've beat this obstacle. That's how we're going to get home. One step at a time.

IRELAND

I sit at the edge of the opening. No one thinks it's wise for me to go far, seeing as how I don't move fast, but the longing for fresh air screams from my core.

"Let's make our plan." Vicky taps one finger on her other wrist like someone checking a watch. "The morning is half over, and we can't just sit here waiting for those guys to get back with the trailer."

A shiver passes over me. "These kind of men would kill us to preserve their secret. I've met groups like this while protesting. They're the kind who come back in the middle of the night. We've got to get out of here. At least you two do."

Jenna shakes her head so hard she looks like she's trying to dislodge a crab from her ear. "We don't go anywhere without you. We're a family. Family sticks together."

"Not my family," I say.

"Ireland, enough. You're part of my family, like it or not. And I don't care what kind of stunt you pull, you're not getting away from me again." Jenna crosses her arms in front of her chest. "Now, what is our plan?"

"I've been thinking." Vicky paces in her five-foot section of barn. "Those men aren't interested in these cows for any reason besides making a buck. Their plan is to haul them out in the middle of the night, right?"

Jenna nods. "That's how I understand it."

"Well, then. If they're busy here, loading the cows, who's at the farmhouse?"

"Could be a wife or someone," I say.

Vicky's forehead wrinkles. "Yes, there could be others. I hadn't thought of that. But there might not be. There must be a phone up there. And if there's a woman, she's likely going to have some compassion for our situation."

The smile that spreads across my face is tight under my chapped skin.

Jenna reaches for my hand. "I hear what you're saying, but how do you expect to make it to the house without being seen? How do we get past the men?" She pulls my fingers straight and the piece of wood in my palm feels like it's cutting deeper.

I breathe in, stretching my diaphragm, blowing out the used air through circled lips as I count to five.

Jenna pinches the exposed end and wiggles it, moving the sliver partway out.

My stomach wobbles, threatening to expose my vegan failure.

Vicky keeps pacing, avoiding any eye contact with my medical situation.

"We hide around the back of the barn after dark. When they go inside, we go to the house. How long will it take to load the cows?"

Jenna squints at my palm. "I'm not sure. Probably at least twenty minutes." She gets a better grip then pulls hard, the sliver of wood coming free followed by a flow of bright red blood.

I clamp my palms together, trying to embrace the pain as a sign that I'm alive, but the room begins to spin as adrenaline courses through my pounding veins. Three cleansing breaths and I regain partial control. I'm finding my center. I'm leveling out. "Thank you." I can't take my gaze away from my clasped hands.

"It's a risky plan." Jenna pats my arm. "But I don't have another."

"Then this is the plan we work with," I say. "We have to make this place look like we haven't been here. We'll need the time. No more milk. Those cows need to look like they're more than ready for a milking."

"Easy for you to say." Vicky tosses me a conspiratorial wink.

Jenna scoops up grain from our pile, and fills her pocket. "We'll need to have a look at the road to the house. Is there anywhere we can hide if we need to?"

Vicky moves to the door. She pushes it open an inch, her eye pressed to the crack. "I can't see much from here, but we have a problem no one has mentioned."

Jenna steps toward her. "What?" There's terror in her voice.

"We're locked in."

JENNA

There're only two options and breaking the door open isn't a good one. That leaves us with door number two, a window at the top of the hay pile. I let my gaze settle on our only escape route.

"I don't like what I'm seeing." Vicky drops onto a hay bale.

"It's not so bad." I pull straw from my hair. "In fact, it's a better option. Less chance of being spotted." I climb the layers of bales until I reach the opening. It's wide enough to easily pass through, and there's a rope and pulley for hoisting hay up. "We can do this. No problem."

With the plan in place, we wait for the sun to sink and the darkness to give us cover.

The time passes with too little to do. I've started rubbing cream onto Ireland's foot. It did wonders for Vicky's rash, so I figure it won't do any harm.

The skin is still red, but I thank God that there doesn't appear to be any black spots. I remember my first-aid class well enough to know that's when it's really bad. A few blisters have formed, but she has more than her fair share of those on the good foot too.

Ireland flinches as I rub over a raw patch. "Jenna, when did you know you loved your children?"

The question is so far from what I'm expecting that I suck in a quick breath.

"I'm sorry. Maybe that wasn't a sensitive question."

"No. You just caught me off guard." I sit back against a bale with Ireland at my side. "I think I loved them from the moment we decided to have children. Or that could have been just the idea of them."

"What made you want them so much?"

I notice Vicky's ear tipped to catch our conversation, but she keeps her gaze away. "I think it was my mom. I missed her so much, and I wanted to get her back. I wanted to feel the mother-child kind of love again. You know, as I'm saying it, I understand it so much better than I ever did before. It's part of my holding on so tight. I'm afraid I'll be alone again." I'm slightly sickened at this. I've used my kids for my own comfort. Sure, I love them for themselves, but too much of my love has been about the hole they fill for me.

I shake my head. "I've held on way too tight. It's a mother's job to love her children and protect them. Teach them. But it's also a mother's responsibility to set them free and rejoice in the independent people they've become."

"You wanted children because you wanted to be like your mother." Ireland inspects her injured hand. "I walked away from River because I was afraid I would be like my mother. It's ironic really." Ireland wraps her index finger around one frizzy gray curl. "I wish we would have stayed in touch. Maybe you could have helped me be a mom."

"I would love to do that still. River is young. You have time to build a relationship."

Ireland smiles, but it's sad, broken.

"I think I get what you're both saying." Vicky's eyes remain glued to the wall. "I started off wanting to be different. I wasn't going to cut my kids out. But then it became easier to hold them at a distance. Love and relationship is messy. It's dangerous. There's no better way to get your heart broken. I wish I'd taken the risk."

I link my fingers with Ireland's. "It's not too late for any of us. We're not dead."

One of Vicky's cheeks rises in a crooked smile. "No, not yet."

"Listen to us." I stand. "Can you imagine how hard it was for Hope to know she'd be leaving Em motherless? We haven't talked about our responsibility to Em. We need to get ourselves home and love that girl. Someday, she's going to get married. We need to be there. She'll have children, and they're going to need three great-aunties. That's us." My pulse is firing, and I'm ready to take on that horrid rancher with my bare hands. This fight is nowhere near done.

Chapter 26

JENNA

The one thing I've missed by watching life play out on television is the actual feelings that come along with the action. We've crouched on the very top layer of hay, the window cracked so we can see movement at the house up the road. A long stock trailer pulled in about twenty minutes ago, right after the sun set. My legs burn with the effort to stay still, while at the same time, the cold that pushes through the shutters freezes me to the bones.

"Ireland, how's the foot?" Vicky asks.

"It's good."

She's lying. There's no real point in asking Ireland how she's doing. She'll always say what she thinks we want to hear.

In the distance, metal clanks and an engine growls. As if they've received their cue, the cows begin to moo. Their voices rise into a chaotic mix of hunger and panic. I didn't anticipate this. Now we're without the benefit of hearing what's going on outside. I press my eye against the slight opening. There's still no one in sight, and the sky is as dark as it's going to be with a nearly full moon. "We should go now." I turn back to Vicky and Ireland.

Fear is evident in Vicky's wide eyes. "What if they see us?"

"The last guy is in the house now. If we wait until they start driving this way, we don't stand a chance. It's now or be caught."

Ireland nods her head. She lifts the rope with our pack already tied onto the end. The other side is fastened to a beam above us.

I take another look, searching the area by the house and following the road all the way to our barn. I can't see anyone, but I could be wrong.

Opening the shutters, I motion Vicky forward. She has to go first for our plan to work out well. Once she's down, I'll help Ireland get out the window and then Vicky will help her land without soaking her foot in the mud.

Vicky lets the rope fall to the ground then swings both legs out the window. She lays with her stomach on the edge, her hands tight around the rope and a glare piercing me. "If I get shot on the way down . . ."

"What, Vicky?" Ireland says. "What will you do to us if you get shot?"

Vicky's expression softens. "I don't know."

"Chances are we'll be right behind you." I squeeze her hand. "You've got this. Now." My skin is damp with perspiration and my heart races like I've run all the way home. This is the beginning of the end.

Vicky wraps her arm around the rope and lowers herself the ten feet to the ground. A groan travels back up to the window when her feet hit the mud. She unties the pack and flicks her wrist, sending a wave up to us as a signal.

"All right, Ireland. Try not to put your foot in the mud when you get to the bottom."

"No problem. I can balance for ten minutes if I have to." She grins. "Yoga." The bright t-shirt we used to wrap her foot seems like a mistake now that it's waving outside the barn window like a come-get-us flag. She's down in a matter of seconds, and it's my turn.

I'm not a climber. I don't even like glass elevators. My house is a one-story, and that's how I like it. Just looking out this window gives me a quaking stomach and wobbly legs. Below, Ireland and Vicky are waving frantically. A light moves in the distance, cutting the darkness at the farmhouse as the door opens. It's now or never, cliché or not.

I wiggle my legs out, grip the rope, and push myself over the edge, but I'm too much weight for my arms to manage the lowering. In panic, I cling to the siding, my muscles burning and shaking, my bones crying to break. Then I lose my grip, and I'm down. The air is forced from my lungs with the impact. Mud splashes up around me, plopping onto my face, my arms, my chest.

"Get off me." Vicky cries in a desperate blend of yell and whisper. "You're breaking my leg."

I roll to the side, my arm squishing into the mud. "Sorry."

She mumbles something I don't think was meant to be forgiveness.

Ireland grabs my hand and pulls me up then does the same for Vicky. The bandaged foot is sunk so far into the muck, it isn't visible. So much for hygiene.

I tug them toward the side of the barn. "Let's get around the corner until they get down here. There's a lot of movement at the house." Each step we take sounds like the gross way Calvin used to swish pudding around in his mouth. I can hear his sisters screaming at him to stop in my memory. I hope I get the chance to be irritated by little things like that again.

We lean against the back of the shed, the moon lighting the field in front of us. The mud is cold, but nothing like the freezing we felt as we made our way to this barn.

Behind us, the clank of metal echoes through the night, joined by the shouts of men. They may be moving the cows under the cover of darkness, but they're not good at stealth. The rumble of a diesel engine is close, only the width of this barn from us now. I nearly trusted these men with our lives. My skin crawls. It could have been me that killed the three of us.

Ireland nudges me with her elbow so hard it stings. "What's that?" She points into the field.

Something is moving this way with a slow strutting gait. As it moves closer, the silhouette becomes clear, the steam rising from his nose, the beefy hump along the top of the neck and shoulders. It's a bull, and we're trespassers in his pasture.

VICKY

I open my mouth to scream, but Ireland saves me by slapping her hand over my face. That monster with the eyes that almost glow in the moonlight is staring straight at us. We must look like dinner. My heart beats so hard is takes the full expanse of my chest and cuts off my ability to breathe. What's the proper reaction to this situation? Do we play dead, or run for our lives?

He moves closer. Stops. Digs his front foot into the ground.

My decision comes easy. We run.

I grab Ireland by the hand and pull. The mud holds tight to my feet, slowing my movement and endangering my life more than the outlaw ranchers with their shoot-now-ask-questions-later attitudes.

Around the corner, I find the fence securely attached to the wall of the shed. I grab the round wooden fencepost, put my toe in the web of metal and throw my other leg over the top. Pain zaps through my body, tossing me to the ground along with a section of metal fencing that comes down with me. My head buzzes and my stomach is a tight ball.

Through the bent section, Ireland and Jenna climb out. They kneel at my side. "Are you okay?" Jenna asks.

"What just happened?" Inside the shed voices are yelling and cows moo over the chaos.

Ireland looks around, her head moving like a nervous owl's. "You knocked out the electric fence with your body."

"That sounds about right for how I'm feeling." I rub my fingers into my temples.

Ireland yanks me up, but I'm not ready. She and Jenna hold me under the arms. "That surge made the lights go out in the barn. They'll be here in a minute to see what happened. We have to move."

About ten yards farther away from our destination of the farmhouse is an old pickup that looks like the owner parked it there in 1860. We crouch behind the rust-mobile waiting for the men to come out. One finally does. He opens a compartment on the side of the shed wall, pulls a switch and lights snap on again.

As soon as he's back in the shed, Jenna tugs my arm. "We've lost a lot of time. If we don't get to the house quickly, we won't have time to make our 911 call before they come back."

I know we need to cover the open area fast, but my legs won't respond to my commands. Each step is clumsy and off center. Ireland is making better progress than I am, and she's hopping on one foot. We stay to the edge of the road, in the shadows.

At the side of the overgrown yard, we leave the road and scoot our way around the back.

Shouts ring up from the shed. Then the sounds of metal bending and men cussing burn the air.

I peek around a tree. The boy we saw this morning is on top of the truck, the bull gouging the door with his horns. "Do you see that? I let out the bull. What if he kills one of them?"

Jenna squeezes my shoulder. "They're ranchers. I'm sure they can manage. That just gives us more time to get in the house. Let's go."

She's right. Maybe this is God's provision. It never looks how I imagine.

Barking startles me as we close in on the house. A dog that looks like a mix of hyena and lion stares at us, drool dripping from his sagging lips. He lunges, but the chain that ties him to the porch yanks him back. "We're not getting in that way."

"I've never been to a house that didn't have a back door." Ireland hobbles on.

We skirt the yard. In the back it's dark, the trees cutting out much of the moonlight. Three cement steps lead to a back door with a dilapidated screen. I feel like I should knock, maybe call on the graces of the wife.

Ireland pulls the gun from the pack. "If we meet someone, there's no harm in them thinking we have bullets."

I grab tufts of my filthy hair. "No harm unless they decide to shoot us before we can shoot them."

Ireland tucks the gun close to her side as she pulls open the door. It whines as if purposely calling attention to our presence.

I catch Jenna's eye. Her mouth hangs open, her ear tipped toward the house.

Ireland eases open the back door. Country music drifts out from a radio, but I don't hear the sound of anyone singing along. We each step into a mudroom where dirt crusted work clothes form piles alongside a rusty washing machine. I reach my hand out and stop Ireland from going any farther. "We'll track mud," I say.

"So?" Ireland shrugs me away. "What do we care?"

"It's like leaving a trail. If we find a phone and make the call, we'll still have to hide until help gets here."

"She's right." Jenna starts to strip off her pants and boots. She pulls a garbage bag from the shelf and deposits her clothing into it. "Here. Everything in here until we leave. We can hide it outside."

The bruise that runs from Jenna's hip to the outside of her knees makes me cringe. I pull off my mud-covered clothes and put them in the bag, leaving me bare-legged with only a pair of ripped running shorts to make me decent.

Lord, if you're after my pride, I think you've got it.

When the bag is filled, I take it and our pack outside, push them into the dirt along the cement steps, and cover the top with leaves. Within the next hour we should be safely traveling down the road with all our things in a patrol car. We'll be heading home.

Chapter 27

IRELAND

This place is all about beef. The cows they stole from a neighbor, the bull in the field behind the shed, and I'm sure there's a whole lot more cows on this ranch that we haven't met yet. And then there's the smell of stew that permeates the walls of the house. They must cook up the stuff by the gallon. We creep through the living room. A television plays in the corner, the sound down, the picture fuzzy like I remember it being when I lived in a foster home that had a rabbit-ear antenna. Two recliners, worn at the arms, face the screen. I don't see any computers or tablets lying around. These guys are old-school.

The twang of Johnny Cash filters through from the kitchen where we find the stew. I touch the cast-iron pot. It's still warm, but the burner's been turned off. Dishes are piled in the sink, not even rinsed. Beer cans line the chipped orange counter. Brown and yellow linoleum peels at the edges, dirt collecting near the vents. There doesn't seem to be anyone left in the house. And honestly, I can't imagine a woman who could tolerate this kind of life.

"I think the coast is clear."

"No kidding." Vicky holds her nose and drops a half-eaten shriveled hot dog into the trash.

I reach my hand out in front of her. "No cleaning."

Her face reddens. "Any sign of a phone?"

"There's none in the hall," Jenna says as she joins us. "I found an old jack, but no phone."

I move things around the counter and find the same. "Looks like our low-tech guys are cell phone only. Could be a phone upstairs."

We start to move toward the hall when a man shouts outside. "Only take me a minute to get the rifle."

A voice scratches something back on a radio.

Adrenaline buzzes through my body as I watch the doorknob turn.

"Hush, Killer. We've got bigger problems than your need for a bone."

Jenna grabs my arm and pulls me around the corner. There's a door behind us, but I hear the man enter. It's too risky to make a move now.

I hold the gun in front of me.

The smell of him—sweat, smoke, and alcohol—weaves through the house. An interior door clicks open, then the sound of a gun cocking, and another, and another.

My heart beats so loudly it's only the nonstop barking of the dog that keeps me from being heard.

A voice scratches over the radio. "Three of those cotton-pickin' cows are coming up your way. Shoot 'em before they get past the house."

Jenna draws in a quick breath, and I feel the man hesitate.

"Did you hear me? Hurry!"

"Got it." He slams the door on his way out.

All three of us slide down the wall, holding each other in a huddle on the floor.

The door opens again, banging against the wall. "You get on in there before you cause us more trouble." The wall behind us shakes as the man goes out.

The click, click, click of toenails pattering along the floor is followed by a low grisly growl.

VICKY

"Maybe he won't come this way." My arms clasp around Ireland's leg.

"I wouldn't count on that." Jenna claws her way back up the wall. "He's a dog. He'll smell us even over the stew."

I'm shaking, my whole body giving in to one of my greatest fears. When

I was only five, a dog got free from his owner at the park where my brother practiced soccer. The nanny had let me play on the swings, out of her reach but within her sight. I was wearing my pink tutu, having just been picked up from ballet, and I felt like a princess gliding through the breeze. But the dog thought I looked like prey. He ran by, jumping into air and pulling me off the swing by my leg. The pain cut through me, his eyes, they burned with hate.

It must have been only seconds before the dog was pulled off, but the memory has remained clear for over forty years. That was the day my favorite nanny was fired, leaving no one to hold me when I woke with nightmares. My mother did come in after she heard my screams, but only to tell me to quiet down and not to worry. She was going to get that man for all he was worth, her attorney had guaranteed it. I didn't understand what she meant, but I knew it didn't sooth my fears.

What would I have done if that had happened to one of my children? Jenna would have slept the night beside her little girl, always there when the child woke up scared. I wonder if Brooklyn will let me brush her hair when I get home. I wonder if she still has room for me.

There's a crash in the kitchen and the beefy smell gets stronger.

"Here's our chance." In one quick motion, Ireland is up, swinging the door to who knows where open.

We rush through, Jenna tripping on the unexpected stairs and tumbling down into the darkness. Something crashes followed by her moan.

"Jenna?" I feel around the wall for a light switch but Ireland grabs my hand.

"No lights. They'll see them through the windows."

A tiny glow of moonlight filters in along narrow windows near the ceiling. As my eyes adjust, I'm able to see shadows but not much else.

"I'm okay." Glass scratches along cement. "I don't think I'm cut, but you'll need to be very careful coming down here."

Behind me the dog's nose sucks in air from the crack under the door. This basement isn't inviting but it is better than the alternative. I make my way down wood-plank stairs until my foot falls on the landing where Jenna is righting herself.

Behind her I can just make out a shelf of canned goods. Real food. Running my fingers over a jar, it comes away with a mound of dust. These could have set on this shelf since the pioneers came over the trail. Holding one up to the moonlight, I see the murky invitation to botulism. Not my favorite dinner guest even in this circumstance.

From the landing, stairs go down to the left and the right. I choose the right.

"Well, this is just great." Ireland's breath is too close to me, and she's in dire need of a mint. "We just keep trading one problem for another."

"Don't you think we know that?" I wave my finger in her face. I hope she can see it. "Why don't you get on the horn with the universe and see what's up?"

"Whoa." Jenna puts her hand on my arm, but I shake it away. "Come on. We can't turn on each other."

"Whatever." Ireland unfolds the top of a cardboard box on the shelf.

"What do you think you're doing?" I say.

"Looking for anything that will help us get out of here."

Jenna joins her. She holds an apron up in the moonlight. "There was a woman here at one time. I wonder what they did with her." She makes a creepy sound.

My stomach shrinks. "That's not funny."

"Vicky, nothing is funny in your tight life. Loosen up." Ireland holds up a child's book. "Nope. Nothing here."

I need some space from these two. That night in the hay fort was about the last straw for my patience. I feel my way along the wall until I come to hooks piled high with coats. Below these are an assortment of boots. "Ireland, I think I found something you need."

I pick up a rubber boot and something scurries away toward the corner.

"What was that?" Jenna wraps around my arm as tight as a boa, and I stand as much chance getting her free. Although I'm just as happy to have her here. Whatever that was probably doesn't live alone.

"Enough of this." Jenna stomps. "I want to go home. Now."

"Okay." Ireland's voice is cracked but steady. "But how do we do that?"

"We know where the road is now. We just have to get to it." Jenna's voice breaks and she starts to sob into my shoulder. "I can't do this anymore."

I push her away. "Yes, you can. You've led us through some really desperate times out here. Pull yourself together. It's time to get home." I yank a thick coat off the wall and lay it over Jenna's shoulders. The scent is worse than dust or even cow manure, but it will keep her extra warm. "Ireland, let's find you some boots that will work. Do you think you can walk with the condition your foot is in?"

"It's doing remarkably well. Mind over matter."

"Then we got this." I point toward the wall by the furnace. "See that? It's a wood chute. We'll climb out that way as soon as we know it's safe."

JENNA

Curled up with Vicky and Ireland in a dark corner, I've tried to sleep while the scrapings of rodents makes me sweat. I thought I wanted to get home before, but this is a whole new level of need. Every time I start to drift off, I imagine one of them climbing on me, chewing. I shiver even in the heat of my borrowed coat.

The days are getting shorter, but I imagine the guys upstairs are not the type to sleep away the morning. They didn't bang into the house until what had to be well past midnight. Maybe that will buy us a few extra minutes. I nudge Vicky.

She moans and wipes a string of drool from her face. "What time is it?"

"How should I know? It has to be close to dawn. I think we need to get out of here."

Ireland stands with a cringe and a low yelp. She reaches high, taking long slow breaths, then folds over, laying her palms flat on the cement floor.

I can't even brush my toes with the tips of my fingers. Looks like age can't take the blame for that one.

There's more light coming through the window than is comforting. My heart starts to pound. I think this is the day we get home. And who will I be now? I want to go back, but not to the person I left behind.

Vicky unlatches the wood chute and pushes the small doors to the sides of the house. Cool air rushes in. "We'll need something to step up on."

Ireland situates an ancient wooden ladder against the wall. "That should do it. Time to go." She looks around in an almost sentimental way.

Vicky is up the ladder and outside in under a minute. She squats near the opening, her gaze going one way, then the other. "Looks good," she whispers.

Ireland braces the bottom of the ladder. "Your turn."

On an impulse, I hug her, then start my short climb. The rungs bow under my weight. I'd hate to survive all this time to die in a freak ladder accident. The opening is wide but short. I slide my head out and see the sun rising over the trees. Fresh earth sinks under my hands, the scent reviving me after a night in a musty basement. One step higher on the ladder, I try to squeeze through, but my stomach wedges tight. Even after this crazy wilderness diet plan, I don't fit through small holes.

"Hurry," Vicky whispers.

"I'm stuck."

"What?"

"Stuck. You know, it means I can't get through."

She grabs my hands and pulls, but that only forces all my weight down on my middle and the edge of the opening cuts into my flesh. This is going to leave a mark.

Vicky presses her face to my side. "Ireland, you're going to have to push."

I've become Winnie-the-Pooh. And I didn't even get a lick of honey. Ireland presses on my backside, while I wiggle side to side, my flesh scraping against rough wood.

"I hear them," Ireland says.

I wiggle faster and Ireland pushes harder. Finally, I make it past the tight spot and roll onto the wet ground.

Ireland pops through like one of those circus dogs through a hoop. She closes the doors and Vicky rolls a rock in front to hold it down. "We've got to move quickly. They'll be in the basement to put wood in the furnace any second."

My arms go numb. They'd be within their rights to shoot us. We're intruders. I get upright, and we rush to the trees at the side of the yard. From here we make our way to the edge of the driveway and follow it without speaking, Ireland between us, leaning on our shoulders for support.

It must be over a mile before we get to a mailbox and intersecting road. A road. It's an actual road. I haven't seen one of these in so long. I drop to my knees. "Thank you, Lord, for this road."

Ireland pats me on the back, her face is bright with a grin, but her eyes are tight, like they're holding back unspeakable pain. "Come on. Let's get you back to your family." She pulls me up and starts down the road, limping but not complaining.

"Wait." Vicky twists around. "How do we know this is the right way?"

Ireland shrugs her shoulders. "We don't. We just have to trust our instincts."

"So we're throwing out logic?" Vicky kicks a rock.

"No, Vicky. We're not going to trust logic, or instinct. We're going to trust that God will take care of us just like he has through every other struggle."

She doesn't answer, but she does follow.

"What do you miss most about home?" I ask.

"Moisturizer," Vicky says. "No, really I miss my kids. It's not unusual for them to be gone for weeks at a time to camps and things, or for me to travel. But I've never missed them like I do this time. I hope it's not too late for us."

"What about you, Ireland. What do you miss?"

There's a long silence. "I don't know. I miss eating when I'm hungry. And I miss a safe warm bed. But other than that, my life doesn't have much in it to miss. When I get home, I still have the situation with my job to deal with. My word against that kid's. But I think I'll fight it out, and then I'll leave on my own terms. That's what I'm looking forward to. I want to go back to Carrington."

"Will you look up Skye?" Vicky asks.

"Maybe. It's been a long time. I don't want to cause more damage."

I think of the way my father never really came back into my life. That scar still marks me. "I think your son needs to know you're willing to try. If nothing else, you wanted him."

Ireland looks to the side, her hand wiping across her face. "Maybe."

An engine growls from somewhere ahead of us.

Vicky clasps my hand.

As the pickup rounds the corner, Vicky and I wave our hands over our heads. But it drives past.

Chapter 28

IRELAND

The truck skids to a stop, backs up, and drives toward us. I can hardly breath as the possibilities wash over me.

A man wearing flannel and a baseball cap hops from the driver's side. "You folks seen any cows wandering this way?" As he comes closer, he pulls the cap from his head and scratches his scalp. "My goodness, you all look like you've had a rough time. You ain't the missing ladies are you?"

Jenna wraps her arms around my waist squeezing me tight. My tongue, drier than my most dehydrated moments, can't form words.

"We are." Vicky covers her heart with both hands, her eyes shining.

"Well, there. Let's get you into town. There's quite a crew out looking for you." He guides us back to the truck where he opens the passenger door. He whistles and an Australian shepherd bounds down from the seat. "You get on in. I'll take you right to Dr. Martin. The sheriff will find you there." The tailgate whines open, and the dog jumps into the back.

Vicky wraps her hand around mine. "We're not leaving you," she says.

My face warms. The instinct to pull my hand away is strong, but I'm going to fight this time. I'm going to hold on to the people I love even if it ends with me getting hurt. Because it hurts when I walk away too. And the pain doesn't go away. In my life, it's about the only company I've maintained. I lay my other hand over our clasped ones and rest my head on Vicky's shoulder. It's boney but comfortable all the same.

The man climbs back in the cab. He starts down the road in the direction he came from. "There's a lot of people who'll be glad to see you."

I wonder, will there be anyone to welcome me back to civilization? Not likely. My colleagues find me cold, because I am. My neighbors think I'm weird. I know this is true because I keep my bedroom window cracked open year round. I've heard them talking. And maybe that's how I've presented myself on purpose. The oddity seems to keep people away.

I've lived most of my life like I've been waiting for it all to end. If the mountain didn't kill me, I may just be here for a while yet. Maybe it's time to make a home for myself.

The truck pulls into a circular driveway of what looks like a large house. In the front is a sign, Pioneer Mountain Hospital.

"Sit tight. I'll go in and get Jacob." The man leaves the truck running and heads inside the extra-wide French doors.

A moment later, a man and woman rush from the door, each with a wheelchair. The man who picked us up follows behind with another wheelchair.

Both truck doors open. "Aren't we glad to see you. Johansen says you're the missing group. News came through this morning about your guide." He runs us through a battery of questions about our injuries as we get seated in the chairs and pushed into the hospital. Jenna and Vicky are taken into one room, and I'm delivered into another. Alone.

The nurse takes my information after helping me into a bed. Her hands never stop moving.

There's an empty bed on the other side of the room. She pulls a gown from a dresser by the door. "I'm going to help you get out of these dirty clothes, then we'll have you wear the gown. Dr. Martin will want to give you a full exam before we get you cleaned up. Is there anywhere I should be particularly careful?"

My foot has throbbed in rhythm with my heart since we woke up this morning. Now that our journey has come to an end, the pain seems unbearable. I blow a breath out and tap my fingers on the oversize rubber boot.

"All right, then." She tries to gently remove the boot, but my foot has swollen inside. "I think we'll go ahead and cut this off if that's okay with you."

"No problem. They're not even mine." I probably shouldn't be confessing to burglary right now. One thing at a time.

With blunt ended scissors, she works the rubber until there's an opening along the outside of my leg.

I wince as she removes what's left of the boot. Blood stains the t-shirt wrapped around my foot. I lay my head back. I don't want to see what happens next.

Apparently it's as bad as I imagined. "I think we'll have Dr. Martin take a look at this right away. He may be able to give you something for the pain before we go any further."

I nod. That's exactly what I need. Something for the pain.

JENNA

"I'm a few hours out, but I'm on my way." Mark's voice trembles in my ear.

I hold the telephone closer.

"I'm so grateful you're alive. I love you, Jenna."

Tear rush over my cheeks. I'm losing fluid as fast as the IV in my arm pumps it in. "I love you too. I'm really sorry."

"None of that." The connection gets scratchy. "We're headed through the pass, I'm going to have to say goodbye before I lose—"

"Mark? Mark?" It's like waking from a beautiful dream and finding yourself alone in the hospital. I hold the phone to my chest, against my heart.

"What happened?" Vicky's face is slathered in some kind of pink ointment that makes her look like she's doing facials at a slumber party.

"We lost the connection. He's on the way."

She smiles, but her eyes are sad.

"Any word from Daniel?"

"No. Not yet. He didn't answer my calls. Neither did the kids."

Guilt takes over. I don't have any words to encourage her. Nothing to give her hope that her husband, who I know she still loves, will walk through those doors and all will be right again. Because that may not be Vicky's happily ever after.

I look up as a man in uniform knocks on the door frame. He pulls a notebook from his breast pocket. "I'm Sheriff Collins. I'm going to need a few questions answered. The doctor said you'd be up to that."

My jaw drops. We may not have seen the end of our troubles.

VICKY

I just want to sleep. The sheriff asked a hundred questions. Then he asked the same questions in other ways. Did they really think we had some kind of nefarious motives? Did they think we wanted to die? When Jenna explained about the cows, the look on the man's face went from bored to irritated.

I turn toward the wall, pull the blankets over my shoulders and close my eyes. After the sheriff left, Jenna brushed her hair and teeth. She showered for twenty minutes. All she can talk about is Mark getting here. And my biggest dread is Mark getting here.

Maybe I can pretend to sleep through his visit. Maybe I can manage to never see him, and to never remember how he used to be my boyfriend. And how I rejected him. And how he's happily married to a woman I love as a sister.

It's not that Mark is so special, at least not to me. It's the happily married to someone who loves you thing. I want to figure a way to take back the last ten years of super-independence and revive what Daniel and I had. But I don't know if he even wants to work on our marriage, and I don't know if I can ever forgive him.

Heavy footsteps enter the room. I pull the blanket higher, over my ears. I just can't watch their reunion.

A hand warms my shoulder. The gentle feel of a finger pulls back the hair at my temple. I know this touch, but I can't open my eyes. Tears squeeze through my closed lids and a whimper creeps up my throat. I grip his hand, holding it tight, praying that Daniel and Cori were some kind of horrible nightmare my imagination created.

He gently rolls me onto my back, but I keep my head turned away, until his rough fingers press against my crusty cheek, forcing me toward him. "Vicky, look at me, please."

My lower lip quivers. This moment is worse than any I faced on the mountain. Deep within me I know he is a part of me, and I am a part of him. I'll never be whole without him. But I can't live with his heart divided between me and her. "I can't."

As much as I long to fall into his arms, I can't make the journey.

"No more avoiding. We've got things we need to talk about. The kids will be here soon."

It's a punch to the gut. A final kind of statement. And I can't go there. I'll never be ready for what I know he's about to say.

"Vicky, we need to talk about Cori."

I cover my face with my hand. "I can't."

"I'm sorry. We have to. Jenna went to sit with Ireland. We have the room to ourselves."

"I don't want to be alone." My eyes snap open. "I don't want to hear what you have to say. I don't want any of this."

"I fired her."

I blink. Did the doctor drug me? That wasn't what I expected to hear.

"She was coming on to me." He throws up a hand. "No, that's not fair. I gave her every indication I was interested." He sits on the edge of the bed facing away from me, his elbows on his thighs, his hands clutching his gray-brown hair. "I really messed up here. Things between us are not good. I know you think everything is under control, but I feel like an actor in a movie you're directing. What happened to us? I was so scared when I thought you might not be coming home. How do I get you back?"

For days I've been asking myself this same question. How do I get Daniel back? Now he's asking me? "I guess this is a start. We've got to be honest. I read your email to Cori. That's what motivated me to go on this crazy survival trip. I wanted to manipulate you into loving me again. Sick, isn't it?"

His shoulders jump, and I'm not sure if he's crying or laughing. Clasping his hands, he looks up at the ceiling. "What are we doing to each other? You could have died out there. I could have been the cause. A woman gave me a little attention, and I jumped right in. I can't stand who I've become."

"I can understand that. There was a lot of time to think out there. No distractions. I am not proud of my half of our relationship either."

"It doesn't change anything, I know, but I promise, I never touched her."

I thought those words would bring me joy, but they don't. There's still a betrayal sitting between us. And I can choose to be bitter and walk away, like what happened with me, Jenna, Ireland, and Hope, or I can choose to walk through the muck with Daniel until we find solid ground.

I take his hand. "You're right. It still hurts. And I'm sorry for the ways I've hurt you."

He turns to me, scooping my head into his hand and pulling me into his chest. The beat of his heart drums against my ear as his tears run over my cheek and down my neck.

"Mom?"

I peek over Daniel's shoulder. My children stand in the doorway. "Come here," I say.

Brooklyn sits behind her father, using him as a wall between us. I recognize the move. It's something I would do. I want her to come all the way to me, to hug me, to let me smell the freshness of her hair and hold her close, but that's not the relationship we have.

Cameron walks to the head of my bed. "Glad you're okay, Mom. That's quite a trip. What are you going to say when the press gets here?"

"They can wait. I'm not giving interviews."

"Because of your hair?" Brooklyn sneers.

"No, because I want to spend time with the three of you." But I can't help it, I touch my hair.

Chapter 29

JENNA

They've given Ireland something to help her sleep, but she's still restless, her face grimacing as she cries through some awful dream where I can't help her.

Daniel and the kids are still in our room. I don't want to disturb them. There's a lot of healing that family needs. But I'm so tired my eyes won't stay open. I brush back Ireland's curls, saying a soft prayer. The thought of her going home to an empty house cuts me deep in a way I thought I could only feel for my children.

I've dwelt on the rejections in my life, but they're nothing compared to what my friend has suffered.

Dr. Martin comes into the room. "Shouldn't you be resting?"

"Vicky has visitors, and I wanted to see how Ireland was doing. Is she going to be okay?"

"I'm not allowed to discuss her condition with you. But, she did refer to you and Mrs. Cambridge as her sisters right after we gave her the sedative. No details, but I think she'll be fine. There's a toe we're keeping a close eye on, and we're dealing with infection, but this could have been so much worse." He stuffs his glasses into his front pocket. "You know that already. I heard about your guide. Sounds like you're three brave women."

"Not so much. But we're blessed."

He nods but doesn't make eye contact, then he leaves the room. Machines fill the space with hums and clicks so loud, I can hardly stand it. For the first time in my life, I desire silence. Peace in which to sort through the things that have happened to my body and to my soul.

A tear leaks from Ireland's eye, trailing down her cheek and spilling over her chin. Pulling back the covers, I climb in beside her, weaving my arm around her. Shallow breaths turn deeper. Her chest relaxes. I'll stay here as long as it takes for Ireland to feel the love we have for her. Even if that's forever.

❖ ❖ ❖

I'm startled awake by a man standing at the edge of the bed. He's familiar, yet completely a stranger. Scruff colors his jawline. His forehead is tense, forming a river of lines. His mouth is tight and turned down.

"Can I help you?" I push myself up, tucking the blankets snug around Ireland's arms.

"No. I just wanted to see her." He crosses his arms in front of his chest. "I should go."

As he turns I'm overwhelmed by the feeling that I shouldn't let this stranger leave. "Stop. Please."

He does, his right hand braced on the doorframe, his face turned away from me.

"Do you know Ireland?"

"I used to. But that was a long time ago. A different life."

"I can understand that. Please stay. It would mean so much to her to have a visitor." I stand, wanting to grab his arm to stop him from taking another step.

"She wouldn't want to see me."

Realization thunders down on me. "Skye?" My question is quiet, hesitant, but the shudder spreading across his shoulders tells me I'm right.

"Is she going to be okay?"

"Yes."

His chin dips, then he squeezes the trim around the door. "Thank you." Without another word, he's gone.

I wrap my arms around myself. How will I tell Ireland he was here?

How will I tell her he left? Turning back to my friend, I see how foolish my questions were. She's staring past me to the place in the hall where he walked out of sight.

I take her hand and sit there in the relative silence, letting the moment sink in.

VICKY

My family has gone, and with them went the last of the illusion of our perfect family. I saw the gaps and scars, the wounds and loneliness etched into each of them, into me. I start to make a list in my mind, the most effective actions to fix this problem, but I have nothing.

Facing my own death has left me vulnerable rather than empowered. It's left me with no doubt that I am insufficient. It's a fascinating place to be for a woman who's touted God's all-powerful nature to the masses. And a woman who's never surrendered even her grocery list to him.

The room is too empty with Jenna off somewhere and my family gone. Just me. I used to value time alone. Time for productivity and uninterrupted work. But today the stillness makes the pounding in my head louder. I'm afraid. Purely scared of what comes next. And I don't want to face it alone.

Slipping my feet into disposable slippers, I take hold of my IV stand and start down the hall to Ireland's room, hoping to find Jenna and Ireland together.

Ireland lies still in her bed as if she isn't really there anymore. Is it possible to come this far only to die in a hospital?

"Hey, there." Jenna joins me in the hall. "Ireland just drifted off again. Skye was here. It really shook her up."

I put my hand to my chest. "I'm sure it did. What did he say?"

"That's the thing. He didn't say anything. Just took a look at her and left." Jenna scratches at her temple where the edge of a bandage is peeling free.

There's a squeal, and we both swing around to see its origin. A young woman with long, flowing hair runs down the hall toward us. She halts inches from Jenna, then wraps her arms around my friend. "Mama. Are you okay?"

Jenna gently scoops strands of hair over the girl's ear. "I'm great. Nothing that won't heal in a couple weeks."

Jenna's other daughter arrives. They're all a tangle of arms grasping their mother and her taking stock of each one, a mother hen checking her chicks.

Then there's the last of them. Mark. A man who at our last meeting was my recent ex-boyfriend. He doesn't seem to even notice me, his eyes trained on the pile of people beside me. "All right. Let me in there." His voice is firm but his mouth tips up in a playful grin.

The girls loosen their hold, but don't let go.

"Baby, I'm so glad to see your beautiful face." Mark holds Jenna's jaw with his forefinger and thumb, tipping her head up and staring down into her eyes. "Calvin couldn't get loose, but they got word to him this morning that you'd been found safe." He just looks at her for the longest time, then leans in, fully kissing her on the lips.

"Gross." One of the girls shakes her head, but she has an almost identical smile to her father's, and it plays on her lips in contradiction to her words.

Here's a family that may not have had all the benefits a million-dollar ministry can afford, but they're not lacking in the one thing my family is missing, connection.

Watching them is both fascinating and heartbreaking. Maybe this is one of the reasons I stayed away. I think I've known what I couldn't provide for a very long time, I just didn't want to see it. Without saying anything, I duck into Ireland's room. I can hide here.

JENNA

Nighttime in the hospital is almost as bad as it was in the wilderness. I sent Mark and the girls to the one hotel in town, though he really wanted to stay here with me. The hurt etched in Vicky's face was enough to give me the strength to say no.

There's a television on a cart in our room. It doesn't get many channels, and even those are in and out. And the clock on the wall—it ticks like a time bomb.

I can't sleep, though my body is thoroughly exhausted. I just lay here on this overly soft mattress listening to the ticking until the sound builds tension that will have to blow.

Shaking out my arms, I try some of Ireland's deep breathing techniques. In—two three, four. Out—two, three, four. Great, now I'm breathing to the ticks.

I can't take it anymore. I slip out of bed, careful not to wake Vicky, and head out into the hall. The doctor and the nurses here have been beyond kind, and I'll be released to go home tomorrow. Vicky will likely be released too, but Ireland, she's in worse shape than Vicky and me.

Peeking into her room, I hear the soft sounds of her breathing. And I thank God that she is still alive. The injured foot is wrapped and held up in a sort of hammock. Ireland's chemical-free body is wasted on pain and sleep medications. She's a zombie. What if she wakes up and we're gone?

Tears punctuate my feelings. I wipe them on the front of my gown, and shuffle down the hall.

Having left the environment of survival, my body is now in angry mode. Each tiny step is agonizing. The mixture of bruises and cuts, along with muscles that have been worked far past their ability, all equal pain.

The hallway opens into a foyer that appears to be an old living room. There's a couch on one wall with a coffee table in front of it. I plop down on the rough sofa and finger through the reading material. A stack of books in the corner catches my eye. It's a series about the legends from the Cascade wilderness. I feel like one of those legends right now.

Picking up the set of six thin books, I lean back into the couch's shoulder and start to read the back covers. Number three halts my breath.

Alongside the words, there's a drawing of a rugged sort of caveman, dressed fully in furs. He's a lot like how I'd picture Bigfoot. He's tall and broad, his features chiseled and rough.

The description goes into detail about the man who some believe lives in the wilderness, highly sensitive to anything man-made. I flip to the first page. The legend of the wildman. This is a story I own a piece of. Maybe I'll write what happened to us. Is that actually something I can do?

Insecurity tackles me, then I look at my bare leg, a bandage covering the outside of my right calf. I just made it through over a week in the wild without any experience and without a guide. Yes, of course I can write a story. How hard could that possibly be?

There's action outside the double door. Light, more and more by the minute. I stand and walk to the window, gazing out into the night. There's a flash, then more.

A nurse grabs my arm. "Come on, Mrs. Savage. Let's get you back to your room."

"What was that?"

"It appears the media has arrived. I'm sorry."

I look down at my attire. Great. That's just what I want to have printed in my local newspaper.

IRELAND

The fog in my brain hangs on like it does in the valley, leaving the sky gray and the people wishing for some sign of spring. I hear the doctor talking about me to the nurse. They've just checked on me. I pretended to be asleep. It's easier to avoid their prying questions.

Now they're outside my room. The man says he wonders what happened on the mountain that left me mentally broken. The woman's voice responds. He thinks I'll need therapy.

He has no idea. It wasn't the mountain that broke my spirit. It was the life before the mountain.

Living each day to survive and get Vicky and Jenna home to their families was the closest thing I've felt to actual breathing in years.

❖   ❖   ❖

There's a tap at the door.

I turn my head, slowly because there's a knot the size of an orange in the right side.

Vicky and Jenna are dressed in street clothes. Not their own, that's certain. Vicky is in a pair of off-the-rack jeans and a t-shirt advertising a business that sells farm implements. Jenna wears capris that make her look like her legs were cut short, topped with a red hoodie.

But it's not what they're wearing that concerns me. It's the fact that they're dressed, and I am not.

Jenna eases toward me, her hands clasped and her lips tight. She doesn't have to say a word. They're leaving.

Before the horrible news is out of their mouths, the same nurse who checked us in yesterday floats into the room. "I'm so glad you're awake. We didn't get to finish our paperwork, you were so exhausted yesterday. You only gave me the phone number to contact your employer. I'm sure that was a mistake. We need the number for a family member. Someone who will take care of you while you recover. The doctor wants to make sure they understand the situation with your foot, and he also would like to conference with the physician who will take over your medical care."

Her eyebrows lift, her fingers ready with the pencil to jot down the information I don't have.

The room falls silent aside from the buzzing of the heater under the window sill.

"Her mother lives in Canada." Vicky eases onto the chair in the corner of the room. "I'm sure she'd be willing to come help out for a bit." She looks to me, and I turn away from her gaze.

"No." Jenna's voice rings firm into the sterilized air. "That's not going to happen."

Vicky's chair squeaks as she rises. "Why on earth not? You're a mother, Jenna. Wouldn't you drop everything to come care for your daughter?"

"Of course I would. We're not doing this any longer, are we, Ireland?"

My leg is pinned up in a sling that won't allow me to do what I need most. To run away.

The nurse taps her pencil. "Ms. Jayne. I just need a name and phone number."

It's like a pressure cooker in here, and I'm a piece of meat these three are planning to eat for dinner. I can't take the constriction. "My mother doesn't live in Canada, Vicky. It's a lie. I don't have a mom."

Jenna skirts the bed and comes to the side where I've been boring my gaze into the wall. There's a smile on her face, and I can't understand what's behind it. "Ireland will be coming home with me. I'm her family."

My mind replays a scene from a book where the empty-nest mother takes an innocent bystander as a hostage to care for.

"I think I can take care of myself, can't I?"

The nurse shakes her head. "It's a week with someone else to help you out, or a week at a rehab facility."

Now I'm remembering the things Jenna yelled at the mountain man. I can't do a week in a nursing home any better than he could take a year in prison. "I'll go with Jenna."

"I want to go too." Vicky lays her head on my shoulder.

I thought I was going to be the one left behind.

Chapter 30

VICKY

I pull my legs under me on the hospital bed. Jenna is seated on the edge of the other one. She's already tucked in the blankets, even though I'm sure she knows the nurse will strip it down as soon as we leave.

"So, that's the story. Ireland never had a mom in Canada. She never really had parents at all." Jenna clasps her hands and gazes down at the floor.

The truth turns my stomach into knots. "I can't believe she never told us."

"She has now. That's what matters."

"No. She told you."

Jenna shuffles toward me. The bed sinks to the side as she sits down.

I stare at her hand over the top of mine. It's warm, and I don't pull back.

"She would have told you too."

Loud voices come closer until Brooklyn and Cameron explode into the room.

Brooklyn plops down onto a chair. She hasn't even looked at us, but keeps her gaze securely fastened to her cell phone.

"Mom, are you ready?" Cameron's hands are tucked deep into the pockets on his jacket. "I need to get out of Hicksville. This place could syphon the intelligence out of Stephen Hawking."

How did I manage to ignore the attitudes of my children for so long? These are the people I'm releasing out into the world. People who I was charged with raising. They're supposed to make the world a better place, but they're self-absorbed. Like their mother.

My shoulders slump.

Jenna reaches an arm around me and squeezes. In her position, I would have left my friend with a supersize serving of my judgement. Jenna gives me comfort.

"Well?" Cameron's eyebrows rise.

Daniel steps into the room; his hair is messy and there's a scowl on his face. "Enough, Cameron. Not another word from you."

"Come on. You can't possibly like it here. Did you hear what they were talking about at that hole-in-the-wall restaurant you took us to for breakfast? Cattle thieving. Like that's even a thing." He pulls the hood of his sweatshirt over his head and pushes in earbuds.

I stare at Daniel, my mouth open, but I have no idea what to say.

He shakes his head. "I've made arrangements for you and the kids to fly from here to Portland. From there, you can catch a flight home. It's only an hour or so to the first airport, but you'll have to take a small plane. They don't fly the big ones out of here."

My face buzzes with a flush. "What about you?"

"I have the truck. I started this way as soon as I talked to Mark. I was worried when I didn't hear from you all weekend. Then you didn't come back on Monday, and I knew something was wrong. Mark told me about the survival week. He's a great guy. I really like him."

My heart rate fires up in my chest. "I want to go with you." It's sudden, maybe the fault of a healing concussion, but I want to go the long way home, with my husband.

Daniel examines the floor tiles. "No, you don't. I came in the old truck."

"All the better. It will be like old times." Butterflies flitter in my stomach. I look at the kids. "And when we get home, there will be some changes."

Neither of them look away from their devices. I hope it isn't too late.

IRELAND

"I don't understand. Why do we all have to do this press conference? Aren't the reporters just here to get a photo op with Vicky?" The throbbing pounds in my foot as the nurse lowers the sling.

"You're all big news. Three untrained women making their way through the wilderness to safety. That's not how these stories usually end." She rolls a wheelchair next to the bed and sets the locks.

I tug at the synthetic sweater they brought me. It's too short and the fabric has the texture of woven plastic. I can almost smell the petroleum. But there isn't anything else aside from a drafty hospital gown to choose from. We came away from the ranch with only the clothes on our backs. Everything else is tucked under the porch of some men I hear are in the local jail. Maybe we could ask the sheriff to retrieve our bag. But what's in there that we can't live without now?

"Ready?" Vicky breezes into the room, her face coated with cosmetic spackle. "It's time to get this show going."

Behind her, Jenna trails like an overwhelmed mascot.

"Can't you do this without us?" I'm sure I can get a different answer from our personal celebrity.

"They asked for all of us." Vicky's shoulders fall back into a relaxed position. "Listen, I don't want to do this either. I lost my edge somewhere in the mountains. And I'm not sure I want it back, but there's a crowd out there, and we have to get through them if we want to get home."

I nod. "I'll go, but only if you agree to chisel your face out of that mask first. You look much better without the goop."

"That's what I've been telling her for the last hour." Jenna lays back on the bed I just vacated. "Wash your face, Vicky."

Behind the veil of cosmetics, I see the fear in Vicky's eyes. This is a new world for her, scarier than the Cascades could ever be. "How about we just wipe off some of the foundation?"

Her chin bobs in short nods. "All right. I can do that."

It's the small steps that sometimes mean the most.

Vicky runs a washcloth under water at the sink near the door. Rubbing it over her face, the terrycloth becomes a solid beige, but even under the fading rash and bruises, Vicky glows. The confidence and false image I've seen on television washed off with the makeup.

I wheel over to her and hold her hand. It's not a natural move for me, but she's stepping well out of her comfort zone. I can take a step to join her. "Come on. Let's show them how wonderful you really are."

Vicky moves behind me and takes control of the wheelchair. As we head down the hall toward the buzz of the reporters, I feel like a human shield.

Cameras flash as we enter the foyer. There's a small table set up at the back of the room where we're to sit and answer questions. The scene is pretty much what I was warned it would be. Vicky wheels me into position and sits in the middle seat, Jenna on her other side.

We just sit and take the hits from cameras for what feels like months. Finally, a man I haven't met steps up in front of us. "These women have been through a lot, and this is a quiet town that doesn't appreciate a lot of media craziness. You'll have ten minutes to ask your questions, then this circus ends. Am I understood?" He nods toward the sheriff and three deputies stationed at the side of the room.

Questions about Vicky's skin and will she require cosmetic surgery come at her like daggers. She answers with the vagueness of a pro.

Then one reporter points his microphone my direction. "Dr. Jayne, reports tell us that you've been suspended for improper behavior with a student. What do you have to say about that?"

My stomach plummets. I should have seen this coming. But McCormick Wilson has been out of my mind for the last few days. *Lord, I don't know what to do.* The cry of my heart shocks me. I wonder if God is having a similar reaction.

Tapping my toe on the floor, I let the tension fall from my shoulders. Vicky reaches my hand under the table and holds it tight. "To answer your question, I plan to fight the allegations." Strength is running through my body. The battle begins here. "Mr. Wilson thought he could grow a story that would allow him to get his way without having to do the work other students manage. He thought making an allegation against me was going to bring him an easy victory."

I pull my hand free and press both into the top of the table. "One of the worst things a human can do is wage a false accusation against another person. In this world, there are true crimes and assaults. Each of those is minimized by the manipulating ways of people who choose to use this kind of accusation to get their way. I will not allow it to happen on my watch."

As I lean back in my wheelchair, my body begins to shake.

Jenna stands. "That's all. Thank you for coming." She pulls my chair back and follows Vicky down the hall.

In the quiet of my room, I hear the thumping of my heart. Now, I'm ready to go home.

JENNA

The frightened look on Vicky's face as she and Daniel pulled out of the driveway with the kids and Vicky squeezed into the cab of the truck makes me want to go after them and get her back. But I've learned my lesson. Hiding from a problem does not make it go away. It's like fertilizer. The trouble grows roots and vines.

Mark and the nurse help Ireland into the back of the rented Suburban. We decided driving home would be more comfortable for her because we could keep her foot elevated while we travel.

The girls left this morning, back to their separate colleges. And it didn't hurt as much this time. I think I was even a bit happy for them. This is such a great time in a young woman's life. It's a time when lifetime friendships are formed and relationships bloom.

"You ready?" Mark holds both of my arms in his large hands.

"So ready." I step forward, molding my body into his chest, listening to the dialogue of his heartbeat. "You're a good man."

"Only because I have a good woman beside me." He kisses the top of my head.

How beautiful to have another chance to love my family and my friends. This is truly a blessed life.

Chapter 31

IRELAND

My office smells musty and the woodwork is dark and suffocating. It's hard to believe this was my sanctuary only a few short weeks ago.

I lean my crutch against the wall and look out over the sea of students making their way from one lecture to the next. Academia is a beautiful creature. The thirst for knowledge exists at our core. I love being a professor. And I'll love it even more if I can do it somewhere besides here.

There's a rap at the door. I expected as much. I'm sure I was spotted walking through the main hall. Since the end of our survival experience, people have been bold with questions. And for once, I don't really mind answering them.

"Come in." I pull the ball out from under my desk, think again, then push up with my good foot to perch on the desktop.

Dr. Doogan crosses his arms and takes two steps in. "So it's true. The survivor has survived another ordeal."

"If you mean I made it off the mountain, yes, it's true. But I won't be signing up for that adventure again."

"Sure. Leave the extreme stuff to the youth. They're still foolish enough to enjoy a good life-or-death kind of vacation." He comes farther into the room, then leans against the window sill, his arms tight against his chest. "What's next, Ireland?"

"Professor?" This position, with my feet dangling, has started the damaged foot throbbing again. I slide down. "What do you mean?"

"Will I have to replace you? Is it time for you to make another run?" His head cocks and he observes me over the top of thick-rimmed glasses.

"You were right to call me out on that before I left. I came here to hide, and this place was a wonderful retreat from reality, but"—I pull my new glasses off my nose then rub the bridge with my thumb and first finger—"not every leaving equals running."

His hands grips the wood ledge behind him and his gaze studies the wall. "You're a difficult person, you know that?"

"I do."

"And you shouldn't run away from a fight. You're stronger than you give yourself credit for."

I nod. "I think you're right about that too. I'm not running from Mac's accusations. I fully intend to fight him all the way to the Supreme Court if that's what it takes to get this kid to tell the truth, but I can fight from Oregon. I have another fight, one that's so much bigger, with consequences that are more than career-threatening. That one requires my presence. This one does not."

"If you leave, what's to stop the board from giving Mac what he's asking for?"

"Good sense. A backbone. Doing what's right." Now I cross *my* arms. "We all know the accusations are false. It's a matter of standing up to them, when the media may, and probably will, take another angle."

"So, we can count on you to testify, if it comes to that?"

I rise to my one good foot and snag my crutch from the wall. "Absolutely."

Dr. Doogan's face brightens with a smile. "That's what I was hoping you'd say. But there's no need."

My shoulders sag. "The university gave in?"

He pushes off from the wall and walks toward me. "Nope. Mac did. The boy dropped all charges against you. I guess he realized he'd met his match."

I shake my head and wag my finger the way Jenna would. "I can't believe you let me go on, all the while knowing this nightmare was over."

"I had to make sure you were leaving for the right reasons. Dr. Jayne, you're a strong woman. Stay that way." He pats my shoulder. "And take care of that foot." Dr. Doogan turns and walks out of my office.

It's time to pack.

VICKY

My stomach turns as we make the final corner. The house we're searching for is located in an older neighborhood in one of the Dallas suburbs. The sidewalks are ever so uneven, but trees line the streets, giving the area a comfortable feel that masks the dilapidation characterizing the facades of these homes.

Daniel drives slower than the residential speed limit. I appreciate the added care for the children that seem to pop out of nowhere along the way. Our six-month-old SUV stands out like a limousine here. A boy of about seven grabs the arm of his friend and points in our direction.

There's still so much for me to learn about the world and loving the people in it. My first reaction is to paste on that Victoria Cambridge smile and turn the dial on my Texas charm up to twelve.

The GPS startles me from my self-reflection. "You've reached your destination."

Daniel pulls over to the curb and cuts the engine.

It's the smallest house on the block, probably less than a thousand square feet, but the yard is well kept and flowers still bloom pink and purple from the cedar window boxes.

Without warning, my nerves begin to buzz. I'm not sure what I'm doing here uninvited. This felt like the thing to do. Like this was God's leading, not mine for a change.

I pull down the visor and review my face. Pockmarks cover my once smooth cheeks and a scar runs along my right eyebrow. I reach for my purse and remove a compact of powder, but Daniel covers my hand.

He says nothing, but gently shakes his head, restoring my confidence and bringing a tear to my eye. "You look beautiful."

My stomach tickles with butterflies so much like he gave me when we were newlyweds. I inhale the savory scents that permeate every inch of the vehicle. My marriage isn't healed, but there is a mending, a slow stitching back together. And like my face, there may be scars that endure, but I'm not sure I would change that. Without this lasting evidence of the struggle, the only thing that would remain is an open wound.

Daniel pops his door.

In a moment of spontaneity, I reach for his hand.

He turns back to me, and our eyes meet. There's so much meaning in this moment. So much understanding of where we are and where we want to someday be. The counseling has been hard, brutal at times, but good. "You've got this." A half smile tweaks his features.

His fingers squeeze mine then he lets go. In too short a time he's at my door, opening it and standing aside for me to climb out. "Don't worry. I think this will be a good surprise."

"I hope you're right. Because if it isn't, I don't know what I'll do."

He angles his elbow out, and I wrap my gloved hand into the hole he's created. I don't know if I could follow through with this crazy plan if it weren't for his nudging. I want to tell him that, but I can't get my mouth to do the work. This is something new for me.

At the door, he rings the bell, and we wait.

Finally it opens and a man stands in the entry, a toddler on his hip and an apron tied around his waist. "Can I help you?" His eyebrows knit together and his chin tips. "Aren't you that lady from television?"

My mouth falls open.

"I'm so sorry. That was rude." He bounces the little girl who clings to his shirt.

"No. It's okay." I stretch my hand out to him. "I'm Vicky Cambridge and this is my husband, Daniel."

"Nice to meet you. I'm Nathan, and this little one is Carlie." He looks around behind us. "Should I have been expecting you?"

"No. I met your wife on a flight. Bridgett is your wife, right?"

"Yes. She'll be home any minute now. Carlie and I are trying to help her out with Thanksgiving dinner, but I'm afraid we may have done more damage than good."

"We'd like to help with that. Our Suburban is filled with food and decorations. With your permission we'd like to give Bridgett a break."

He leans out the doorway. "Is this some kind of television special?"

"No." I wave my hand in front of my chest. "This is personal, no cameras, no press. I feel like I owe this to Bridgett."

His lips curl between his teeth and the skin between his eyes wrinkles. "That would be wonderful." His jaw bobs in tiny nods. "She's been so worried. I told her it wouldn't matter if we had bologna sandwiches off paper plates for dinner, but she wants to show my mom that she's capable. And now her flight is delayed. She'll barely make it home." He turns his head to the side, blinking.

"We've got this." Daniel turns back to the SUV. In a minute his arms are filled with boxes of Thanksgiving essentials.

"Let me help you." He motions to me with Carlie. "Would you mind?"

"Of course not." The little girl comes into my arms willingly, but she gives me a thorough examination before settling against my chest. Soft hair that smells of baby shampoo tickles my neck, and I instantly feel the pangs of missing my own babies.

Since returning home, I've cut my schedule in half. I've made simple dinners and attended every school event. The kids seem happy I'm home, but what I see most often is caution, like they're waiting for me to rebuild the walls. I understand, because each day for me is like an addict trying desperately to recover. Those old ways, the keeping everyone at a distance and burying myself in work, are hard to let go.

Nathan and Daniel come up the walkway with their arms full. They're already laughing together. My husband has a way of making friends in seconds. I love that about him. One of my assignments is to tell Daniel the things I admire in his character rather than holding them back. I shift Carlie to my hip and send myself a text so I'll remember this detail.

Inside, the house actually seems smaller than I had expected. The space is clean and uncluttered. A tiny living room extends from the dining room. Though the house itself is simple and ordinary, the furniture is exquisite. The table is rustic, natural, and filled with character. I run a hand over the sanded top, feeling the grooves and textures of the wood.

Carlie leans from my arms and mimics my motion.

"This is a beautiful table, isn't it Miss Carlie?"

Her face bursts to life with the most precious one-toothed grin.

Daniel sets a box down. "You're right about that." He leans over, inspecting the craftsmanship. "This is quality." Standing, he knocks a fist on the surface. "Nathan, where did you get this piece?"

The young man takes his daughter into his arms like a child would hold a blanket for comfort. "It's mine. Just something I put together for Bridgett." His gaze remains on Carlie.

Daniel turns toward him. "This is incredible. Have you made anything else?"

I can see by the passion in my husband's eyes that his Thanksgiving attention is lost for the time being. "Why don't you two talk wood, and I'll get going on dinner?"

Daniel winks at me, and it sends a pleasant shiver through my body.

"Are you sure that's okay?" Nathan asks.

"No problem. I'll holler if I need anything."

Nathan leads my husband out a door on the other side of the dining room.

The first thing I do is take in the tiny kitchen and evaluate the best plan of attack. The turkey is wrapped in a roaster I plug in to keep it warm and give the skin that perfect brown color. This takes up a great deal of the meager counter space.

I've brought a variety of tablecloths, not knowing what size the table would be, but now that I see it, I decide to abandon that plan and simply set it with placemats. On these I stack two plates, the top slightly smaller, and drape the middle with a maroon cloth napkin. In the center of that, I place a perfect pear. With the added touches of crystal glasses, real silver utensils, and a centerpiece designed with tiny pumpkins and gourds, the table goes from beautiful to elegant.

Standing back, I take in the scene I've created. I have no idea how many people are coming, so I've probably over-set the table, but it's lovely. There's just one thing missing. From the box on the floor I pull the hand-written card that will sit in the middle of the centerpiece. It reads: It's not the décor. It's not the food. It's the love that makes a family.

I remove Nathan's turkey from the oven. It's still nearly raw, no way it will be done in time. Just as I put the potatoes in to heat and remove the plastic wrap from the last of the side dishes, Daniel and Nathan walk back into the room.

"I'm sorry we were gone so long." Nathan's smile shines bright on his face. "How can I help?"

Carlie is nestled in Daniel's arms now. She reaches up and runs her hand over the stubble on his cheek. That man will make a fine grand-father someday. "Vicky, that table is perfect. You're amazing."

"I hope Bridgett will like it. She really touched my heart. I want her to feel blessed."

The door swings open. "Nathan, I'm home." Bridgett doesn't look up. She pulls off her coat and hangs it in the closet then heads to the kitchen, pulling her apron off the hook as she turns and freezes.

"What's this? Did you do this?" She finally notices the four of us standing side by side. Her mouth drops open.

"Surprise," I say. "I hope this is more helpful than that ridiculous advice I gave you on the airplane."

Bridgett covers her mouth with one hand. Her eyes brim with tears. "I've been up for twenty hours. It was all I could do to get home. I thought Thanksgiving was ruined. I kept begging God for a miracle." She steps closer to me. "Why did you do this?"

I can't answer her. It's too deep, and I'm too grateful for the privilege of this day. Instead I pull her into my arms and love her. This woman I didn't even know was the beginning of my trip home. How can I thank her?

"What time are you expecting your company?" I ask.

She steps back and looks at the clock. "Oh no. Nathan's parents and brother will be here in less than an hour."

"That's perfect. You go get cleaned up, and I'll put on some coffee."

She squeezes my hand, her eyes sparkling and alert, then takes off down the hall after kissing Nathan and taking Carlie.

In the corner, Daniel and Nathan bend over a wood-crafted end table.

Within ten minutes the earthy scent of coffee mixes with the Thanksgiving smells. Bridgett is back, her hair tied up in a loose bun. Carlie has been changed into a ruffled dress which she pulls up and chews. I've packed up the extras in a box, ready to take back to the car. "Daniel, are you ready?"

He nudges Nathan. "Just about. I'm trying to get Nathan here to give me a chance as a boss. He's a great craftsman. I could use him on the team."

Now I see where God was going with this, and I'm even more grateful to have been blessed to be here. "I think that sounds wonderful."

Nathan beams. "What do you think, Bridgett?"

She walks into his arms. "I think that's perfect."

A hard knock sounds at the door and breaks the celebration.

Bridgett's face grows serious. "That's them."

"So early? I wanted to be out of the way first." I take Daniel's hand and we step back into the kitchen. I don't want to be the first thing they see.

"Happy Thanksgiving." Bridgett's voice has a hint of nerves in it.

"Thank you for having us. I see you've set the table." A woman with a tight bun and fluffed bangs steps into the dining room. "Interesting. No table cloth."

"I think it's perfect, Mom. Let me take your coat," Nathan says.

"It's the little touches that are important not to forget. At least that's how I was raised."

I step forward. "That's an interesting perspective. Though I believe what's truly important is the way a mother loves her family."

The woman turns to see me. Her eyes round, and there's no doubt that even in my recovering state, she recognizes my face.

"Bridgett is such a treasure, don't you think?" I tilt my head.

"Well, certainly." The woman wrings her hands, her forehead tense with woven lines.

"Bridgett, I have an opening for an assistant. I hope you'll consider applying. And since Nathan is working with Daniel, it would allow you to spend more time together. Of course, that's only if you're interested in a new career."

"You want Bridgett working for you?" The woman raises an eyebrow. "You're Victoria Cambridge, aren't you?"

"Yes. Bridgett, you give it some thought and call me after the holidays. We've got to get home to our kids and our Thanksgiving." I give Bridgett a hug.

"You don't have to do this," she whispers in my ear.

"It's not a favor. I really want you there. And bring Carlie." I step back.

Daniel and Nathan work out a few details for the next week.

Outside the air is cool. Daniel puts his arm around me as we walk to the SUV.

JENNA

By the time Mark gets out of bed, I've written a scene, taken the dog for a three-mile walk, and flung open all the blinds in our house, letting in the bright morning sun. Next week we'll move the clocks forward, and I'll miss this time outside before the rest of the neighborhood wakes.

Ireland left two weeks ago. Her trip to our home was extended not because of her injuries, but because Mark and I really enjoyed having her here. I think Ireland enjoyed it too. I miss her, but we have new adventures on the horizon, and the three of us have to keep moving forward.

"Hey there, Sunshine." Mark shakes his hair still wet from the shower. "How about meeting me at the school for lunch today?"

"Can't. I have a writer's lunch." A shiver runs up my spine. I still can't believe I'm a writer. When the article I wrote was accepted by a national magazine, it legitimized what I've been doing since the adventure. And the check didn't hurt either. Secretly, I copied it and have the image tucked into my right-hand desk drawer.

"Great. I guess that's more important than lunch with the old husband." He plants a kiss on my cheek and ruffles my sweaty hair. "I'm proud of you."

I know he is. And it's not because I'm writing the story of our time in the wilderness. I think Mark is truly proud of me for coming back to him after all the years of drifting further away.

I'm proud too.

Last week I spoke at a women's retreat. Me. The timid one. The woman who hated to even leave her home. I talked to the group about the value God places on each of our lives and how the devil tries to steal the security we have by realizing how precious we are. I told my story, all of it, and I wasn't rejected. I was revived.

Chapter 32

IRELAND

In the courtyard behind the vacant house, I elevate my feet on the edge of a brick fire pit. Closing my eyes, I envision the scene to come. Girls gathered around with marshmallows browning over hot coals. Their laughter filling the space between young women who came here as strangers and will leave as sisters.

The house is not the same as the old Emery House. Emery 2.0, as I refer to it when I talk with Jenna and Vicky, is smaller, a touch more quaint. There are thirty beds in the sleeping porch, a vast change from the original house with its fifty bunks. We've managed to obtain the historical mementos from the original Emery. Tonight we'll hang portraits from all the years past. And this place will take on the memories from the old house.

I don't walk the short way from here to my new office. That path leads past the Emery of my youth. It's been stripped to the studs inside, soon to become, of all things, office space. The university's plans to tear it down and build a sky-high dorm have been put on hold. For how long, I have no idea.

I tip my head back and let the end of summer sun warm my skin. The fragrance of blooming jasmine floats over me. And I breathe deep from the life I have here, dreaming of the newness of what is still to come.

Skye has allowed me three meetings with River so far. These have been closely monitored, and I don't hold that against him in the least bit. The man who never wanted to be a father has turned into a protective daddy. I thank God for that.

River will be with me alone on Monday. My heart pounds, and I smile at the thought. I've bought a few things to make this a home for him when he comes. And if I have trouble being a mother, I'm sure the thirty girls in the house will give me pointers.

In less than a month, I will not only be a mom to my son, but a housemother to the new generation of Emery Girls. It's more than I can breathe in. It's more than I thought I deserved. It's a chance to have a family again in a way that doesn't look traditional, but in the center of me, feels so right.

"We're here," Jenna yells from the foyer, and my heart races.

I jump up and run to the entryway, throwing my arms around the two of them.

Vicky is wearing jeans. I hold her back and check out the university t-shirt and tennis shoes.

"What?" Her face is bright with a smile that catches in her eyes.

"You're as beautiful as you were in college, maybe more."

A blush creeps over her face. "Whatever, you crazy hippie."

Jenna sucks in a breath then bursts out laughing. "This is going to be just like the old days except now we have the house to ourselves. It's a slumber party."

"I have something." I rush to the slots where the mail will be divided for the residents and pull out three worn envelopes. "Here are our letters. Em delivered them this morning. Hope had them all along."

"What should we do with them?" Jenna holds hers to her chest. "All our secrets are out in the open."

Vicky waves hers in the air. "I think we open them, and answer the same three questions again. Then we put them together in a new hiding place to be retrieved in twenty-five years."

Where did you come from?

Where are you now?

Where are you going?

It's agreed. And all the answers will be different this time.

Acknowledgments

A huge thank-you to my husband, Jason, who puts up with my endless string of what-ifs, encourages me to keep going, and tells me he's proud of me. You're the best man for me.

To my kiddos, thanks for being the crazy group of wildly individual people you are. I love each of you with my whole heart.

Thank you to my agent, Karen Ball, who is the one who reminds me why I write and never pushes me to write anything but what God puts on my heart. Karen, you've been a beautiful friend to me as well as a mentor. Thank you for giving me a chance and believing in my abilities when I didn't.

I could not have asked for a better editor than Dawn Anderson. Dawn, you made the editorial process fun and easy. You made me a better writer, and I'm so grateful. Thank you!

Noelle Pedersen and the marketing team at Kregel made me feel welcome from the very beginning. Thank you for putting up with my newbie questions and caring about my book.

My endless love and thanks go to the sisters I gained through the writing journey. If I received nothing else from this career, it would all be worth knowing Jodie Bailey, Kimberly Buckner, and Donna Moore. A special thanks to Jodie for being my accountability partner. These words would not have been written without your encouragement and hounding.

To Marilyn Rhoads, Heidi Gaul, and Karen Barnett who tell me when I'm not making sense, when I've abandoned all commas, and when my writing becomes a long river of thats, verys, and justs. You three make me readable.

Deborah Raney was one of the very first people to read my fiction writing. From the beginning she has been an encourager and a positive presence. Deborah, you can't possibly know how much your words have meant to me over the long years of trying, trying, and trying again. Thank you.

I have so many wonderful friends who've supported my crazy writing life with their patience, love, and support. Thanks to all of you.

Thank you, Erik Simmons, for sharing a wild story with me that sparked the idea for this book.

And most of all, thank you to God who put wonderful people in my path, gave me stories to write, and honored me with a life so wonderful and undeserved.